PRAISE FOR THE NOVELS OF
CHANEL CLEETON

"A sexy fighter pilot hero? Yes, please. For anyone who's ever had a *Top Gun* fantasy, *Fly With Me* is for you."

—Roni Loren, *New York Times* bestselling author of *Off the Clock*

"A sexy hero, strong heroine, delicious romance, sizzling tension, and plenty of breathtaking scandal. I loved this book!"

—Monica Murphy, *New York Times* bestselling author

"A sassy, steamy, and sometimes sweet read that had me racing to the next page."

—Chelsea M. Cameron, *New York Times* bestselling author

"Fun, sexy, and kept me completely absorbed."

—Katie McGarry, author of *Nowhere But Here*

"Scorching hot and wicked smart, *Flirting with Scandal* had me hooked from page one! Sizzling with sexual tension and political intrigue[...]Cleeton weaves a story that is as complex as it is sexy. Thank God this is a series because I need more!"

—Rachel Harris, *New York Times* bestselling author

"Sexy, intelligent, and intriguing. Chanel Cleeton makes politics scandal-icious."

—Tiffany King, *USA Today* bestselling author

CHANEL CLEETON

BERKLEY SENSATION, NEW YORK

BERKLEY
SENSATION

An imprint of Penguin Random House LLC
375 Hudson Street, New York, New York 10014

INTO THE BLUE

A Berkley Sensation Book / published by arrangement with the author

ISBN: 9781101986981

PUBLISHING HISTORY
Berkley Sensation mass-market edition / July 2016

PRINTED IN THE UNITED STATES OF AMERICA

10 9 8 7 6 5 4 3 2 1

Cover art by Claudio Marinesco.
Cover design by Danielle Mazzella di Bosco.

Penguin
Random
House

*To the fighter pilots who dedicate their lives
to serving something bigger than themselves . . .
and one in particular . . .*

Thank you to my wonderful readers and all the bloggers who signal boost my work. Your passion for books makes our community a wonderful place to be. You're the best!

Thanks to my fabulous agent Kevan Lyon and editor extraordinaire Kate Seaver for making my dreams come true. Big thanks to the team at Penguin and Berkley for all their hard work, including my publicist Ryanne Probst, Jessica Brock, Katherine Pelz, and the AWESOME art department for giving me such amazing covers.

I couldn't do this job without the support and encouragement of my family and friends, especially the amazing people I've met in the book community who make me laugh throughout the day, are always there when I have a question or need a sounding board, and keep me sane.

And as always, thank you to my husband, my heart and my best friend. You're incredible.

ONE

BECCA

I walked into the bar, already feeling about ten years past my prime. Columbia was a college town, especially the closer you got to the University of South Carolina campus, and while Liberty Tap Room managed to straddle the line between students and young professionals fairly well, tonight the place was packed with fans celebrating the Gamecocks' latest football win.

I pushed through the crowds wearing garnet and black, my gaze peeled for my friend Rachel's distinctive red hair. I neared the bar, spotting a flash of red through the crowd. Rachel and her friend, Julie, sat on bar stools, locked in conversation with three guys.

Whoa.

Two of the guys had their backs to me, but the view was pretty spectacular. They were both tall with impressive muscles that tapered down to lean waists. The third was something out of a magazine ad—tall, blond, tan, panty-dropping blue eyes, and a shit-eating grin with a body to match. He leaned into Rachel, whispering something in her ear, bracing his muscular forearms on the back of her chair.

In all the times we'd come to Liberty, we'd met some cute guys, had our fair share of successes, but this was something else entirely. This was like an alternate reality. This was karma making up for one failed engagement that resulted in my heart as emotional road kill and the series of less-than-spectacular relationships that followed.

Rachel spotted me, her lips transforming into a wide smile that gave me a pretty good indication of how the night was going.

I lived in my hometown of Bradbury, South Carolina, population twenty-five thousand, and while I loved it there, most of my friends had married long ago and started families. At thirty-one, I was one of the few singles left, so when I needed a night out, I made the hour-long trek to Columbia and Rachel. We'd met at a law school alumni mixer a few months ago, and she and her friends had adopted me into their group.

She waved me over, the guys turned, and my ovaries exploded a bit as three sexy smiles flashed back at me. Rachel closed the distance between us, leaving the hottie behind at the bar. She wrapped her arms around me in an enthusiastic hug that suggested I had some catching up to do.

"Ohmigod, Becca. You got here just in time. We hit the jackpot," she hissed in my ear.

I grinned. "So I noticed. Which one isn't taken?"

"The dark-haired one in the blue sweater."

I pulled back slightly, studying the guy who was apparently "mine" for the night. Cute, and not in the same intimidating way the blond was cute. The dark-haired guy shot me another friendly smile and my heartbeat kicked up a notch.

Rachel led me over to the group, making the introductions, her voice nearly at a shout to be heard over the conversations around us and the pop music blaring from the speakers.

The blond guy introduced himself as Easy, the other one as Merlin, and the dark-haired guy who was "mine" told me his name was Bandit between pulls of beer.

I blinked.

Boy band? Professional wrestlers? Guys reliving their high school years?

My gaze swept from Rachel to Julie and back again, wondering why I seemed to be the only one concerned about the fact that a group of thirty-something-year-old men had just introduced themselves by such bizarre monikers. Were they part of some preppy motorcycle gang?

"They're fighter pilots," Julie announced with a grin, her body angled toward the one called Merlin.

Oh, hell to the no.

Considering Shaw Air Force Base was only an hour away from Columbia and two hours from my hometown, I'd always considered it a stroke of good fortune that I'd managed to avoid meeting any of the F-16 pilots who called South Carolina their temporary home.

Apparently, my luck had changed.

I'd known one fighter pilot in my entire life, and since that experience had left me completely and utterly fucked— and not just in a screaming orgasm sort of way—once had been enough.

"Why don't you sit next to me?" Bandit asked, patting the seat of an empty bar stool.

Rachel and Julie flashed me encouraging smiles. One of the great things about making new friends was the fact that they didn't know your every failure or all of your flaws. But that meant they also had no clue that this was basically my own personal version of hell.

One night. I'd just wanted one night to go out, have fun, meet a cute guy, and maybe get laid. Okay, so sex was definitely off the table considering lady town had gone into lockdown mode at the term "fighter pilot," but that didn't mean I still couldn't have a good time. I mean, it wasn't like Eric was *here*. And how many F-16 pilots could there be in the world? Maybe they didn't even know him.

I climbed up onto the bar stool, a lead weight settling in my stomach. I'd stay for a drink. Then all bets were off.

"Can I get you something?" Bandit asked.

"That's okay. I'll get it." I turned and caught the bartender's attention, ordering a glass of wine for myself, feeling like I'd brought the group's mood down. Everyone was in full-on flirt mode, the couples clearly paired off for the night, and I felt badly for the one they called Bandit for getting stuck with me.

I turned back to face the group while I waited for the bartender to pour my glass of wine, pasting a smile on my face.

"So how long have you guys been stationed at Shaw?"

"I've been there for a year." He gestured toward Easy and Merlin. "They're visiting from Bryer Air Force Base . . . here for a buddy's bachelor party last night . . ."

I heard Bryer and my world came to a crashing stop.

Motherfucker.

The world really was way too small.

I wasn't one of those girls who kept in touch with her exes—not *the* ex, at least—the one who took my heart and shattered it, then ran over it with his car, and for an encore set it on fire. We weren't friends on social media, everyone who knew me from before, who'd known *us*, knew better than to bring him up with me. But at the same time, we were both from a small town, and even though he hadn't come home for the better part of a decade, he was the local boy who'd hit it big, the troublemaker who'd turned it around, joined the military, and become an officer and fighter pilot. So I'd heard that Eric was living in Oklahoma. That he flew F-16s there. And despite all of my best intentions not to keep tabs on him, he was frequently in the back of my mind. I'd waited for years, my heart in my throat, wondering when someone would mention in passing that he'd gotten married, mentally steeling myself for the inevitable blow that never came.

Then again, he'd made his choice clear a decade ago when I'd lost out to a hunk of metal. Maybe he didn't wear a wedding band on his finger, but he'd promised 'til death do us part all the same.

It was on the tip of my tongue to ask if they knew Eric—I figured the fighter community was pretty small, the F-16 community even smaller, and Bryer its own little world—but I wasn't sure I wanted to know the answer. On the one hand, didn't everyone want to win the "who's doing better" contest after a breakup? I didn't want him to be suffering or anything, but if he was desolate in my absence, had developed a weird fetish where he'd stopped clipping his toenails, and had lived a hermit's life for the last decade, I wouldn't exactly shed a tear.

"We were going to head over to Tin Roof and see if there's any music playing. Want to come?" Bandit asked.

"Yeah, maybe I'll come for a bit."

I could just casually mention him. No big deal, right?

"We're just waiting on our buddy, Thor," Bandit whispered in my ear, a flirty smile on his face. I had to give the guy some credit—I had the personality of a wet mop tonight and he was still looking to score.

"Okay." I took a sip of my wine, making an effort to smile, feeling a little guilty for ruining this guy's shot at getting laid. Would it be weird if I casually mentioned that nothing was going to happen? It would give him a chance to find someone else for the night, at least.

But what should I say? "I'm already in a relationship" was a blatant lie that Rachel and Julie could easily debunk. And I didn't want to hurt his feelings and make him think it was something wrong with *him*. And, "Sorry, but you have the same job as my former fiancé who I have not managed to get over in a decade," sounded really fucking sad.

"Listen—"

"There he is," Bandit interjected.

I would later appreciate the irony as Taylor Swift filled the bar, singing about a guy being trouble, at the exact moment—

I swiveled in my chair, my world stopped, and my wineglass hit the ground.

Eric—heart-crushing, would-rather-slide-inside-a-jet-than-me, one-that-got-away Eric—stood in front of me, his arm draped around the shoulders of a stunning blonde.

He was just as tall as I remembered—tall enough that it was an effort to look up at him. His reddish blond hair was the same—or was it just a touch lighter? His blue eyes seemed more intense than I'd remembered, which was just stupid because of course they hadn't changed—maybe it was just me and my reaction to him. Or that the way he looked at me had changed. Before, his gaze had been heated and affectionate; now, it just looked . . . I didn't even know. His shoulders were broader, his body much more impressive than I'd remembered, but I figured that came with the territory and his job.

He looked good. Really good. Better than the mental

image I had kept tucked away in the recesses of my mind, which was a pretty impressive feat considering I'd had some vivid memories to keep me company in his absence.

His hair fell over his forehead, his gaze boring into me, and his teeth sank into his bottom lip—a lip I'd sucked over and over again—and a little wave of light-headedness hit me. Or maybe it was the sexual drought finally hitting me full force, or the wine, or the loud music, or the fact that my heart hammered in my chest.

More likely, it was the force of Eric. Six-feet-two-inches of Eric.

Fuck me.

THOR

No fucking way.

I blinked, convinced I'd somehow hallucinated her, that Becca Madison couldn't possibly be *here*, standing a few feet away from me, Bandit's arm brushing against her side.

The sound of breaking glass shattered the haze, everyone around us scrambling to pick up her dropped wineglass. *We* didn't move; it was like time stood still for the two of us while the world went on.

"Becca?"

I had to say her name, as though somehow that would confirm that this wasn't a case of mistaken identity or a dream, that she was really here, in front of me.

She looked different and somehow the same—maybe that was the effect of ten years. Her dark hair was up, exposing the curve of her neck and highlighting the deep V between her breasts. Glasses perched atop her nose, dark frames that somehow complemented her deep brown eyes and made her even more beautiful. She'd never been in-your-face sexy; instead, she'd cornered the market on the sexy librarian fantasy, the good girl you wanted to play with until she turned bad.

And considering how many times I'd had her naked, my body sliding into hers, drowning in her tight, wet heat, I knew just how mind-blowing the sex could be.

"Do you guys know each other?" the girl next to me—Mandy or something—asked.

"Yes."

"We used to," Becca answered at the same time.

I took a step away from Mandy, still feeling like I was in a dream.

"I can't believe it's really you."

She didn't answer me, her gaze unwavering, assessing. I struggled not to flinch under the weight of her stare, the measure of all that I'd lost.

"How have you been?"

Had it really been ten years? Did it feel like less because there hadn't been a day when I didn't think of her? When I didn't wonder where she was or what she was doing?

And now she was here, looking up at me with those big brown eyes that I was helpless in the face of, her presence a punch in the gut and a knee to the balls as she knocked the wind out of me.

Finally she spoke, her voice making me ache.

"Good. Great, actually," she squeaked.

"Good. Good." I swallowed, losing a bit of myself as I stared at her. "You look great."

A flush of color spread across her cheeks. "Thanks."

I heard Easy calling my name, felt the blonde tugging on my arm, watched as Bandit slipped his arm around Becca as though he could somehow claim the girl I'd fallen in love with when I was seventeen fucking years old.

I wanted to reach out and hold on to her, wanted to keep her in front of me even as I felt her getting ready to pull away, wanted to fall to my knees and fix the mistake I'd made a decade ago.

I swallowed again, trying to steady my voice, wondering if I sounded as desperate as I felt.

"Do you want to get out of here—"

"I'm going to go." Becca lurched off of her chair, her gaze darting around the group, looking everywhere but at me.

Look at me. Please. Give me a chance.

"Becca—"

She didn't look at me, didn't react. It was as though I hadn't even spoken, and after a hasty good-bye—swallowed up by the white noise rushing through my ears—she was gone as quickly as she'd crashed back into my life, her brown hair gleaming, bobbing through the crowd until even that disappeared and I was left standing by the bar, feeling like I'd just been hit by a Mack truck, surrounded by six pairs of curious eyes and one pissed-off blonde.

TWO

THOR

I ordered another tequila from the bartender at Tin Roof, bracing my elbows against the bar, regretting my decision to stay with the group rather than just going back to my hotel room. I'd lost the blonde approximately ten seconds after I'd lost Becca.

"What was that back there?"

I turned as Easy settled into the space next to me, signaling to the bartender for another beer. I downed the shot of tequila in front of me, needing the liquid courage before I answered him, setting the glass down on the bar top.

"How did you know the girl? Becca, right?" he asked.

God, her name sliced through me.

"Yeah." I stared down at my hands, laced together over the scarred wood. "We were engaged."

I didn't have to look at Easy to know I'd shocked him. Some guys knew I'd been engaged, but it wasn't something I'd advertised, either. Easy and I hung out together, had probably become closer in the last few months considering what we'd been through—the night we'd both been flying and lost our friend and squadron commander, Joker—but we didn't talk about our feelings and shit.

"Fuck, man."

That about summed it up.

"How long ago?"

"Ten years."

We'd been in our early twenties. Kids. Kids who'd been together through high school and college. We'd been everything to each other. Family, best friends, a fire that had burned hot and bright until it flamed out.

"What happened?"

Me. I happened.

"I wanted to be a fighter pilot. She wanted to go to law school. We started fighting about our future, wanted different things. In the end, I left."

"Shit." He took a pull of his beer. "You looked like someone hit you in the balls."

"Pretty much."

"I asked the girls. Apparently, she's a lawyer in a town near here. Bradbury."

I'd heard through the grapevine that she'd stayed; I wasn't sure if that was why I'd made it a point never to return, but considering my family ties were tenuous, excluding my grandmother, it hadn't exactly been a hardship.

"It's where we grew up."

"And you haven't seen her in ten years?"

I nodded.

"You thinking about changing that?"

I shrugged, unable to talk past the lump in my throat.

"You're an idiot. Bandit was all over that. She's fine. Seriously, fine. Got that sexy librarian thing going on. If I'd seen her first . . ."

I glared, all too familiar with Easy's warped sense of humor and uncanny ability to get under everyone's skin. "Fuck off."

He flashed me a cocky grin. "I'm just saying, if you don't get in there, someone else will."

The idea had occurred to me approximately one million times in the last decade. It wasn't like I didn't want her to be happy, but at the same time, the idea of Becca with someone else, hearing about it . . . yeah, I wasn't sure I was ready for that one. Another reason why I hadn't exactly been eager to go back to the place where I'd grown up. I figured one day I would return and I'd see her walking down the street, or going into the grocery store, a baby on her hip and a ring on her finger, and I'd know unequivocally that I'd lost the best thing that had ever happened to me. But she'd been out tonight and I hadn't seen a ring . . .

"You saw how she acted. She hates me."

"Come on. You said it yourself—it's been a decade. She doesn't know you. Are you the same guy you were ten years ago?"

If I'd been any drunker, I'd have fallen off my bar stool. Apparently, Easy was doing deep.

"No."

Ten years ago I'd been struggling to scrape together a future for myself, trying to become the kind of man who deserved someone like Becca, only to fuck everything up spectacularly beyond repair. Now I didn't know what I was.

"I chose F-16s over her. Ended our engagement. Decade or not, I don't think she's going to forgive or forget that easily."

"If you had the choice to make all over again, would you still choose flying?"

Had it all been worth it? I'd wanted to serve my country,

wanted to do something with my life, to make a difference, and I'd thought I'd find all of that behind the stick of a jet. And now that I looked at the scales of what I'd given up and lost, and what I'd achieved, I didn't know which one won out.

I'd gone to combat; I'd done my part, had supported the guys on the ground, but I couldn't ignore the doubt inside me that recognized that we left one place just to return years later under a different operation name, a different spin, even when the mission sure felt like the fucking same. It was a rinse cycle—go to the desert, come back from the desert, go to the desert again. It was losing good guys, guys like Joker, and for what? We were called to fight, to risk our lives to defend our country, to fight for those who couldn't fight for themselves. And we did it. But it never felt like we got anywhere, like we actually made things better. And in exchange . . .

It was dangerous to let the losses consume me, but when the stakes were as high as they were with our job, the ramifications of fucking up were catastrophic.

I'd been on his wing.

That night in Alaska, the night we'd lost Joker, I'd been number two in the formation—Easy and our buddy Burn, who'd since moved on to Korea with his new wife, Jordan, rounding out the four-ship. I'd been Joker's wingman when the spatial D hit, when he became disoriented and crashed his plane into the cold ground. I'd heard the radio call, that last sound of his voice that I'd never forget, and then nothing. He'd just fallen from the sky.

I'd hugged his widow, Dani, when we all returned from the TDY to Alaska, minus the most important member, had sat through his memorial service, had presided over the piano burn where we marked his sacrifice, and still, through all of it, I couldn't wrap my mind around the fact that he was gone, couldn't quiet the questions and doubts that kept me up at night, wondering if I'd fucked up somehow, if I'd failed him—*I was on his wing*—if I should have noticed his spatial D, if I could have saved him. The accident investigation board had cleared all of us, but I couldn't quite manage to clear myself.

I wished I had an answer to Easy's question, but right now it sure as fuck felt like our losses outweighed our successes, and despite the heroic spin of my job, I wasn't sure I could point to one instance where I'd actually made a fucking difference, especially in the face of the glaring loss of my friend.

I turned and held Easy's gaze, flinching a bit as the bleakness in his eyes hit uncomfortably close to home. I definitely wasn't the only one trying to outrun my troubles tonight at the bottom of a glass. We'd never spoken of it, but I'd seen the despair in his eyes enough times to realize that losing Joker hit close to home for Easy—after all, he had the added guilt of being in love with Joker's wife.

"Do you ever regret being a pilot?" I asked him.

"Not for a fucking second."

There were guys who flew F-16s and guys who were fighter pilots. Easy was a fighter pilot through and through. He lived and breathed the lifestyle, pissed jet fuel, and got off on the high of pulling G's. He bedded women, partied hard, and sucked every inch of life. He was a throwback to what it had meant to be a fighter pilot in the olden days, a dying breed of men who looked up to Robin Olds as their own personal hero and were happiest on the edge. And he was a fucking killer with the stick. One of the best pilots I'd ever known.

I was good, damned good, but I still didn't know which I was. If flying the 16 was what I did or who I was.

I was just drunk enough to ask—

"If you had to choose between flying or a woman . . ." My voice trailed off.

Easy looked away, staring off into the distance. "Hell if I know." His jaw clenched. "Let's just say, I didn't exactly have a choice. But if it came down to a choice between the Viper and . . ." He took another swig of his beer. "Yeah, no contest."

There was no need to fill in the blanks; his feelings for Dani were quickly and dangerously becoming an open secret in the squadron. I imagined most men would agree with him. There weren't many women like Dani. Or Becca.

Easy got a lot of shit in the squadron for being a bit of a whore. The stereotype of the love 'em and leave 'em fighter pilot was slowly becoming eclipsed by the carpool brigade, guys who were more about family than pussy. Easy saw more action than any guy I knew, and he never made a secret of it, so it wasn't like his reputation was undeserved. But at the same time, as someone who'd had *the girl*, the one you'd turn yourself inside out for and work yourself to the bone to please, and been so fucking stupid as to blow it, I knew that sometimes it wasn't about not caring who you were with as much as it was not caring who you were with because for some guys, once they'd met the one, there wouldn't be anyone else who mattered.

I pushed back from the bar. "I'm going to go."

Easy's brow rose. "You sure? You fucked it away with the blonde back at Liberty, but this place is full of hot undergrads."

"You don't think a ten-year age difference is too much? Even for you?"

"What the fuck else am I going to do?"

I opened my mouth to speak and then closed it again, figuring I was the last person who should give anyone romantic advice. It'd be overstating the obvious to admit that we'd been living on the edge before, neither one of us the poster child for healthy decision making, but at the same time, it was also impossible to ignore the feeling that Joker's death had killed a part of us that night and we were both hurtling through life, trying to hold on to anything that would make it bearable, anything that would make us okay—

If we ever found it at all.

BECCA

The cursor hovered over the "Add Friend" button. I swallowed. I moved the cursor away like a kid caught with their hand in the cookie jar.

Fuck me.

I took a sip of merlot, questioning my sanity for the four hundred and fifty thousandth time since I'd fled Liberty.

I hadn't been prepared to see him. Understatement of the year, and yet, the brutal truth. I'd had a decade free from Eric Jansen, and in one evening the Band-Aid had been ripped off and all of my feelings—pain, and anger, and confusion—had slapped me in the fucking face.

And even though I knew I should just be glad that the whole thing was over, there was another teeny-tiny undeniable part of me that wanted to redeem the fact that I'd come off looking horrendously awkward at best, and totally crazy at worst.

I could friend him. No big deal. Maybe send him a message that said something like:

Nice to see you. So sorry I had to run. I had an appointment I couldn't miss.

No, a date. A date sounded better. *Yes.* Let him think that I'd moved on, that I had a fabulous new boyfriend who was a doctor . . . no, wait, an accountant. That sounded stable and not thrill seeking. Like the kind of guy who would be happy to come home for dinner at a reasonable hour, who wouldn't get tired of living in the same place, who didn't flinch or flee at the idea of putting down roots. I could totally see myself with an accountant. Except, I had dated an accountant, and he'd had the unfortunate habit of jabbing at my clit like it was a key on a calculator until I'd finally had to break up with him before he broke my vagina.

Whatever.

I took another sip of wine. Okay, a gulp. A big fucking gulp of get-your-head-on-straight-and-forget-you-ever-saw-Eric-Jansen liquid courage.

I clicked on "Message" instead.

A message was safer. No need to actually friend each other and make that commitment into each other's lives. I mean, yes, I was friends with my old hairdresser, but surely ex-boyfriends, hell, ex-fiancés, were held to a more tenuous standard.

My fingers shook as they hovered over the keyboard, pressing down on each letter like it was a wire connected to a bomb . . .

Eric,

It was nice to see you tonight. I'm so sorry I had to run, but I had a date. I hope you're well. Take care.

Becca

That was nice, right? Maybe a little crazy, but at this point I figured I had nowhere to go but up. And it was probably an improvement over what I wanted to type, which was basically a variation of, *Fuck you, fuck you, fuck you, fuck you for breaking my heart.* It got the point across, but probably wouldn't do a lot to help me in the sanity department.

I stared at his profile picture. He looked good in his green flight suit. He wore a blue cap on his head that I figured was part of his uniform and covered up his thick Prince Harry hair. He stood in front of an F-16, looking like every girl's fantasy. And even though I didn't have a pilot fantasy, I had a whole lot of Eric fantasies, and more than that, I couldn't ignore the twinge of pride for the man he'd become.

He might have broken my heart in the process, but it was impossible to deny that Eric's transformation from the boy who'd been in and out of juvie before we got together to a captain in the Air Force—one of the elite few who flew fighter jets—was impressive to say the least.

Once upon a time I'd been his biggest fan, had believed he could do anything. We'd had dreams—I'd wanted to go to law school at the University of South Carolina and he'd still been figuring out what he wanted. I'd been surprised when he told me he wanted to join the military, but so proud of him. I hadn't thought about what it would mean for us then, just felt excitement that he'd found something he was passionate about, something that could give us the future together that we'd envisioned.

And then, little by little, the fights had started.

The military meant that he couldn't control where he was sent; it meant overseas assignments, and as he slowly explained to me, it meant moving every couple of years, sometimes as frequently as every year. It meant that being an attorney—a difficult enough goal to accomplish—would be that much harder, that I would struggle to find a job that would be willing to take a chance on someone as transient as me, that if I passed the bar in one state and then we were moved to a state that didn't offer reciprocity, I'd be forced to take the test all over again, studying for months and months only to repeat it again the next time the Air Force moved us, that all of a sudden my future started to look like it would always come second to his.

We'd tried long distance when he went off to basic training, but even then the cracks had begun to show. We'd both been under so much pressure—me in my first year of law school, working my ass off just to keep up with the nightly reading, forget doing what I needed to in order to excel— him going through the process to become an officer and then getting ready to leave for pilot training in Texas. In the end, it had been too much and he'd given up and left. Or maybe I'd pushed him away. I didn't even know anymore.

I clicked "Send" before I could chicken out, figuring I owed us this at least. And then I was alone again in my apartment, the connection to Eric somewhere out there.

I'd gone out tonight hoping to have fun, to get my mind off of work and my overwhelming caseload, thinking that maybe if I was really lucky, I might meet a guy and maybe get laid. Instead, the past had caught me in its talons and I couldn't shake loose no matter how badly I wanted to or how hard I tried.

THOR

I read over Becca's message three fucking times Monday morning before my flight, not to mention all of the times I read it between getting the message and landing back in Oklahoma on Sunday afternoon, trying to decode it and coming up short every single time. She hadn't reached out to me in ten years, and now this . . . Did she want me to respond? But if she did, why hadn't she sent me a friend request? My finger hovered over the "Add Friend" option, and then I pulled back.

Shit.

I seriously contemplated messaging Burn and his wife, Jordan, to get a female opinion on this, needing someone to sanity check my next move, but I did a quick mental calculation and realized that with the time difference it was the middle of the night in Korea, and I figured there'd be no end to the shit I'd get from the guys if it got around that I was this pathetic.

Flirting with women had never been this difficult. It was Becca who always made me feel like I came up short.

I could respond, but with what? It wasn't like she'd left me much—*any*—room to maneuver. And I didn't want to get into some awkward pen-pal relationship with her—talk about rubbing salt into the wound. But that was the problem. I didn't know what I fucking wanted from her.

I stared at her profile picture, my heart clenching at the sight of the smile that had made me feel like the luckiest guy in the fucking world every single time it came my way.

My finger hovered over the "Add Friend" option again, telling myself she wouldn't have sent me the message if she completely loathed me. I mean, yeah, she'd said the line about the date, but I'd sort of skimmed over that part, preferring to focus on the fact that after nearly a decade of silence, she'd reached out to me. Maybe this was her way of telling me the ball was in my court.

I clicked the button, watching as the message, "Friend Request Sent," appeared on the screen.

Fuck.

I raked a hand through my hair, sliding my phone into my locker, removing my patches, and putting my combat name patch on my left arm. I slipped on my G-suit, then my harness, affixing my lineup card to my right knee, grabbing my helmet, and slipping it into the helmet bag. I draped my earplugs around my neck, grabbed the bag with my flight pubs and in-flight checklist, swung it over my shoulder, and walked to the vault to get my classified materials.

I left the vault and made my way to the step desk to get my step brief, the tension and anticipation building inside me as I got ready to fly, Becca temporarily pushed from my mind.

Time to go to work.

BECCA

I downed my fourth cup of coffee for the day, cringing a bit as the lukewarm liquid hit my mouth. Definitely a Monday.

I flipped through the case file again, skimming the words contained there. The First Appearance was scheduled for later in the week.

Our circuit bled right up to Columbia, so we occasionally got some students who lived in between the two cities, taking advantage of lower-cost housing in exchange for a slightly longer commute. This case was a DUI, a college student who'd driven home after a night of partying too hard and throwing back too many beers. He'd been pulled over and failed both his field sobriety test and a Breathalyzer. He was a kid, but he was a kid who'd made the same mistake one too many times, and since this was his second offense, we were going after a harsher sentence than he would have received as a first-time offender.

Luckily, he hadn't injured anyone—or worse.

A lot of the cases that came across my desk were difficult reads. I'd seen more of the horrible things people could and would do to one another than I'd ever imagined before I started working at the Solicitor's Office seven years ago. The ones with children were the worst. I'd lost count of how many times I'd cried in private reading about some heinous act that had been committed, how many times the anger burned inside me, hot and bright.

It wasn't supposed to be personal; I understood the reasons behind it, at least, but sometimes nothing gave me greater satisfaction than watching someone pay for the evil they'd wrought.

This case wasn't the worst, not by a long shot; on its face it was mundane, even.

Just not to me.

I wanted to scream at this kid that he had no fucking business getting into a car after he'd been drinking. None. I couldn't, of course—*it isn't personal*—but God, I wanted to.

I wanted to ask him if he thought the seven beers he'd consumed were worth the damage they could have caused, weighed against a life.

I was ten years old and my parents were driving back from a wedding in Columbia when a drunk driver heading in the opposite direction crossed over the median and hit them head-on. My dad died at the scene, my mom a few hours later in the hospital from injuries sustained at the accident.

The driver survived with little more than a few scratches.

I'd gone to bed that Saturday night, my head full of my parents' promise to take me to the beach for the day the next morning, dreaming of sun and waves, wondering if I could convince them to take our old Labrador with us. I'd woken up to tears and the stark reality that there would be no more family trips anywhere, because one person's careless mistake had taken my family away from me.

I'd gone to live with my mom's elderly mother, moving from a house full of laughter and love to a quiet space where our grief swallowed us up.

The driver received ten years in state prison and a twenty-two-thousand-dollar fine for what the court called a felony DUI, also known as killing both of my parents. Five years and eleven thousand dollars per parent. He was out in six.

I went to law school.

Twenty-one years later, my grandmother long gone, I was still angry. Maybe I should have been forgiving. Maybe that would have been a sign of my growth. But forgiveness had never come easily for me, so I stayed with angry. I couldn't right the wrong done to my parents, but I sure as hell could do everything in my power to protect others from the same thing happening to them. There were hard cases, ones we lost that we should have won, times justice eluded me, but for the most part I genuinely felt like I helped people.

My e-mail pinged, adding to the seventy-five unread e-mails filling my box, and I groaned, already reaching for the bottle of pain relievers I kept on my desk.

My hand froze midway as I read the words on the screen.

Eric Jansen has sent you a friend request.

Oh, holy hell, I definitely should not have sent him that message.

I'd spent all day Sunday obsessing over why he hadn't answered, whether I wanted him to answer, whether I *should* want him to answer, and finally concluded that he had realized it was opening a can of worms and he was being the wise one, whereas my judgment had clearly failed me.

He'd sent me a friend request. That one was a game changer.

I stared at it for what felt like an eternity, wondering if accepting would be a sign of personal growth or enabling my crazy. It had taken me years to get over him, years to get to the point where the sound of his name didn't send a dagger through my heart. Why would I risk that again?

Adulting was fucking hard.

I picked up my cell and hit the first number on my speed dial.

Lizzie had been my best friend since we were kids who'd bonded over our disdain for naptime in pre-K. She'd been there with me throughout the totality of my relationship with Eric and, more importantly, had held my hand—and occasionally, my hair—as I'd struggled to move on from the devastation he'd wrought in my life. She was happily married now with a little boy, and if there was anyone whose opinion mattered, it was her.

She answered with a weary sigh and yelled, "Dylan, do not stick the action figure up your nose. Dylan . . ."

I grinned. My six-year-old godson was a little terror, and I meant that in the best possible way. I babysat frequently so Lizzie and her husband, Adam, could go on date nights, and I had quite a few gray hairs that hadn't been there before thanks to Dylan's antics. Of course, he always ended the night cuddled in my lap, his expression that of a perfect angel, so he pretty much had me and all the females in his life wrapped around his finger.

"Okay, I'm back. Sorry. I cannot *wait* until Adam comes home."

"Daddy!" Dylan yelled in the background.

"Yes, Daddy is going to come home soon and you should *definitely* show him all of the tricks you learned at your Aunt Caroline's."

I grinned again. Adam's younger sister was notorious for teaching Dylan pranks that drove Lizzie nuts every time she babysat.

"Okay, I'm really back this time. He can run in circles around the yard for a while and burn off steam. Mama needs a break."

I winced. "I shouldn't have called you during the day. I know you have your hands full. Sorry. It was stupid."

"Please. It was a break from pulling little green Army men out of my son's nose. You calling is pretty much the best thing that's happened all day. What's up?"

I took a deep breath. "He friend requested me."

There was no need to explain who *he* was. I'd already told Lizzie all about my awkward run-in with Eric and my stupid message.

"Ohmigod."

"Yeah."

That was the best thing about our friendship—we might have been in different places in our lives, but she was always right there when I needed her, and she always understood how big things were for me. She'd been the one to hold my hand through my parents' funeral, even as we were both children struggling to deal with our grief. Lizzie's mom took me shopping for my prom dress; she taught me how to do all the things my mom would have shown me if she'd been alive.

"What are you going to do?"

Lizzie was also the best because she didn't pass judgment, even when she probably should have.

"I don't know." *Liar.* "Accept it, I guess. I mean, I have to, right? It would look petty if I didn't."

"You want to."

"I don't know. Maybe. Yes."

"Where do you think this is going to go?"

"I don't think it can go anywhere. He lives in Oklahoma. He's in the Air Force. Who knows where they'll send him next? I'm here and I have no intention of leaving."

I'd worked hard to become a deputy solicitor—essentially South Carolina's version of an assistant district attorney—and I loved my job. All of the reasons I hadn't wanted to give up my career to follow Eric around the world still remained. Except there were moments . . . moments when I cuddled Dylan in my arms and wondered if I'd made a mistake going with my head over my heart. I was thirty-one and my most serious relationship to date had ended when I was barely legal to drink. It was hard not to feel like I was going backward in some ways, even as I advanced in my career.

"So why do you think he friend requested you?"

"He could have been trying to be friendly. Or maybe he was curious."

"Or maybe he saw how fabulous you looked on Saturday night and regretted his decision to let you go."

This was why everyone needed a best friend like Lizzie— she made you feel good even though you'd made an ass of yourself in front of your ex.

"Highly doubtful." I sighed. "What should I do? Do I accept the request, or is that just opening me up to a world of hurt?"

"At this point, could it get worse?"

"Probably."

"Then do you want my advice?"

"God, yes."

"Sit on it. Take a few days and think about whether or not you want him back in your life, even in a limited way. He wasn't just some guy, wasn't just some ex. It's going to be hard to let him in, even peripherally. So take the time."

I *really* loved Lizzie.

"Has anyone told you that you give amazing advice?"

She laughed. "Just tell my son that the next time he tries to stick something up his nose. Yesterday it was Play-Doh."

"Let me know when I can take over babysitting duty. I'm happy to help."

"I will definitely take you up on that. I just want to go to a movie with my husband and make out in a dark theater."

"Done. Name the time and day, and I'm there."

We talked for a few more minutes and then I hung up the

phone, deleting the e-mail, already feeling better. Maybe time did heal all wounds. Or maybe I was just delaying a date with destiny. Either way, I had a three o'clock deposition and bigger things to do than worry about Eric.

I almost believed it myself.

THOR

The night sky was inky black as I stared out the canopy at my surroundings.

Lightning flashed, static filling the radio from the electricity of the thunderstorm.

My hand gripped the stick, heart pounding.

I'd never minded flying at night before, had always loved the calm and peace of the dark sky. Until the night Joker died . . .

I was doing a FLUG ride at the range, serving as an instructor for Brick, one of the younger wingmen in the squadron who was trying to get certified as a flight lead for his night close air support sortie. He was a solid lead, but we were strafing at night, and the weather was shit, not helping the nerves ramming through my body.

I kept my eyes on Brick, my night vision goggles giving me a good view of his jet, five nautical miles from the target area. We were in a right-hand turn, two miles apart from each other, his covert strobe flashing on my NVGs.

The joint terminal air controller on the ground called in and requested a strafing pass over the radio, passing us a nine-line over the frequency.

"Nine-line Charlie. This next attack will be a Type II bomb on target. Attack. Lines one through three NA. Line four three hundred and fifty feet. Line five enemy personnel in the open . . ."

He went through the remaining four lines, giving us our targeting instructions, adding in the remarks and restrictions.

Brick read back the lines and gave his brief.

More lightning flashed at my three. More static filled the radio. I gripped the stick even harder, my mask suddenly feeling too tight, my chest growing heavy.

The JTAC gave the clearance.

"Cleared hot."

We went in for the attack, my eyes on Brick off to my right, banking and rolling into a twenty-five-degree dive. A green explosion of fire flashed on my NVGs as Brick employed his gun.

Green fire.

Just like Joker. The same fucking image burned into my brain.

My hand shook on the stick.

I began the roll in for my attack, the jet in a thirty-degree right-hand turn, going forty knots, looking over my shoulder.

Another bolt of lightning to my left jolted me from where I'd locked on to Brick.

I gave the radio call, my words eerily echoing the last call I'd ever heard Joker make that night on the range in Alaska.

I overrotated, pulling four G's, looking over my shoulder.

A secondary explosion came from where Brick shot the gun, just as I was about to squeeze the trigger. The light washed out my night vision, blinding me for a second.

I froze, my heart pounding, chest tightening.

Fuck. Fuck. Fuck.

The JTAC called out, "Abort. Abort. Abort," over the radio, and ice filled my veins, taking me back to that fucking night, to the same three words I'd heard right before Joker had crashed into the ground.

I could hear Brick over the radio, breaking through the whoosh of white noise in my ears.

"Snake two! Recover! Snake two! Recover!"

A solid, steady tone sounded in my headset. *Mmm. Mmm. Mmm.* The jet lurched up on its own, until I suddenly got light in the seat as the jet leveled off, a couple hundred feet off the ground.

Spatial fucking D.

Sweat rained down my face, my chest hammering like I was about to have a fucking heart attack, my hand, which used to be so steady on the stick, trembling and shaking like a leaf.

I hadn't realized where the jet was in the sky—between the secondary explosion washing out my night goggles, the bad weather, and the fact that I'd been too focused on Brick's jet—on watching my lead—I hadn't even noticed that I'd been flying toward the ground.

Just like Joker.

With one noticeable difference—

I had the Auto Ground Collision Avoidance System installed in my jet, a recent upgrade to the F-16 that alerted us to spatial D and recovered the jet when we lost control. Joker had been two months away from his death being avoidable, from his flight playing out the same way mine had.

One upgrade away from coming home to his wife in a jet rather than a coffin.

No matter how hard I tried, I couldn't stop the trembling in my body, couldn't catch my breath the entire flight back to Bryer. There were ghosts in the jet with me, and if I didn't get them under control, I'd kill either myself or someone else.

The wheels touched down on the runway and I could finally breathe again.

The new squadron commander, Loco, was a good guy whose biggest flaw was unfortunately the fact that he wasn't Joker. He did a pretty decent job of navigating a squadron still grieving while simultaneously preparing for a looming deployment to Afghanistan, but it wasn't quite the same.

I'd had my range of commanders throughout my military career—some were dicks, more concerned with getting ahead in their own careers than the guys they were responsible for; others were marginally better, guys who meant well and tried to connect with their people, even if it felt forced. And then there were the commanders like Joker. He might have been the boss and we'd all respected the shit out of him, but he'd been one of the guys, regardless of the rank on his shoulder. He'd been a fighter pilot first, a commander second, and in a squadron like the Wild Aces, street cred like that went a long way.

I stood outside Loco's office, trying to find my balls, not sure what I was even going to say. Everyone in the squadron had already figured out that I'd lost my shit a bit in Alaska. And now it was fucking with my flying.

Loco opened the door and waved me in, sitting down behind his cluttered desk. He gestured for me to sit in one of the empty chairs. "What happened?"

I sat, trying to come up with the answer he wanted. The truth came out instead.

"I think I need some time."

"Since the accident."

I nodded.

"The investigation board ruled on it."

"It did. But I was up there with him. We were friends. I was on his wing." I swallowed, feeling like a pussy, but needing to get it out there just the same. "It feels like he's in the cockpit with me every time I fly. I can't shake it. Tonight was bad."

Because it was a night flight. Because I was number two again. The green fire. Because it had reminded me of before, and now it didn't matter how many flights I'd flown in the Viper; the one when we'd lost Joker was the monkey on my back that I couldn't shake.

"You haven't talked to anyone."

I didn't bother answering that. Getting flagged with a psych issue would be a bitch with my security clearance and career progression. The military fully encouraged us to get help, but we knew how it would look if we did. Besides, I didn't see Easy sitting in here, bitching about his feelings. Burn was kicking ass at Osan. *I* was the one who was fucked up.

"I just need a few days off. Just need to get my shit sorted. I went from Red Flag, to Alaska and Joker's accident, and I've been flying my ass off these past few months." I felt like the biggest loser in the world for bitching about flying *too* much when all I'd ever wanted to do was fly, but at the same time, it was like no matter what I did, I couldn't catch my breath. I needed to hit pause on everything. Needed to breathe again.

"You've been flying a lot because we're undermanned. You're one of our strongest instructors. We need you here, getting the younger guys ready for the deployment."

"I know. And I will be. But right now, my mind isn't where it needs to be to get the job done."

I could go through official channels and get medical leave to get my shit sorted out, and then he'd really have a manning problem. And I didn't think he was trying to be a dick about it; I'd been to the schedule buys—we definitely needed more bodies in the squadron. I'd seen the inbound list and we had some older guys who were already qualified as instructors—IPs, like me—before we left for Afghanistan, but in the meantime, they needed me.

"How long?" Loco asked with a weary sigh.

"Three weeks?"

He made a face.

"Two and a half? I already have leave to go to Reign's wedding in South Carolina. I could just extend it a bit."

Reign and I had gone through pilot training together and had bonded over busting our asses flying T-38s and trying to make it to the big leagues. He was friends with Easy and Merlin as well—the F-16 community was a tiny fucking world—so we'd all flown out to Columbia for his bachelor party this past weekend and had planned on making the trek back to South Carolina for the wedding since we were all groomsmen.

"And you think this will fix the issue?"

God, I hoped so. This wasn't exactly a normal request, and if the circumstances were any different, there was no way I'd get to take time off with this short notice. But we were in a bit of a weird situation here, and I figured Loco was trying to do the best thing for his squadron. No one needed a rattled pilot up there.

"Yeah, I do."

He sighed. "We'll work out the manning. Take the leave."

Relief flooded me. "Thank you."

I felt like an asshole because me being on leave would mean that everyone else in the squadron would have to pull longer hours, but this had become more of a necessity than an option, so I figured I was all out of plays here.

"If you need to talk . . ."

I nodded. "Thank you, sir."

I got up from my seat and headed to the door.

"Thor?"

I turned.

"Are you going to be in the local area while you're on leave?"

I hadn't even thought of it, hadn't considered my options besides hoping that he granted my request, so no one was more surprised than I was when the words left my mouth—

"No. I'm going home."

FOUR

THOR

Ten years was a long time to be gone, but at the same time, part of me felt like I'd never left.

I drove through downtown Bradbury, surprised to see that some of my old favorites were still in business: Casey's Diner where I'd taken Becca on dates in high school, the ice cream shop where she'd always ordered scoops of salted caramel ice cream, the hardware store where I'd worked my senior year of high school. Other places were long gone, windows boarded up, "For Sale" signs in the window. A fast-food chain that definitely hadn't been there before sat on the corner.

But more than that, Becca was everywhere I turned, on every street, in front of every building, the ghost of us floating around me, reminding me of why I hadn't come home before.

I hadn't really thought through what I was doing once Loco granted the leave—just gone on my computer and booked a flight to Columbia for the next day, renting a car to drive the rest of the way to Bradbury. I'd managed to book a room in one of the three hotels in town, thrown some clothes into a suitcase, including my mess dress for the wedding, and then I'd been off. Now I was here, pulling into the grocery store parking lot, wondering if I'd lost my mind.

I'd told Loco I was coming home to get my shit under control, not stir up a hornet's nest. The town was too small to avoid running into Becca, and with the gossip chain being what it was, she'd definitely hear about my return. I told myself it would only complicate things, even as a part of me wanted to see her again.

I was a mess, felt cracked and broken inside, and she'd always been the one I'd counted on. It seemed like my entire adult life had been spent either running from or to this one girl. She was the compass when I was so lost I couldn't find my way.

So I'd come here. To a place that held so many memories for me. My parents were gone, my father leaving first for parts unknown when they divorced the summer before my freshman year of high school, my mother for Florida a year later, but I still had my grandmother. Still had friends that I'd mostly lost touch with over the years.

I wasn't a fighter pilot here. And I didn't know if it was something in the air, or the sensation of coming home, but I couldn't help feeling like I could breathe again.

I parked the car and walked into the grocery store, planning on grabbing a few things to keep in the mini-fridge in my room. Part of being in the military included regular fitness tests, so I made a point of eating healthy and working out daily. Sometimes it was tough to fit in with our schedules, but I'd lived with the habit for so long that it was tough to break. My hotel had a small gym that would make do for the next few weeks, and I still remembered some of my old running trails from high school and college.

I grabbed a basket, walking toward the produce section, figuring I'd pick up some fruit and vegetables. And some flowers. I'd called my grandmother on the drive over from Columbia and told her I'd be in town. I figured flowers weren't nearly enough of a peace offering, but it was better than coming empty-handed. I'd seen her at holidays over the years, the few times I'd spent Christmases and Thanksgivings at my mother's home in Florida with her new husband and kids, but I'd never made it back home.

"Eric? Eric Jansen?"

I jerked in surprise at the sound of my name, realizing how long it had been since anyone had called me anything other than Thor.

A pretty blonde with a baby on her hip stared at me with a big smile on her face.

"It's Katy Russell. Well, I was Katy Muller. From Bradbury High?"

It took me a second to place the name and face, but I remembered her. She'd been a cheerleader and we'd had bio together. We'd hung out a few times, and when I'd left Bradbury for the University of South Carolina with Becca, Katy had been dating my buddy, John. And by the last name, she'd married him.

I returned the side hug she gave me, careful to keep from jostling the baby on her hip, surprised by how good it felt to see her. We hadn't been close or anything, but I had solid memories from high school.

"How are you? How have you been?"

She grinned. "Good." She lifted her hand and flashed a diamond. "I married John Russell."

"That's awesome. How is he?" I gestured at the baby on her hip. "And who's this little guy?"

"John's great." She beamed. "This is Cory. He's one now."

The baby waved his chubby fist at me and I couldn't resist the urge to reach out and take his hand. He clutched my finger tightly before something else distracted him and he let go.

"How about you? You're in the military, right? Army?"

"Air Force."

"I bet that's exciting."

"It has its moments."

Her gaze turned coy. "So is there anyone special in your life? Are you married? Kids?"

I swallowed, the baby flashing me a smile and making a noise that sounded like something between a laugh and a gurgle.

"No, it's just me."

Her eyes widened. "Really?"

I nodded, knowing full well that every single person in this town knew about my past.

Her voice turned sly. "So how long are you in town for? Do you have plans to catch up with anyone . . ."

She let the last part linger; we both knew exactly who she meant.

I wanted to see Becca, but I wasn't sure I wanted the entire fucking town to play matchmaker. I still hadn't ruled out the possibility that she'd knee me in the balls if I tried to get close to her again, and that was not something I was looking forward to having an audience for.

"A few weeks, maybe," I hedged. "I'm not really sure. I'm going to a friend's wedding in Columbia."

"Did you call your grandmother?"

I grinned despite the interrogation. My grandmother was much beloved in Bradbury, having served as the town's librarian for nearly fifty years.

"I did."

"Did you call anyone else?"

"No, I haven't had a chance. I just got in a couple of hours ago."

Katy grinned. "I have a feeling things are about to get very interesting around here."

BECCA

I barreled into the grocery store on a mission. I had an hour before my favorite show started, and I was in desperate need of a comfort food fix. It turned out my Tuesday hadn't been any better than my Monday, and I'd barely made it to yoga class after a court appearance had run late and then I'd realized my cupboards were bare.

I hurried down the aisle, heading toward the pasta section, mac and cheese the cure for a shitty day. I waved at a few of my neighbors, the downside to living in a small town the fact that it was impossible to "sneak" anywhere, and that meant everyone saw me in all of my sweaty, faded, much-loved Introverts Unite T-shirt and yoga pants glory. Whatever. Despite what legions of romantic comedies had told me, I'd yet to find true love in the grocery store.

I stopped for a moment to talk to Megan, one of the other yogis in my class.

"Comfort food?" she asked.

I nodded with a rueful grin. "I always walk out of there feeling like I should be eating—*drinking?*—wheatgrass or something. Unfortunately, this week has already turned itself into a five-alarm-need-fatty-goodness kind of week."

She groaned. "Tell me about it."

Megan had taken over Casey's Diner when her mother retired, and every time I went in there for coffee, she was behind the counter, looking ready to drop from exhaustion. The place was an institution in Bradbury and had the business to reflect it.

We chatted for another minute or so about our class and the new instructor.

"Make sure you head over to the produce section," she added with a parting wave.

I made a face. "Is that where they keep the wheatgrass?"

She laughed. "No clue, but that's where I spotted Katy Russell talking to a mysterious hottie."

I grinned. "Well, why didn't you say so? I'm not sure what would appeal to him more—the sweat-smudged makeup on my face or the hole I discovered in my T-shirt. I better go over there and sweep him off his feet before someone else does."

"I'm just saying. Billy Crandall just got engaged. We're down to slim pickings here. Speaking of, how was your big night out in Columbia?"

I snorted, ignoring the twinge of panic as I remembered that I still hadn't responded to Eric's friend request. "Trust me, you don't want to know."

She sighed. "Then give the hottie a look. I couldn't see his face, but I caught his profile and the back view, and let's just say he's the kind of guy who looks pretty fine walking away."

"Just the way I like them," I joked. "Well, I was planning on putting chives on top of my mac and cheese to go along with the heap of bacon to save me from a coronary event, so maybe I'll check out his assets. Covertly, of course."

"Trust me, it's worth it."

I found myself grinning as I went in search of chives and a fine ass, deciding that I was going to convince Lizzie to round up some of our friends and do a girls' night. Since my plans in Columbia had been thwarted by Eric's appearance, I'd missed out on the night I so desperately needed. It felt good just to laugh and forget about work for a bit.

I grabbed some Oreos on the way to the veggies, my basket growing fuller and fuller. *Never shop on an empty stomach.* I turned down the produce aisle, my gaze peeled for Katy Russell and—

Megan hadn't been exaggerating about the guy—I got the same impressive view of height, back, and muscular ass, dressed casually in a pair of jeans and a T-shirt that she had—but I also took notice of a few things she'd clearly missed—like the copper-colored hair, light dusting of freckles on skin that was on the pale side of gold, and the fact that it was my motherfucking ex-fiancé, not in Oklahoma where he belonged, but *here.* In my hometown. Our hometown. Twenty or so feet away.

Apparently, his ten-year vanishing act had ended, and he'd chosen tonight—when I looked like shit and probably didn't smell much better given how much I'd sweated at hot-fucking-yoga—to return.

Kill me, now.

I backed up, my heart pounding so hard I feared I'd have a heart attack, ready to escape without him seeing me, when suddenly my back collided with a precariously placed display, cans of French onion soup hitting the ground in a series of thuds that sounded like cannon fire, startling me enough to have the basket slipping from my hands, and the entire produce aisle turning to face me.

Including *him*.

I stood next to the ruined French onion soup display, my body frozen in horror.

And then he was just there, bending down in front of me, putting groceries back into my basket, grabbing dented cans of soup.

I said a silent prayer for Mother Nature to take pity on me and for a sinkhole to open up right then and there and swallow me whole.

No dice.

"Are you okay?"

I blinked, staring into Eric's blue, blue eyes before he straightened his body, rising to his full height, both of our grocery baskets looped around his arm.

I swallowed, not sure what answer to give, and at the moment, not really caring. It had been dark in the bar on Saturday night, and I'd been so thrown for a loop that I hadn't had a chance to really look at him beyond the basics. Not like I wanted to, at least. So even though this ranked up there as one of the single most embarrassing moments in my life—likely accelerated by the presence of the man staring back at me—I looked my fill, because Megan hadn't been exaggerating in the slightest—he really was easy on the eyes.

He wasn't necessarily hot in the conventional sense—yes, he was tall and muscular—but it wasn't his looks that were lethal. It was his personality. He carried himself like he was in on a joke no one else knew about, mischief dancing in his blue eyes, the naughty smile on his lips making him look both playful and like he was about to press you up against a wall somewhere.

And wasn't it a bitch that he'd only improved with age?

"Are you okay?" Eric repeated, concern in his gaze.

I nodded, still not trusting my voice.

Everyone in the store gave us a wide berth, clearly wanting to stay away from the crazy lady and the hottie who'd unnerved her. And still, I heard the murmurs of recognition, saw the looks being flashed our way; pretty soon most of Bradbury would know Eric was back and that, in under a minute, he'd knocked me on my ass.

"What are you doing here?" I croaked, figuring that took precedence over any embarrassment I felt over my appearance. Worry filled me. "Is your grandmother okay?"

I saw his grandmother around town occasionally. Despite my issues with Eric, she'd always been sweet to me, and it was impossible to miss that she was a little lonely, her only daughter having moved to Florida and her eldest grandson traveling all over the world.

"I'm here for a visit."

My jaw dropped. He hadn't visited once in ten years. It had been an unspoken rule that in the demise of our relationship, I'd gotten custody of Bradbury.

"For how long?"

"A few weeks."

What the fuck?

"Is that okay?"

I froze, everything becoming way too surreal for me to handle.

"Why?"

"Why what?"

"Why are you back? Why here? Why now?" I struggled to keep my voice calm, realizing I likely failed miserably.

I'd needed time to deal with the friend request—hot yoga or not, *this* was beyond my ability to be Zen.

"I needed a break from work. Things were bad. I needed to sort everything out."

"And you thought you could do that here?" I didn't bother keeping the incredulity out of my voice. We had a town's worth of unresolved baggage and I couldn't imagine anything less soothing than throwing us together again.

"I wanted to come home."

I felt the first stirring of anger, breaking through the haze of awkward. It hadn't been home ten years ago when he'd decided to leave. He'd described it as a weight around his neck, told me the town was dragging him down, that he wanted to get the hell out of South Carolina. I remembered every single thing he'd said with stunning clarity, because for all that he'd been talking about Bradbury and our life here, we both had known he'd also been talking about me. He'd been restless, not wanting anything to tie him down, and all I'd wanted was to put down roots, to have the home he'd promised me since we were kids.

"And if I said it wasn't okay?" I kept my tone cool, my gaze boring into him, daring him to look at me.

He'd broken up with me in the female version of a Dear John letter; he didn't get to slink away now.

His gaze met mine and held, and for a moment I was knocked back by the shadows there.

"I'm not leaving. I can't."

"Why?"

"We need to talk."

If not for the shock I'd already been through this evening, *that* would have knocked me back.

"Please tell me you aren't here for me."

"I don't know. I don't know why I'm back."

"That's a cop-out and you know it."

"Jesus, Becca."

My hands fisted on my hips, throwing major attitude his way and having only so many "fucks" to give.

"You don't just get to come back and crash into my life and expect that I'm going to let you. That I'm going to be okay with it."

I moved forward, jabbing a finger at his rock-hard chest. *God*.

"You left. You made your choice. You want to come back here and do the right thing by your poor grandmother who has missed you for the better part of a decade, that's one thing. But if you coming back here has anything to do with me, you need to give up now. You see me walking down the street and want to nod at me, *maybe*, smile, fine. But that's all you get. You threw everything else away a long time ago."

I didn't bother to wait for a response—*couldn't* wait for a response. I just turned and fled, leaving Eric staring after me—and no doubt an audience staring at *both* of us. It wasn't until I got to the car that I realized he still held my groceries in his hand, and if I didn't have enough reasons to be pissed off with him, he'd just bought himself another one.

THOR

Well, fuck.

Of all the ways I'd imagined that going down, I hadn't quite captured the essence of how much she loathed me. Hell, maybe "loathed" was too tame of a word. I was less concerned with whether I'd nod or smile at her if I saw her on the street, and more concerned with the possibility that she'd be driving when I saw her and run me over with her car.

Katy came up behind me, the baby growing fussy. She gave me a sympathetic smile and squeezed my arm.

"Give her time. It has to be a shock seeing you again."

I nodded, not sure I could speak past the lump in my throat. It wasn't undeserved, not by a long shot, but I couldn't help hating the fact that Becca hated me.

"Will you come over for dinner sometime? I know John would love to see you."

I nodded and forced a smile even though I felt like shit inside. "That would be great. Thank you."

We said our good-byes, and I watched as she walked toward the checkout lanes, the baby on her hip, the lump in my throat growing as I imagined another woman in her place, as I envisioned Becca running to the grocery store with *our* baby, coming home after kicking ass in court. I imagined sitting with them at the dinner table, laughing, talking to Becca about our days and then climbing into bed with her at night, the memory of her body curled into mine hitting me like a punch to the chest.

What was so bad about that? What the hell had I thought I'd find away from her? And why had the idea of settling down, starting a family, just being together—day after day—been so terrible?

"Hey, Eric?"

Katy turned back to face me, a smile playing at her lips.

"She goes to Casey's every morning for coffee and break-fast before work. If you want to try to talk to her, if you want to fix things, that's a good place to start."

*   *   *

I dreamed of her that night. Of crashing cans of soup, green fire, brown eyes, of Joker's voice, over and over again, making that last radio call. Of dancing under a starry sky a decade ago, feeling like the world was ours for the taking. Of looking up at the same sky that had taken my friend, that had the power to keep me or throw me back down to the ground on any given day.

I awoke to the numbers on the alarm clock next to the bed flashing a green 5 a.m., my naked body covered in a thin film of sweat, my chest feeling like someone had dropped a fucking anvil on it.

Most nights I slept well, but every once in a while I had dreams of the accident, and I woke up like this—feeling like death clung to me and refused to let me loose. It wasn't as much that I was afraid of dying as it was the sensation that I'd come so close, that we'd all been assessed, our lives weighed and measured, and somehow the ax had fallen on Joker. I didn't know if I felt guilty for having survived, or like I'd dodged a bullet, or guilty for feeling like I'd dodged a bullet.

Either way I felt like I was falling, reaching out with nothing to hold on to, the girl whose hand I wanted to grab, just out of my reach.

IVE

BECCA

I took a sip of my coffee, the hot liquid going down my throat at the exact moment that Eric slid into the booth, taking up the seat across from me.

"What are you doing here?" I sputtered.

He looked like he'd been out for a run—his skin flushed, hair mussed. He'd dressed casually in a T-shirt and athletic shorts and a pair of sneakers. It was a nothing-special outfit, and yet he wore it well. I kind of wanted to lick him, even as I wished he'd get back in his car, drive his ass to the airport, and hop a plane back to Oklahoma.

I'd been angry last night. This morning I felt like I'd gone through a spin cycle, and I wasn't sure I'd made it out whole.

Eric grinned, looking a little unsure of himself. "I wanted to catch you for breakfast. I heard you had a morning ritual." His dimple popped out. "I didn't know what time you came, though, so I've been sitting in the corner for a while." He shifted in his seat, his legs jostling mine under the table.

"Excuse the energy; I couldn't sit here without ordering something, so I've had a lot of coffee."

I bit back a smile. He did look like he was bouncing out of his skin a bit. He'd always been like that—sugar, caffeine, too much and he turned into a hyper boy in a man's body.

I struggled not to laugh.

This was what he did. He was cute and charming and he hooked you with little to no effort, and it always started with a smile. Then a laugh. Next thing you knew, he'd ripped your heart out and left you for dead on the side of the road.

Or something like that.

"Did you miss everything I said yesterday? I'm not interested in rekindling anything. I'm not even ready to be friends. I don't know why you came back, and it's not my business—"

"There was an accident. I was flying in the formation. My friend died."

Oh my God.

He didn't say it like he wanted sympathy, just matter-of-factly, as though that kind of danger was a daily part of his life.

There had been many times over the past few years when I'd found myself wondering if he was okay, times when I'd turn on the news and see stories about combat operations in the Middle East, see pictures of F-16s flying over war zones, and my heart would jump into my throat as I'd wonder if he was there, if he was safe.

"I'm so sorry."

I knew better than anyone how loss could turn you inside out.

He shook his head, running his hand along his jaw. "I didn't tell you for you to feel sorry for me, or anything other than to explain to you where I am right now. I needed a break from everything. Needed to get away."

"So you came here?"

Our gazes locked and he nodded. "Yeah."

I wanted to ask him *why*, but at the same time, I wasn't sure I wanted to know. There were too many feelings pinging inside of me right now, too much between us for me to know where we could go from here. I didn't know how to start over and I didn't know how to just be friends, and I was terrified to let him past the electrified manned-by-vicious-man-eating-dogs fence I'd built around my heart.

But—

We'd started out as friends, had been each other's family, really, for such a long time. So even as I couldn't entirely let go of how angry I was with him, I also couldn't push him away. Not like this.

"I had a flight on Monday." He looked down at his hands. "Something about it fucked with me. I freaked out in the cockpit." His voice grew strained. "It's dangerous and irresponsible to be up there if I'm not in the game. I owe it to the guys I fly with to be better. To get my shit under control." He looked up, leaning back in his seat, his hands back at his jaw again, his body full of restless energy that came from either the caffeine or the topic of conversation. "We have a deployment coming up in the next several months."

"Where?" I asked, trying to keep my voice steady when the word "deployment" brought a sinking feeling to my stomach.

"Afghanistan."

"I thought combat operations had wound down."

"Not for us. We're deploying regularly, doing close air support. There's still a job to do there, a duty to the guys on the ground." He shrugged. "You just don't necessarily hear about it on the news all the time. It doesn't fit the narrative, but yeah, we're still there."

Even as he felt so familiar, I registered all of the differences now, unable to shake the sensation that the man in front of me wasn't quite what I remembered. There was a weight to him now, an invisible bulk he carried on his shoulders, the burden of fighting for everyone else.

I was hurt and angry, but it was impossible to deny that he was dedicating his life to serving others. A hero in the truest sense of the word, ready to give his life for the freedoms we all enjoyed.

"What's it like?" I asked, surprising myself with how much I wanted to hear about his life, driven by the desire to understand what it was that he found in the plane that he hadn't found anywhere else, that he hadn't been able to find with me.

Smile. Laugh. Hooked. Fucked.

He didn't answer me for a moment, and I wondered if I'd asked something that I shouldn't have, if I'd picked at a scab that wasn't healed.

I took a sip of my coffee, not sure how my morning had ended up here, how I'd gone from determined to stay away from him, to sitting across from him, hanging on his every word, getting sucked deeper and deeper into his world.

It had always been like this between us. When my parents died, my world had narrowed to a small group of real friends and a lot of acquaintances, to school, and to books. Boys hadn't even been on my radar. And then he'd smiled at me junior year and that had changed.

Eric gave me a wry smile, a wave of nostalgia hitting me. How could someone feel like an old friend and a stranger at the same time? Was it my own wishful thinking imagining a connection that no longer existed, or was it possible that even with the time apart, there was still a piece of me that he held in the palm of his hand?

"I wouldn't even know where to start."

"What do they call you?" I asked.

"What do you mean?"

"You know, your pilot name?"

His smile deepened. "My call sign?"

I nodded.

"Thor."

And then I remembered Bandit saying something like that before I saw Eric and everything else just stopped mattering. It fit him perfectly. Maybe it was the red hair. Or the way he carried himself. He had the whole warrior-god thing down pat.

"Is it weird that I don't call you Thor?" My lips twitched. It somehow seemed wrong to call a thirty-two-year-old man by such a moniker, but at the same time I remembered how all of the guys had introduced themselves by their call signs.

"Not weird at all. I like that you call me Eric. No one else does anymore."

I didn't know what to say to that one, but I guessed if anyone could claim an intimacy with him, it made sense that it would be me.

"Is it everything you thought it would be?"

I tried—and probably, failed—to keep the bite out of my voice.

"No."

I took another sip of my coffee, gripping the ceramic cup, needing something to hold on to.

"It's all-consuming," he answered after a beat. "It's not just your job; it's everything. It controls every aspect of your life, and you never leave it at home. You're always on call essentially, always waiting to see where you'll be needed. It makes it hard to remember to live at times, to just enjoy the moment, because you're always looking forward, always preparing for the next deployment, the next TDY. Always leaving, always going, never just standing still."

He'd just described a good chunk of my fears ten years ago.

"It sounds exhausting."

"It can be. In the beginning, the first few years, it was so fucking cool. I mean, I fly F-16s for a living. You can't get much better than that. But then, little by little, it starts to chip away at everything. It's hard always being 'on.' Easy to forget why I do it in the first place when I get so caught up in the minutiae of it all." He steepled his fingers together, his elbows resting on the table. "I think I lose sight of the big picture, of my role, because I'm just trying to get through the day to day. Because I'm so fucking tired." He grimaced. "Sorry. I don't mean to sit here and unleash my shit on you. I know I'm lucky to have a job that, for the most part, I love. Lucky that I make a good living at it. I don't mean to complain."

Megan came over and set my cinnamon roll on the table in front of me and a bowl of oatmeal in front of Eric. She wiggled her eyebrows suggestively at me, and I fought the flush spreading over my cheeks. I figured she'd recognized him by now.

We both dug into our food, silence settling over the table. I tried to tell myself that it was an uncomfortable silence, but we knew each other way too well for that. We'd always been able to talk to each other about anything, and even though I didn't know much about the military, it was hard to resist the urge to want to be there for him. Did he have anyone in his life he could talk to? The other guys? A counselor?

This was not good. He wasn't back a day, and I was already worrying about him, letting him into my life.

Eric set his spoon down.

"So how about your job?" He gave me another one of those stomach-tightening smiles. "Is it everything you thought it would be?" he asked, echoing my earlier question.

"Yeah. It kind of is. I work too much, probably. And there are some cases that are heartbreakers—losses that are tough to get over. But I do love it, and I feel like I'm helping people."

"You work at the Solicitor's Office, right?"

I nodded, surprised he'd managed to keep tabs on me all these years.

"That's great. I'm not surprised at all that you're kicking ass. You were always the smartest person I've ever known. Hell, I never would have passed English without you."

God, that took me back.

We'd officially met our junior year of high school when I'd been assigned as his tutor for English lit. Eric had made no secret of how much he hated reading dense British texts, but our after-school study dates had sparked the start of our relationship. So really, I had *Middlemarch* to blame for my current predicament.

Don't ask me about my personal life. Don't ask me about my personal life.

He picked up his spoon again, shoveling the oatmeal into his mouth with a speed that caught me off guard.

He grinned. "What?"

"Nothing."

His grin deepened. "Sorry, habit. You learn how to eat quickly in the military." He slowed down and I found my gaze drawn to his mouth, his lips, his tanned throat, his Adam's apple bobbing as he swallowed.

Attraction was a funny thing. It pitted unlikely people together, reared its ugly head at the most unexpected moments. Like in a diner at seven thirty in the morning, between two people who'd already played all their cards and lost at love the first go-around.

I definitely didn't want to talk about my personal life, and I'd probably regret asking, but I couldn't help wondering:

Had he met someone after me? Had there been other women, other relationships? I mean, sex, yes, obviously. But the rest of it? Had he laughed with someone the way he'd laughed with me, those little lines popping out around his eyes? Had he slept with someone else's head over his heart? Was there someone now? And if there was, why wasn't he sitting across from her now telling her about his fears, his doubts?

"You haven't accepted my friend request, by the way," he said.

I'd been too angry last night, too confused by this new development to think about it. Now it sort of felt like closing the barn door *after* the horses had escaped.

"I know."

"Are you going to?"

I hesitated, feeling more than a little silly. "I don't know. I haven't decided."

"Why?"

"I'm not sure this is a good idea."

"Why?"

"You know why."

"You mentioned that you had a date in the message you sent me. Are you seeing anyone?" he asked, his voice deceptively casual.

Fuck.

I forced myself to shrug, keeping my expression bland. "No one serious."

"But you're dating," he pressed.

I took another bite of my cinnamon roll, buying myself time. "You know how it is."

"It sounds like you've been pretty busy with work. Has there been anyone special?"

Seriously? *You. You, you fucking idiot, you. You were my someone special.* And after that . . . if I'd had abandonment issues after my parents died, having my fiancé dump me in a letter hadn't exactly helped. Trust was a luxury I rarely afforded myself.

"I've had a few relationships throughout the years," I answered, keeping my response deliberately vague.

His voice lowered, his tone going gravelly. "You never married?"

"Nope." There was no need for him to even ask me that. We both knew the Bradbury gossip would have found its way to him if I had married. So what was he poking at? My gaze narrowed, ready to shift the focus onto him. "How about you? Do you have a girlfriend? A legion of angry ex-wives?"

"Now why do you naturally assume that my ex-wives would be angry?" His tone turned silky. "Maybe I have legions of satisfied ex-wives."

I leveled him with my most no-nonsense expression, the one I reserved for dickwad defendants in court.

"Call it a hunch."

His smile wavered, his expression changing again, his moods mercurial like the weather. I couldn't keep up with what he wanted, couldn't figure out what purpose this breakfast served. Were we supposed to be friends? Was he looking for more? Was it guilt that kept him here?

"I owe you an apology."

And just like that, the storm rolled in.

He sighed. "Maybe an 'apology' isn't the right word. I don't even know what is anymore."

I didn't want to do this. Not at seven thirty in the morning, when I had a full day in court ahead of me.

"It's fine."

Liar.

"Becca."

God, it did things to me when he said my name. I didn't know if it was the familiarity of it, or the way he nearly groaned it, as though he ached the same way I did.

But he didn't get to ache. He broke up with me in a letter. I mean, I suppose I was lucky it wasn't an e-mail, but a letter? We hadn't been going steady for only a week. We'd been together for over five years. Engaged. And he couldn't even have the decency to do it in person.

"Why the letter?"

I'd sworn I'd never ask him. That I would never let him see how much it had hurt. But having him here, in front of me—

His eyes swam with guilt. "Because I would never have been able to go through with it if I did it in person. I knew that if I saw you, it would be impossible to leave."

"Apparently not."

"I'm sorry. I made a mistake. You didn't deserve to be treated like that. No one does. I fucked up. I'm trying to make it better."

"I don't want any apology. I don't want anything from you."

"That's fair. I'm sorry just the same, though. So damned sorry."

I looked down at the chipped Formica tabletop to avoid having to look into his eyes, needing the moment to catch my breath, to get myself under control. It really shouldn't be this fucking hard.

I released my coffee cup, realizing I'd been white-knuckling it, and laid my palm flat on the countertop. My gaze drifted to his palm, inches away, his skin just a shade darker than mine, his fingers long, his hand large. There were nicks and scrapes on his fingers, so different from the guys I usually dated with their buffed nails and soft skin.

Something about the sight of that hand sparked a memory in me, heat settling between my legs, a new sort of awareness flooding my body. It had been months since my last boyfriend, and considering I'd basically been cock-blocked on Saturday night, I definitely wasn't immune to the sight of those fingers that had once played my body like a finely tuned instrument.

I swallowed, telling myself to look away, to think of something else, not to remember what it had felt like to have those same fingers slide inside me, stroking me, teasing me, until I came over and over again.

His fingers twitched, and I swore the distance between us diminished. He was so close . . .

Eric reached out, grasping my hand, winding our fingers together before I even had a chance to catch my breath.

Shit.

$\mathcal{S}$ix

BECCA

Eric's hand felt warm against mine—warm and *big*. He squeezed, and even though he touched my fingers, I swore I felt an answering tightness around my heart, as though the power to crush it lay in the palm of his hand.

I wanted to pull back, had never intended to let him get this close, but here we were, and I *didn't* move. The temptation was just too strong to ignore and it felt too good to have him hold my hand.

"I'm so sorry," he whispered again, his voice and eyes full of an emotion that spelled trouble.

This time I did pull back, too close to losing my heart. Too much time had passed, too much between us. I didn't want to fall into the trap of thinking that this could be something again, of letting old feelings confuse me.

"I need to go."

"Can we get dinner sometime, or coffee, or something?"

"I don't think that's a good idea."

"I know I don't deserve for you to let me in again, not after what I did, but what if we just gave it a chance? If we took things slowly? What if we started as friends?"

I didn't know how I was supposed to answer that one, what "slow" was with people who had the kind of baggage we did. We'd been *engaged*; I didn't know how to pretend we were just two people getting to know each other. At the same time, I didn't really know him. Not anymore. But what was the point of getting to know him if he was just going to leave again?

"What's changed?"

"What do you mean?"

"What's changed?" I repeated. "You're back here, but what's different? What's the point? You're going back to Oklahoma in a few weeks, aren't you?"

He nodded.

"Then what?"

He shifted in his seat, his expression guarded. "Well, we have the deployment coming up, and then I'll probably go on to my next assignment. I don't know where yet."

Yeah, I'd been here before.

"So nothing has changed. Not really."

"I've missed you."

I'd missed him, too. It wasn't enough. It had been ten years. We'd been apart longer than we'd been together. It wasn't like we could just hit "Play" and pick up where we'd left off.

"We still want different things."

He didn't answer me for a beat. "What if we didn't want different things?"

I froze. He knew me too well, knew just how to worm his way back in.

"Don't try to make this about me. Don't come back here with your 'maybes' and your 'what-ifs' and expect me to hang my future on it. I've been here before. I know how this goes. You've been back, what, a day? Do you honestly think that after everything we've been through, I'm going to trust that you want a future together? That you'll actually choose me?

"I'm not going down this road with you again. I've been there and all it did was give me years of heartbreak. I don't trust you anymore. There is no us. Not anymore."

I grabbed my wallet, putting some cash on the table for my breakfast. I got up on shaky legs, not giving him a chance to respond, not sparing him another glance.

THOR

"Have you seen her?"

I sat back in my grandmother's worn recliner, in the house I'd lived in through high school, taking a gulp of the tea she'd poured me, not even a little surprised that she'd lead with Becca.

She'd pretty much raised me in my teens and had been there since the beginning of our relationship. She'd always treated Becca like a member of our family, and when we'd broken up, she'd been the first person to tell me I was an idiot for screwing things up.

"I have."

"How did it go?"

"Not great."

"You broke her heart."

It still didn't get any easier to hear it spoken out loud.

"Yeah."

"She's a tough girl. She's been through a lot, losing her

parents the way she did. You were her only family. And then you left her, too. I'm sure it's hard for her to let you in again."

A lot of Becca's desire to work for the Solicitor's Office was to help people who had suffered similar tragedies in their lives by giving them some small measure of peace. I'd always admired her drive and determination, her strong sense of justice that gave her the conviction to do her job and do it well. Unfortunately, her strong sense of justice occasionally meant she resembled Old Testament God—fire and brimstone, plagues and famine—and right now she was a step away from hurling thunderbolts at me.

She'd let me in for a moment earlier today in the diner, and then the moment passed, and she'd closed me out again. I didn't blame her, but it didn't exactly leave a lot of room for an in with her.

"You're getting older now. Shouldn't it be time for you to think about settling down? Starting a family?" my grandmother asked.

I worked all the time. I was gone all the time, frequently on short notice. Not to mention the deployments. It took a lot of sacrifice and determination to make a military relationship work, and the truth was I'd never cared enough about anyone to put in the effort.

My grandmother was right. I saw what guys like Burn had, had seen the love between Joker and his wife, Dani. I wanted that, too. But every time I imagined myself having a future with someone, it was always Becca.

She'd been there in every relationship. It wasn't fair to all the women in between, but she'd always been the woman I measured everyone else against. There was just a bond there, one I'd never been able to find again.

With her, it felt like we'd gone right back to where we'd

begun, even though ten years had passed between us. Maybe it was how long we'd been together before, the fact that we'd basically grown up together, that I'd always known her better than anyone. Which was also how I knew getting her to trust me again was likely going to be the hardest fucking thing I'd ever done.

And I still wasn't sure what my future held—whether I wanted to stay in the military or get out. For all that the job wore on me, for all that Joker's death had fucked me up, I'd spent a decade building my career, honing my skills to the point that I was now one of the best pilots in the squadron, had already been through my major's board and was just waiting to pin on the rank. It seemed stupid to throw all of that away, to start over at thirty-two in a new career. I'd been a fighter pilot my whole adult life and I hadn't a clue how those skills would translate to the civilian world if I did get out.

As fucking terrifying as it was to white-knuckle it in the jet, the alternative, living my life without a clear path, trying to figure out what I did next when all I'd known, all I'd been good at, was the military, was equally scary.

"You always were a restless boy," my grandmother continued.

I figured "restless" was a polite way of saying that I'd been in and out of trouble for a good chunk of my life. First Becca had saved me, then the military, giving me the structure I needed.

"The two of you were always after different things—you running from home, from the problems with your parents. She always wanted to dig in, to bury her roots deep, to make up for the way her world had been torn away from her."

"I know." At least, I knew now with the benefit of

hindsight and a decade of experience behind me. I hadn't recognized it then, hadn't realized that the more she pushed, the more I pulled away, or understood how much I'd regret having done so.

My grandmother patted my hand, leaning over and pressing a kiss to my cheek. "You'll figure it out. With as much love as the two of you had between you, you'll make it work now."

I hoped she was right.

"What should I do?"

"Figure out what you want. If it's Becca, fight for her. If it's not Becca, then you need to let her go. Give her a chance to find someone who wants to put down roots with her. That girl deserves better than what life has handed her. If you can't be what she needs, then you have to let her go."

"I did that ten years ago."

She gave me a look. "Did you really? Did she let you go? Can you honestly tell me that you gave anyone a chance?" She squeezed my hand again. "Independent of Becca, use this time to get your head on straight. To figure out what's best for you. Have some fun. Visit with friends. You look like you're carrying the weight of the world on your shoulders and you're about to break. Take care of yourself so that you don't."

"I will. I love you. And I'm sorry I didn't come home before, that we just saw each other at holidays in Florida. I should have done a better job."

I called her every week to see how she was doing, but that wasn't nearly enough. When my parents' divorce had gotten crazy, and later when my mother had moved to Florida, leaving me behind, my grandmother had been the one safe haven for me. She'd taken me in even though I'd been a massive pain in the ass, and if I knew what unconditional love was, it was because of her.

I couldn't escape the feeling that I'd failed her, too.

"I love you, Eric. Always. And I'm proud of you."

I swallowed past the lump in my throat. "I love you, too."

"You're home now. That's all that matters."

EVEN

BECCA

I didn't know if it was appearing in court today on the DUI, or Eric's return, but when I got off work, I found myself going to see my parents rather than home.

My parents were buried together on a plot in the center of Bradbury's oldest cemetery. When I was younger, my grandmother brought me here every Sunday after church to pay my respects. When I got older, I came less frequently, but I still tried to visit at least once a month, on their birthdays and holidays. It felt important to remember them and honor them, and somehow my link had become the few memories I clung to and these two stones in the earth.

Not a day went by when I didn't think of them, miss them.

I laid a bouquet of flowers down on my mother's grave first, followed by my father's. I sat down on the bench off to the side of their graves, staring at the words etched there.

BELOVED WIFE AND MOTHER.
DEVOTED HUSBAND AND FATHER.

They'd both been my age now when they died. My mother had worked at a vet clinic, my father as an insurance adjuster. And we'd all been happy. Close. The kind of family that sat down at dinner every night and talked about their day.

That was what I'd missed the most—just having someone to talk to. Having that sense of belonging to someone, of being part of a unit. I missed the big house my parents had built, the one we decorated with white lights and wreaths at Christmas, the kitchen where I helped my mother cook, the wall where my father had marked off my height, recording my growth, the tree where I'd carved my initials.

Maybe that was why I'd pushed Eric to settle down at such a young age, why it had been so important to me that we were building a relationship, that our future included kids, and the white picket fence, and all the things I'd missed out on when my parents died.

For years after they died, I struggled with dreams of death, with the fear that I'd lose the people I loved the most—my grandmother, Lizzie, and later on, Eric. I'd had panic attacks, spent years dealing with the spiral of fear and anxiety at the possibility of losing someone else. And yeah, I'd held on tightly with a clenched fist. And in the end, maybe it was that grip that had pushed him away.

I sat on the bench, talking to my parents, feeling like a weight was lifted off of my shoulders with each minute that passed. And then I saw him, standing a few hundred yards away from me, flowers in hand, laying them down on a grave.

His grandfather's.

We'd accompanied his grandmother out here when we were dating, Eric holding my hand while I visited my parents, us standing with his grandmother while she remembered the husband she'd lost before Eric had come to live with her. Through the town grapevine I'd heard she made sure there were flowers on his grave every single week. It looked like today Eric had made the journey for her.

Our gazes caught across the gravestones and he gave me a little nod, hesitating as though he wasn't sure if he should approach me or not, as if he was waiting for me to make a move, no doubt remembering how we'd left things this morning. Part of me just wanted to be alone, but another part couldn't turn my back on him.

I gave a little nod and he began walking toward me, his strides slow and measured. We didn't speak, but he sat down next to me on the wooden bench, staring at the spot where both my parents lay, in a position we'd assumed so many times before.

I waited for him to say something, but he seemed just as content to sit in the silence as I was, and so we stayed there, close but not touching, a weird sort of peace drifting over me as the beginnings of dusk spread out over the cemetery.

Finally I spoke. "If we're going to be around each other, and let's face it, in a town like Bradbury it'll happen, I don't want to talk about us every time. I don't want to keep rehashing the past. I can't."

"Okay." He was quiet for a minute. "Are you okay?"

He knew me well enough to know my habits, to know that I came here when I was upset, when I felt unmoored and needed to get my bearings.

"I had a bad case today."

"What happened?"

"DUI."

"I'm sorry."

"It's a second offense, but you know he'll just get a slap on the wrist." I stared at those two stones, my vision growing blurry. "But what happens next time? What if he gets into the car with a passenger or he hits someone else rather than a tree? It just seems like we should do more to protect the innocent, like there should be greater consequences for taking a life."

"It has to be frustrating when you don't see justice served."

"It is. I know I'm supposed to believe in the system, have faith in the fact that it works the way it's supposed to, but sometimes it's hard. Sometimes it feels like the system fails the people it's supposed to protect and I'm just a part of it." I leaned back, stretching my legs out, wishing I hadn't forgone yoga. I spent so much time hunched at my desk that by the end of the day I was always sore, my muscles full of kinks. "I shouldn't complain. I'm sorry. It was just"—I kept settling on that word—"frustrating," I finished. "I guess I thought more justice would be served, that being an attorney meant I could help people. Sometimes I feel so impotent."

"You don't have to apologize. Believe me, I get it." He looked up at the sky and away from me. "You don't know how many times I ask myself what I'm doing, why I'm doing it. It feels like we never really accomplish anything, and even when we do, someone just goes and undoes the work. It puts the losses in perspective, I guess.

"My friend's name was Joker. He was a great guy. A really great guy. He was our squadron commander, our boss, but he was the kind of guy who you could have a beer with, who cared if you were having a bad day, if there was shit going on in your life. He was like a brother, and I looked up to him a lot."

"I'm so sorry."

"He had a wife. Dani. She was amazing. Kind of an

unofficial 'mom' to all of us. His death destroyed her. Seeing her like that . . ." His voice trailed off. "It was hard.
Really hard to come back when he didn't.

"With Joker . . ." Again his voice faded, but then seemed
to grow stronger. "I just wonder if his death was worth it.
That doesn't sound right. It's just . . . we go into combat
ready to die. No question. We all want to come home, no
one wants to lose their life, but we assume that risk because
there's a purpose to our missions, the assumption that we're
giving our lives for something bigger than ourselves. But
he didn't die in combat; he died on a training mission. What
did he give his life for?

"When he died, there was this big push in the media, like
we were heroes or something, but the thing is, I don't feel
like a hero. And I don't necessarily want to, either, but I do
want to feel like the sacrifice is worth it, and right now, I just
feel, I don't know . . . like I'm coming up short or something.
Like I spent my professional career trying to make my life
mean something important, trying to make a difference, and
at the end of the day, what have I really accomplished?

"There was an upgrade to the jet a couple months ago.
One that had been in the pipeline for a while, but just trick-
led down to all of the squadrons. It would have saved his
life if he'd had it. Two months made the difference. Where's
the purpose in that? Two fucking months."

I recognized the anger, the grief, the confusion. Understood exactly how he felt. But if he'd come here looking for
some kind of explanation or understanding, I wasn't sure I
had any to give. When I'd lost my parents, I hadn't known
how to deal. I'd gone to counseling, had tried to move past
it, but it hadn't been some enlightening experience; I didn't
learn the meaning of life or anything like that. All I could

say was that I'd come through it to the other end. Somehow. Sort of.

"I wish I had a good answer. Wish I could say something that would make you feel better. I asked myself that question so many times when my parents died. I tried to understand how it could have happened, was obsessed with the idea that if they'd just left a few seconds later, if the guy had one less beer, stayed at the bar two minutes longer, they'd still be alive." I stared at those stones again, at the date etched there. "You go crazy thinking like that, and still, the answers never come."

He reached between us, taking my hand and linking our fingers, squeezing, giving me something to hold on to, even for a moment. It was blurring the lines, but I couldn't resist.

"I'm figuring that out. I just haven't gotten to the letting go part."

"That's the hardest part. The part that takes time. You always carry a part of it with you, but it becomes just infinitesimally smaller somehow. You still have days when it hits you, days when it's harder to deal with than others. But you get through it."

"You were so young when you lost your parents."

"Yeah, I was."

"I don't know how you did it."

I shrugged. "I had to. There were times when I didn't think I could. Times when all I wanted was to be with them. That goes, too, though. As does the guilt. You find other things to live for, to get you up in the morning, other ways to honor them."

"Like you're doing now."

"I hope so. On good days, I feel like my life has some

purpose. Like I'm helping people. On the not-so-good days, I feel like I'm drowning a bit."

He didn't say anything, but then again, he didn't need to. We'd always understood each other, always had this kind of connection.

I didn't know if it was the being raised by grandmothers thing, or the fact that we were both working on ourselves, both searching for something beyond us, both wanting more than what we had that brought us together, but there had been something there that had formed an instant connection, one that had yet to taper off, even as I wished it didn't exist at all. He understood me in a way I wasn't sure anyone else did.

He swallowed, his voice strained. "I'm sorry about your grandmother. I heard she passed away a few years ago. I should have called."

"I didn't expect you to."

"I still should have. I wanted to. I just didn't think you would want to hear from me and I didn't want to make things worse for you, to hurt you more than I already had."

I wondered if his grandmother had kept him in the loop about all the changes in my life, how many times he'd thought of me. I wasn't sure which I preferred—for him to have thought of me often or for me to have been little more than a footnote in his mind.

Liar.

"I should get going." We were drifting dangerously into territory where I just didn't have it in me to go.

I rose from the bench, not looking at him.

"I'll see you around."

He didn't answer me, didn't try to stop me. He just stayed there on that bench while I walked away, leaving the people I'd loved and lost behind me.

THOR

I stayed on the bench long after she'd left, my gaze trained to the direction in which she'd walked away, as if that somehow could bring her back, my mind racing. I felt like the carelessness of my actions kept springing up again and again, the reminders that I'd caused her pain everywhere I turned.

I hadn't come back to Bradbury because I couldn't stand the image of myself that I saw here, the way the town and all of the memories it contained reflected back the worst version I could be, the way she reflected an image of myself that filled me with shame.

I knew the reasons behind why I'd left, remembered feeling like the walls were closing in on a future that I wanted but wasn't ready for, a future that had seemed like a good idea in abstract but, the closer and closer it came, began to feel like a noose around my neck.

The only thing I'd been sure about was her. And for a long time, I'd thought that was enough. That for all the moments when I stumbled, when I didn't know who I was or what I wanted out of my life, she would be there, steady and strong for me to lean on.

But it wasn't enough.

I didn't want her carrying me. Didn't want to end up like my parents—my mother working her ass off supporting us, working two jobs while my father drank himself into a stupor every day until one day he just said fuck it, and left everything behind him.

I wanted to be a man she could be proud of, a man who would be a better kind of father, the kind of father who was there for my kids, who taught them not to make some of the mistakes I'd made, the stupid acts of rebellion that had sent me to juvie and had me repeating a grade in high school. I'd wanted to be someone I had no clue how to be, and the second I spoke to the military recruiter, when he arranged for me to talk to one of the F-16 pilots stationed at Shaw, it was like something clicked. Something I'd only ever felt with Becca. Suddenly, I'd known exactly what I wanted to do with my life, known the kind of man I wanted to be.

Before I joined the military, we'd been the odd couple. Becca had graduated as the valedictorian of our high school class, had gotten into the University of South Carolina on a full ride. In the back of my mind, I'd always known she could have gone to a more prestigious school, but she'd said she wanted to stay close to home—close to me. I'd have been lying if I didn't admit that it had bothered me the way people looked at us like they were just waiting for me to drag her down to my level, like she could have done so much better than me. No guy wanted to feel like the girl he was with had settled to be with him, even though I knew Becca had never felt that way.

But still. It was enough to light a fire under my ass. To make me determined to be someone worthy of her. And then, of course, I'd lost it all anyway, and the irony of it was that I didn't like the guy staring back at me in the mirror much anymore, either.

BECCA

I hit "Accept" on Eric's friend request when I got home that night, feeling like I was sliding deeper into something I wouldn't be able to pull my way out of. Because, of course, it didn't just stop at me accepting his friend request. No, I couldn't resist the urge to go through the pictures, flipping through a slideshow of the last decade of his life.

Mistake. Big fucking mistake.

There were women. Lots and lots of women. Pictures of Eric all over the world with guys from his squadron, looking like he was having the time of his life.

I hadn't exactly been in a convent the last decade, and I definitely hadn't expected that he'd been celibate or anything, but damn, it was one thing to acknowledge it in the back of your mind and another entirely to see it. Over and over again.

I shut down my computer, feeling like an idiot for how easily I'd let him back in, or how I'd let myself hope that we could somehow be in each other's lives again. Whatever he said, I struggled to believe he'd spent the last decade missing me. So why was he back now? Because he knew I would always be there for him when he needed it, despite the past? Was I just a stop for him along the way back to something bigger and better? Was I an idiot for trusting him?

I'd wanted to believe he'd changed, that he'd realized that he'd made a mistake all of those years ago. But I just didn't know anymore, and despite how easy it was for me to imagine falling for him all over again, I couldn't make myself let my guard down with him.

Love was easy; trust was the hard part.

EIGHT

BECCA

It was no small feat to avoid someone in a town as tiny as Bradbury, but somehow I managed it throughout the week, impressing even myself with the level of subterfuge I employed. I caught glimpses of Eric—a flash of red hair, the view from behind while he ran down the street—but I always managed to escape before he could notice me.

I needed time. And tequila. And a night out with my girlfriends. And dancing. Definitely dancing.

"Do you know how long it's been since I've had a girls' night?" Lizzie asked as we walked into Liberty on Friday night.

It hadn't taken a ton of arm-twisting to get her to come out for the night, and because Adam was a truly awesome guy, he'd volunteered to watch the baby so Lizzie could have a night off and be my wing woman. They'd been married long enough for him to fully appreciate the implication of Eric blowing through my life again.

I scanned the crowded bar looking for Rachel and Julie.

The four of us had made the plan to hang out, going back and forth over the best spot for it.

Nightlife in Columbia was pretty much divided into two relatively close sections of town—the Vista and Five Points. The bars in Five Points always had a more college feel to them, and while the Vista was close to the Carolina campus, it tended to attract an older and more professional crowd.

I spotted Rachel and Julie waving at us from a booth and Lizzie and I wound our way through the crowd.

Rachel stood and hugged me. "Whoa. You look hot tonight."

I grinned and said hi to Julie. "Thanks. You guys do, too."

I'd sort of broken the whole don't-wear-white-after-Labor-Day rule in favor of an amazing dress I'd found a few months ago and never had a chance to wear. It was strapless and fitted at the waist, and then it belled out into a flirty, short skirt. It wasn't overly sexy or anything, but it was pretty and fun, and one of those outfits that immediately made you feel better the second you put it on.

Given the week I'd had, I needed something to make me feel better.

We exchanged greetings, Lizzie and I sliding into the booth with them.

Rachel's phone went off and she looked down at the screen, typing something before glancing my way, a nervous expression on her face.

"So that guy from last weekend, Easy? He's back in town for a friend's wedding or something. I guess it's the same guy whose bachelor party he flew out for last weekend. He's with Bandit and Merlin, and they were talking about maybe meeting up with us, but I don't want you to be uncomfortable, so if it's too weird, I can tell them we're just having a girls' night."

I'd filled her in on my past with Eric when I called and apologized for bailing on our night out.

I hesitated, not sure I wanted another night ruined by fighter pilots. But the look on Rachel's face was one I hadn't seen on her before, and I hated to get in the way of her chance to see Easy if she did really like him.

"Is Eric—I mean, Thor—with them?"

"I don't think so. He didn't mention him. Do you want me to ask?"

Fuck being nonchalant. I definitely wasn't in the mood to deal with Eric. It had been another hellacious week at work and I desperately needed things to be fun—and pardon the pun, easy—tonight.

"Yeah, go ahead and ask him."

Rachel's fingers flew over the keyboard. Her phone pinged again.

"Easy says he's not with them."

That was good enough for me.

"Yeah, tell them to come then. I'm in."

Okay, fine, maybe fighter pilots weren't that bad. It wasn't fair to give them all a bum rap just because Eric had broken my heart.

"How did you climb down from the water tower?" I asked, laughing as I took a sip of my margarita.

Bandit, Merlin, and Easy had been regaling us with stories all night, and even I had to admit, they were pretty fucking hilarious. It sounded like being a fighter pilot was basically like joining a fraternity on steroids, with a whole

lot of danger and responsibility added in. I figured it made
sense that they needed to blow off steam once in a while,
considering how crazy their lives were.

Bandit flashed me a wolfish grin. "Very carefully. I was
fucking terrified that I'd fall, and even more terrified that
the wing commander would catch me. Some commanders
are cool about that stuff, other guys not so much."

He draped his arm around the back of the booth, leaning
in to me.

"Do you want to go get another drink at the bar?"

I stared down at my margarita glass, surprised to see I'd
already finished it. I'd pretty much matched the guys drink
for drink tonight, and considering they definitely partied
harder than I did on a regular basis, I was struggling to
keep up.

He held out his hand, a whiff of cologne filling my nostrils, and I waged a little inner war with myself. He seemed
like a nice guy and he was cute, and while there weren't
sparks or anything, the last thing I wanted was to experience
that plummeting-to-my-death, butterflies-in-my-stomach
feeling I got around Eric. Nothing would happen here; I
wasn't going to go home with him, didn't even see myself
kissing him given his connection to Eric, but I figured there
was no harm in being nice or flirting a bit.

I grinned. "Sounds like a plan." I took his hand and followed him to the bar, not oblivious to the envious glances
thrown my way. Between Easy and Bandit, we'd definitely
cornered the market on *fine* at our table.

I stayed close to Bandit while he ordered our drinks at
the bar, my hand still in his. He turned back when he'd
finished, his free hand reaching out to capture a strand of
my hair, twirling it around his fingers, mischief in his eyes.

I shook my head in amusement. "You do realize that I'm not going to sleep with you, right?"

"You say that now. Give me an hour or two."

I laughed. "Are all of you guys this arrogant?"

"We prefer confident."

"I bet you do."

"Are you not sleeping with me because of Thor?"

Way to be direct.

"Not entirely. Okay, maybe a bit. Let's just say that I don't have the greatest track record with fighter pilots. Plus it's weird. You guys are friends. We were together. Ergo, weird."

He grinned. "Ergo?"

I rolled my eyes. "Whatever. You're cute and fun, but I just don't need complicated right now. I wanted to let loose a bit tonight; if you want to go hang out with another girl, I totally understand. I don't want to crash your plans for the evening."

He tugged on the strand of hair, pulling me closer so that our bodies brushed against each other.

"One, Thor and I aren't friends. Our paths have crossed because the F-16 community is small and we have friends in common, but we've never hung out or anything like that. Two, you're cute. So if you don't mind, I have big plans to flirt with you tonight. Even if that's all there is."

No sooner had the words left his mouth than my gaze swept the room and I froze, locking on to Eric standing near the rest of our group, staring at me and Bandit, his mouth in a hard line, his eyes flinty.

Fuck.

And just like that, as though someone had flipped a switch inside of me, I came alive. I'd spent most of the evening with a hot fighter pilot flirting with me, and I couldn't have cared less. Eric walked in and I felt a flash of heat, nerves pinging inside my stomach like a pinball machine. His gaze ran over me from head to toe, each part of my body coming alive as his stare scalded me.

Fine.

Maybe I wanted him to look.

Maybe some part of me that still remembered how it had felt to open that letter, thinking he'd sent me something to let me know he missed me and getting something else entirely, wanted him to see me like this, dressed to kill, flirting with a hot guy. Maybe some part of me that was just a bit petty and mean, and nowhere near over our history, wanted him to look at me like something he'd lost and would never recover.

I wanted him to burn for me, ache for me, wanted to give him the same fucking sleepless nights he'd given me. So yeah, I welcomed that jealous look in his eyes, even if I shouldn't have, because at least I'd gotten under his skin, at least I made him feel like he'd made me feel.

I turned away from Eric, my heart hammering so hard I could barely catch my breath. I forced myself to smile up at Bandit, and he grabbed my hand, tugging me away from the bar and leading me onto the empty space that had turned into an impromptu dance floor.

I swore I could feel Eric's eyes tracking me through the crowd.

One of my favorite songs came on over the speakers in the bar, and I couldn't resist the urge to throw my head back and move my hips, losing myself in the rhythmic beat.

This was what I'd so desperately needed—just to let go and relax a bit. To have some fun. And even though it would likely get me in trouble, deep down I knew, even as I danced with one hot fighter pilot, I really danced for another.

He watched me the entire time.

THOR

I walked into Liberty, my gaze peeled on the crowd, searching for Becca.

Easy had texted me two hours ago and mentioned that she was here, and I'd gone back and forth over whether I should come out at all. It hadn't escaped my notice that she'd pretty much been avoiding me all week, whatever truce we'd reached in the cemetery on Wednesday apparently forgotten, and while part of me knew I should give her the space she needed, another part of me was afraid that she would use the space to keep a wedge between us.

I couldn't apologize, couldn't grovel at her feet, if she wouldn't forgive me. And right now, she was a locked door I couldn't break through. I'd thought I stood a chance, thought that the fact that she still talked to me like I meant something to her, like we were friends, meant we had a shot. But now it felt like that had just been wishful thinking, and I really had blown it with her.

So this was it. My Hail Mary, Hallelujah, final attempt at getting her to let me in. I'd caused her enough pain over the years; I didn't want to keep doing it. If she truly wanted me out of her life, then I'd give her that.

I spotted Easy first, his arm wrapped around the same girl he'd been with the first night—a girl with hair eerily similar to Dani's. Easy saw me across the crowd and waved me over, the girl—Rachel or something—tensing immediately at the sight of me and answering the question of whether she knew who I was to Becca.

I cut through the crowd, still searching for her, nerves rolling around in my stomach.

Easy jerked his head in greeting. "Hey, man."

Rachel looked ready to bolt and warn Becca I was here.

"Hey, how's it going?" I asked, glancing over his shoulder, trying to make out Becca's features in the sea of people. Liberty was packed tonight.

His lips curved. "She's by the bar with Bandit."

Shit.

I didn't know Bandit that well, but we'd been out together before, and if he was with Becca, it definitely wasn't because he wanted to be friends.

Easy shot me a pointed look that irked the shit out of me. "Can you blame the guy?"

Fuck.

My gaze drifted to the bar, and then I froze.

Becca stood in a corner, the lights shining down on her like a fucking halo, the skirt of her dress brushing against Bandit.

She looked so beautiful that I felt it like a pang in my chest, the smile on her face one I'd seen so many times before, aimed at me. The one I'd lost. Thrown away. She looked like she was having fun, and then Bandit leaned in closer and said something that made her laugh, and her whole face transformed, her shoulders shaking, eyes sparkling.

I held my breath as her gaze drifted through the crowd; my heart hammered, waiting for the moment . . .

Our gazes locked, her body stiffening, the smile sliding off her face.

It knocked me back like a blow.

I'd envisioned finding a way to talk to her tonight, maybe dance with her, flirt with her; I hadn't envisioned standing here with my heart in my hand, watching her flirt with Bandit of all fucking people, as what little hope I'd clung to died a bit inside.

I waited to see if she'd acknowledge me somehow, the

plea that she'd throw me one of her smiles—something, anything—battering me inside. A wave, even. Just some sign that she *saw* me, that she still cared, that there might be a chance for us to put the past behind us.

I'd missed her this week, missed seeing her face, hearing her laugh. We'd been apart for a decade, and somehow the glimpses I'd had of her had made everything harder, bringing back all those feelings we'd had for each other with a sharpness that pierced me.

Look at me. Please. Forgive me. Let me in.

I stood there like an idiot, the sound of Easy saying my name over and over again drowned out by the bar noise and the pounding of my heart.

And then she did turn, shifting her body away from me, tilting her face up to Bandit, her lips curving in a smile I knew all too well.

I watched, my feet rooted to the ground, my heart in my stomach, a sick, cold feeling sliding through my veins as Bandit led her out onto the dance floor and into his arms.

It hurt to look at her, to watch her body sway. Hurt to watch her give all that beauty and fire to Bandit. I'd never really liked the guy all that much to begin with—he was too cocky in the air, too full of himself on the ground—but now I really didn't like him. There was no fucking way he didn't know who Becca was to me and the fact that he clearly didn't give a shit about it spoke volumes to how many ways he'd screwed over guy code.

Asshole. I hoped his next assignment had him flying freaking drones out of Creech.

Easy slid onto the bar stool next to me, and I stifled a groan.

The last thing I wanted was relationship counseling from the guy currently screwing his way through heartbreak.

"Go away."

"You're drunk," Easy countered.

I'd passed by drunk three beers ago.

"Do you think this is going to win her over?"

Fucking Easy.

"I'm fine."

"We both know you aren't fine."

I glared at him. "And you are? You want to talk about how many times I watched you make an ass of yourself 'cause you couldn't stand the sight of Dani and . . ." My voice trailed off, the knot in my stomach that had been there since that night growing at the thought of Joker.

"Fuck you. I didn't throw away a good thing because I was an ass."

I flinched as his words hit their mark.

"If I'd ever had a shot with Dani, if things had been different, if I'd met her first, I would have done everything I could, become whatever I had to be to keep her. I wouldn't have been a pussy about it, too afraid to make a move, ready to throw in the towel because things became too hard."

"She hates me," I replied, my voice bleak, ice filling my veins as Becca leaned in closer, her hand on Bandit's chest, a smile on her lips and laughter in the air.

"So change her mind."

"She won't talk to me. Won't look at me." I gestured toward where she was dancing with Bandit.

"So you're saying Bandit has more game than you do."

I glared at him.

"I mean, that sounds like what you're saying. Bandit just swooped in on your girl and you're, what, rolling over and taking it?"

I couldn't help feeling like she was slipping through my fingers if not already gone.

"Do you think she's going to go home with him?"

I shouldn't have asked the question—the words brought a knot in my stomach and another flash of pity on Easy's face—and in that moment, I really got what it had been like for him to watch Dani and Joker together.

You were jealous, even though you had absolutely no right to be, but telling yourself that didn't do a damned thing to make the pain go away. So you stood there, drowning in quicksand, watching as the one thing you wanted remained firmly out of your grasp.

Except I wasn't Easy. And Becca wasn't Dani—she wasn't married, hadn't given her heart to someone else.

So fuck it, maybe *this* was my Hail Mary.

$\mathscr{N}$INE

BECCA

It was exhausting work, pretending you were having more fun than you really were. My cheeks hurt from smiling, my feet had begun weeping, begging me to stop dancing an hour ago, and my arms were growing tired from fending off Bandit's increasing advances. Not to mention the pounding in my head that told me I was either getting sick or had drunk too much—or some combination of the two. I was surprised I didn't have a crick in my neck from how much time I'd spent looking at Eric when he wasn't looking at me, trying to gauge his reaction.

I was too old for this shit.

I didn't know what I'd intended tonight, hadn't really thought my actions through beyond wanting to get a reaction out of Eric, but I was beginning to think that all I'd proven was that I wasn't anywhere near over him. And then I saw him, cutting through the crowd, his gaze trained on the spot where Bandit's arm draped loosely around my waist.

I swallowed a lump in my throat, unable to do anything but stare at Eric, everything else falling away.

God, he was beautiful. There was an art to the way he walked. A lazy, long-limbed grace that ensured all eyes were on him as he parted the crowd. Even now, those blue eyes downcast, his jaw clenched, his shoulders hunched in defeat, there was something about him that screamed, "This one," something that set him apart from every other guy in the room. I'd wanted to hit him where it hurt, to make him feel every inch of his loss, but I hadn't predicted that the sight of him like this wouldn't make me feel like I'd won anything, only like I wanted to soothe the ache inside him.

Maybe I was a fool. I probably was. But the thing with love was that once you felt it, it was impossible to turn it off.

So I'd miscalculated tonight when I'd thought I wanted to bring him to his knees, because at the end of the day, all it had done was bring me right down next to him.

Eric halted in front of us, Bandit's arm tightening around my waist. Eric didn't spare him a glance, didn't do any of those annoying, stereotypical, he-man, I'm-going-to-pee-on-you-now-to-mark-you-as-mine things that guys did sometimes. Instead he looked me straight in the eye and asked, "Can we talk for a second?"

I nodded, the decision already made before he'd even made the journey over.

I turned toward Bandit, offered a shrug, and forced a smile. "I should go. Sorry. Thanks for the dancing."

To his credit, he just nodded and released me.

Eric held out his hand, and I hesitated for a beat, and then I placed my palm in his, letting him lead me through the crowd, out the front door, until we reached the sidewalk. He stopped a little bit away from the entrance, until our bodies were tucked into a dark corner of the building that shielded us from the crowds forming on the street.

For a moment, I just relaxed into the beauty of the night—the slight breeze in the air signaling the transition from sticky summer heat toward leaf-changing fall. I welcomed the quiet, the freedom from the bass and the loud voices, the open air hitting my skin rather than the jab of sweaty elbows. And of course, there was Eric, standing next to me, his hands shoved into his jeans' pockets, towering over me, the scent of his cologne and the faint smell of the beers he'd drunk surrounding me.

I leaned back against the building, closing my eyes, tilting my face up to the sky. When I opened my eyes, Eric stood in the same place, staring at me.

I blinked. Still there.

"It feels like a dream."

"What?"

"You being here. In South Carolina. With me."

"Not a nightmare?"

"It depends on the day you ask me."

He shot me a wry smile. "That's fair."

I swallowed, the butterflies kicking up in my stomach. "It's been ten years."

I didn't know why that felt important to say, but it did. It felt like so much had passed between us, like we'd missed out on so much of each other's lives—really the most important parts of them, the parts when we'd been growing into ourselves, figuring out who we were and what we wanted out of life—and still, he stood here before me, and suddenly it was like nothing had changed. I was at once both twenty-one and thirty-one, and both versions of me—the girl I'd been and the woman I was now—gravitated toward Eric.

"Yeah, it has." He was quiet for a moment, staring down at the ground, and then his gaze was back on mine and another wave of flutters ripped through me.

Freaking butterflies. I would have thought I'd outgrown them, but apparently not.

He cocked his head toward the bar. "Bandit?"

I shook my head, answering his unspoken question, giving him the truth, even if it got me into trouble.

"You."

I didn't know if the alcohol had loosened my tongue, or if it was the emotion on his face and the pain in his voice. Either way, I didn't have it in me to lie.

He let out an oath.

"I should have come back sooner. Should have made things up to you a long time ago."

"Why didn't you?"

I needed to understand. I hadn't given him a chance to explain earlier, had been so focused on my anger that I hadn't been willing to listen to any of his reasons. Maybe I'd been afraid that if I had, he would chip away at the wall I'd erected around myself, the one that crumbled after a few days in his presence anyway.

He didn't answer me for a beat and I liked him more for not being glib, for not just giving me the easy answer.

"In the beginning, I didn't come back because I didn't know what I was missing." He hesitated and I saw the exact moment when he decided to give me the truth, even as it was tough for me to hear. "When we broke up, I missed you, but I went straight into pilot training and busting my ass to make sure I didn't wash out, to ensure that I was at the top of my class so that I could get a fighter spot. I worked twelve-hour days, studied when I wasn't working, and didn't have much time for anything else.

"When I graduated and pinned on my wings, I went straight into the F-16 basic course, and if I'd thought pilot training was tough, that was even harder. I was surrounded by guys who'd all graduated as the best of their pilot training classes, everyone willing to do whatever it took to get to the top.

"You know me. I didn't come from a military background, didn't realize how important that phase of my career was until I was thrown into it and I learned that the impression I made on my commanders would set the tone for my future. So my life became about flying. Being the best pilot I could be. I'd be lying if I didn't admit that I thought of you, dreamed of you, missed you so badly I ached for you, but at the same time, you have to know that my entire life revolved around getting through, because if it hadn't, I never would have.

"Then it was my first assignment, trying to make a good impression at a new squadron, deploying for the first time, more twelve-to-fourteen-hour days, getting up at the crack of dawn and going to work and then coming home when it was dark and rinse and repeat, doing it again.

"I'm not complaining. I fucking loved it. But that was my life. There wasn't a lot of room for me to miss you. A lot of room for anything other than trying to be the best pilot I could be. I dated, but there was never anything other than casual, because that was all I had room for. And maybe, because I didn't have anything left to give. I'd already given you my heart, and even if I'd wanted to, there was no way in hell I could get it back."

I had missed him, mourned him, but at the same time, I'd had law school, and then my career, to keep me busy. Lizzie had tried to get me to date so many times, and even though there had been a string of guys, none of them had even come close to meaning something special to me. I hadn't been willing to prioritize those relationships, to give them the attention and effort they needed to sustain themselves. Instead I'd buried myself in work, not letting anyone get close. So in a way, I understood. That also didn't mean I wasn't wary.

"Everything you're saying is in the past tense. So what changed? Why are you here now? What do you want now?"

What do you want from me?

He held my gaze, looking like he was searching for something there.

"I don't know exactly. I guess it started off gradually at first. It started to wear on me—the coming home to an empty house, landing after a deployment or a TDY and not having anyone there waiting for me. I started thinking about what it would be like to put down roots, to have a home, a family. Started seeing other guys and what they had, and wondering if I was throwing my life away. I don't know. I'm tired. So fucking tired. I've been going balls to the wall for the better part of a decade and I don't know how much more I have to give. And after Joker . . ."

His voice trailed off, the pain there making my stomach sink.

"How long ago was it?"

"Four months. I started to feel this way before Joker, but after . . ." He took a deep breath. "I just started to wonder if it was all worth it, you know? When he died, I wondered what my life was all about.

"There's no one special in my life. No one whose life I make special. Joker had that. He was married and they had this great marriage, and his wife, Dani, looked at him like he was the love of her life. And then in a flash, he was gone, and she was a widow, and I watched her grieve for him, saw how his death rocked her, and while I know he loved to fly, I couldn't help but wonder if he would have done things differently if he'd known how it would all play out.

"The truth is, we don't think about dying when we're up in the sky. Sure, there are moments in sorties when I have close calls, times when my brain just becomes a litany of 'fucks' as I deal with whatever emergency has cropped up in the jet, as I do everything I can to have to keep from fucking ejecting, but it's not real, you know? It becomes so normal, living on the edge, that at times I forget how dangerous it really is. That I could die. It doesn't feel real until it is, and I don't know, I just keep asking myself if it's worth it. When Joker died, he left behind someone who'd loved him, who mourns him. If I died . . ."

I couldn't help it. *Fuck.* I took a step forward, closing the distance between us, hating the words falling from his lips, hating the way he spoke of his life. It was true—this was the path he'd chosen, the decision he'd made when we were young, but at the same time, I knew better than anyone that sometimes you couldn't see your path until you were already so far down it that there was no way back.

"I can promise you . . ." The words stuck in my throat, blocked by a boulder of fear and do-not-go-there-he-will-crush-your-heart-to-dust. "That if something happened to you, *I* would care." I swallowed. "A lot."

My heart hammered, my hand moving to cup his cheek. The second I touched him, his body stiffened, his eyes widening. I was pretty sure his expression mirrored mine since I wasn't sure who was more shocked by the gesture.

And then some part of me gave up fighting it, and I leaned forward, rising to my toes, my mouth colliding with his.

Kissing him felt a lot like coming home.

My hand slid to his neck, threading through his hair, pulling his head down to mine, pressing my body into the curve of his, and then his arm hooked around my waist, his cock brushing against me, his lips parting, his tongue swooping in.

He tasted so freaking good, his lips and tongue laying siege to mine. His mouth contained the kind of hunger I couldn't ignore if I tried, his hands holding me like he never wanted to let me go.

His teeth sank down on my lower lip, drawing it between his, sucking on it, laving my flesh with his tongue as my nipples tightened and my clit throbbed.

It was both familiar and new all at the same time. As though I was kissing a stranger, because there was a desperation to this kiss that hadn't been there before. This was a decade of pent-up unrequited whatever-we-were, and we kissed like we couldn't get enough of each other.

My hands were all over him, gripping his hair, stroking his neck, moving lower to feel his impressive shoulders, going lower, my hands gripping his biceps, holding him close to me. His body felt amazing against mine and I found a whole new appreciation for the physical demands of his job. He'd always been in shape, but he'd never felt this hard against me, his muscles impressive enough to make my mouth go dry and make my body so very wet.

I moaned as his hands gripped my ass, pulling me closer, his leg sliding between mine so that I rode him, the friction sending even more heat through me.

My fingers dug into his skin, and he made a noise somewhere between a moan and a growl, nipping at my lip again, his hips canting toward me so I could feel every inch of how badly he wanted me.

And by the thick, hard length brushing against me, apparently he wanted me a lot.

THOR

Of all the ways I'd imagined this playing out, I hadn't dared to hope that the evening would end with my arms around Becca, my mouth on hers, drowning in the taste of her. And I definitely never would have predicted that the reality of kissing her would blow the memory out of the fucking water.

Whatever doubts and fears I'd had were silenced the instant our mouths connected. I'd been an idiot before and thrown away the best thing that had ever happened to me, but there was no way I was making the same mistake again. I'd wanted an in with her, some kind of sign that hope wasn't lost, and if this wasn't a flashing-light-burning-bush kind of sign, I didn't know what was.

She pulled away first, her lips swollen, eyes wide, her chest rising and falling as she tried to catch her breath. I knew exactly how she felt, because I couldn't have gotten control if I tried. Forget the beers, I was utterly wrecked by her.

I ran my tongue over my bottom lip, capturing the last taste of her while she watched, that familiar look in her eyes that my body instantly recognized.

I took a step back, needing to put distance between us before I did something I'd regret. I wanted her and she wanted me, but as easy as it would be to fall into bed with her again, there was still too much between us for sex to do anything but complicate an already messy situation. I wanted her, but I wanted more than her body, even as I didn't know what I had to offer her in return.

Becca swallowed, my gaze immediately drawn to her mouth.

"That was unexpected."

I couldn't fight the grin at how cute she sounded—as I remembered just how much she hated the unexpected, how she tended to want everything in her life to fit into a neat container that she could label and manage. What she called "unexpected," I called "inevitable," because there was no way we could be near each other, setting off the kind of sparks we did, without something catching on fire.

"Go on a date with me."

She blinked. "Are you joking?"

I stepped forward, taking advantage of the way she just stood there, staggered, and twined my fingers through her hair, pressing my lips to hers.

"One date."

Her mouth opened, her breath mingling with mine, her body relaxing into my embrace.

"No." Her hands settled on my hips, holding on to me as her words pushed me away.

"Becca."

I sucked on her bottom lip as she shuddered against me, the grip on my hips tightening, her body arching forward.

She tasted amazing. So fucking sweet. All soft curves and sex.

"Give me a chance," I whispered against her mouth. "Please."

She stilled and I waited, everything hanging on her answer.

"Maybe."

One word. It wasn't the one I wanted, but it was enough to give me hope, and considering it was probably more than I deserved, I'd take it.

"Okay."

I held out a hand to her, feeling like the luckiest guy in the world when she slid her palm into mine, following me back inside the bar to find the rest of the group.

"Maybe" was a lot to hang everything on, but right now I clutched it in my fist, praying it was enough.

$\mathcal{T}$EN

BECCA

I woke up feeling like death had visited me sometime after I'd fallen asleep. I would have blamed the alcohol and the late night out, but I figured the brunt of it came from the congestion filling my nose and head, the ache in my throat, the watery eyes, the chills wracking my limbs.

I groaned as I studied my reflection in the bathroom mirror—taking in the pale skin, red eyes, puffy face.

Yep. I was definitely sick.

I gave up, crawling back into bed, welcoming the warmth of my sheets and the comfort of my soft mattress. I needed to get up and take some medicine, make myself tea or something, but I felt like shit and all I wanted to do was just lie in bed, every step making me dizzy and weak.

The sound of my doorbell ringing screwed that plan up.

I groaned, contemplating just ignoring it and weighing the odds of whether it was Lizzie, coming to pump me for information on what had happened with Eric last night. She'd ended up driving both of us back to Bradbury, and the silence in the car had spoken volumes. She'd dropped me off with a meaningful look I recognized as code for *spill later*.

I had no clue what to tell her. We'd kissed and I'd sort of reached the conclusion that the likelihood of us eventually having sex was pretty much inevitable. I just wished I could parse out my feelings about the whole thing, that I could separate out the emotion and love stuff and just enjoy what he offered—really great orgasms and a lot of fun. I tried to tell myself we could do no-strings, even as we were connected by more strings than a fucking puppet.

So yeah, best friend or not, I wasn't entirely sure I was ready to have a conversation about this with Lizzie.

The doorbell rang again and I finally gave in, grabbing my bathrobe from the foot of the bed and wrapping it around my body, running my hands through my hair, trying to get most of the tangles out.

I padded to the front door, wincing with each step. I was definitely going to give myself a big dose of cold meds and then go back to bed when Lizzie left. Maybe if I was lucky, I could convince her to make me tea, or soup, or something.

I pulled open my door, prepared for Lizzie, and got someone else instead.

Eric.

Shit.

I didn't know what I'd done to deserve these awkward run-ins, but I would happily settle any bad karma that I'd accumulated in order to clear the scales.

Eric stood on the doorstep wearing a gray long-sleeved tee, the sleeves pushed up to expose his forearms, his reddish-blond hair messy and tousled. His lips curved, something that looked a lot like concern in his gaze.

"Are you okay?"

"I'm dying," I croaked, glaring at how freaking *healthy* he looked. There was a flash of embarrassment over the fact that he'd caught me in my ratty bathrobe, cocooned in a blanket, unwashed hair—*fuck*, I forgot to brush my teeth. I took a step back into the apartment, hoping that put enough distance between us.

Seriously, why did he have to look so perfect all the time, and why did he keep seeing me at my absolute worst?

"Are you hungover?" Eric asked, his gaze raking over me.

I shook my head, wrapping the blanket more tightly around my body. "Sick."

He frowned, crossing the threshold in one smooth stride, the back of his hand connecting with my forehead as his other hand held me steady, his fingers pressing into my skin.

I was pretty sure it was the fever and not the man that made me feel warm all over, the sinus infection that made my breath hitch.

I swayed.

His grip on me tightened, holding me steady.

"You're burning up."

"I told you I was dying," I muttered, my voice sounding peevish even to my ears.

"Come on." He shut the door, leading me into the living room.

I opened my mouth to tell him that I could walk on my own, that I didn't need him here taking care of me, but at the moment, I was too tired to put up a fight.

"Couch or bed?" Eric asked.

I thought about it for a moment.

"Couch. I don't have a TV in my bedroom."

"Do you want a pillow?"

"Please." I pointed to the bedroom door, grateful for the help, even if it did come at the expense of me looking like this. "My bedroom is over there."

He returned a minute later with two pillows. I leaned forward while he adjusted them behind my head, a flush settling over my cheeks.

"I look terrible," I mumbled.

"You do not look terrible. You look like you feel terrible, though. Do you need me to take you to the doctor?" He sat down on the edge of the couch, next to my legs, worry in his gaze.

I shook my head. "Thanks, but I'll give it a day or two. I'm hoping it's just one of those twenty-four-hour things. I felt okay last night." I winced, remembering our kiss. "Sorry. I hope I didn't get you sick."

He grinned. "I don't think so, but if you did, it was worth it."

Well, hell.

I blinked, my head feeling like it was about to explode, my vision going a bit wobbly. "Why did you stop by?"

"You left your phone in the car last night." He pulled it out of his back pocket and set it on the coffee table. "I wanted to make sure you got it back."

Ugh. Definitely had too much to drink last night.

"Thanks."

"No problem."

"Wait." A flash of memory broke through the haze. "Lizzie gave you a ride home. Why didn't you just leave my phone with her? I see her all the time. It would have been easy for her to return it."

He gave me a boyish grin that tugged at my heart. "Because then I wouldn't have had a chance to return it to you." His voice turned husky, sending a shiver through my body that had nothing to do with the fever. "I wanted to see you again."

I didn't even know what to say to that one, and feeling the way I did, the best I could come up with was a weak, "Oh."

I waited to see if he'd get up and leave, but he didn't. He just sat there, staring at me, a smile playing at his lips.

I felt my cheeks heat under his scrutiny, and I burrowed deeper into the blanket.

"I forgot how cute you are when you're sick."

"Are you crazy?"

"It softens you up. You get all cuddly and sweet, and it's probably the only time in your life that you actually let someone take care of you. And as much as I like the fact that you're the kind of girl who doesn't need anyone to take care of her, it's nice to have a chance."

I opened my mouth to say something, protest, anything, but the words died on my lips and I just stared at him, my thoughts scrambled by the feelings filling me up and the sickness dragging me down.

A coughing fit hit me again as I opened my mouth to tell him he could go. Suddenly he was there, his big body surrounding me, his palm warm on my back. I seriously needed air.

The shaking subsided, my eyes watery, nose running.

Ugh. So freaking embarrassing. Well, on the bright side, I'd wanted to put some distance between us and cool things off, and I had a hard time believing this wouldn't do it. *Nothing* about my current appearance screamed desirable or sexy. More like covered in phlegm.

I grabbed a tissue, pausing mid-blow. "You don't have to stay. I mean, I appreciate it and everything, but I'm sure you have better things to do than sit with me and risk catching my germs."

Please have better things to do.

He grinned. "I have a ridiculous immune system, remember? There's no chance you'll get me sick."

I did remember. He never got sick. We used to joke that hopefully our kids would inherit his genes.

"It just feels weird," I confessed. "After everything. After last night. I don't know how to move forward. How to pretend things between us aren't awkward."

"So don't let them be awkward." He hesitated. "That kiss last night—"

"Was complicated."

I grabbed another tissue, blowing my nose loudly, wishing I were firing on all cylinders for this conversation and not hopelessly over my head.

"You can't tell me it didn't mean something to you; that there isn't still a part of you that cares for me."

I grimaced. "That was never the problem."

"I don't know how many times I can say I'm sorry before you'll believe it."

"I do believe that you're sorry; it just isn't enough."

"Then what is? Tell me what I have to do for you to let me in again. Tell me how I can make it up to you, and I will."

"I don't know." Frustration filled my voice, swimming through my body as exhaustion overtook me. "I'm not playing a game here, not trying to be difficult. I just don't know where this is going."

I sucked in a deep breath and told him exactly what was on my mind, because I figured, with our history, we owed each other that much. And I hadn't lied—last night had been about ego, and hurt, and part of me had flirted with Bandit to get a reaction out of Eric, but the truth was, I didn't know what I wanted from him.

"The kiss was amazing, but then again, you know that. Sex was never our problem. And yeah, it's really easy to be around you and to slide into old habit patterns, but that was never our problem, either. No, actually, maybe that is the problem. Because yes, I can see myself letting you in again, but I don't envision this playing out differently than it did before. And as hot as things are between us, as much as yes, I want to go to bed with you again, it can't be like last time. I can't put myself out there again, give you my heart, only for it to be crushed in return."

"That's fair. And I get that. After the way things ended between us, you giving me a chance is more than I deserve." He took my hand, seemingly unconcerned with the fact that I was a disgusting, germy mess. "What we had—what we have—you and I both know it isn't a given. I've never found it with anyone else, never felt the way I do about you. And I think you feel the same way."

I nodded, figuring there was no point in denying it.

"I don't know where this is going. I'm still sorting my shit out, and I wish I could tell you I had all the answers, but I don't. If you don't want to take a chance on that, then I understand, and I'll back off. I don't want to hurt you, don't want to let you down again. But if you want to give this a shot, however you want it, I'm here."

THOR

I hadn't been able to stop thinking of her. She'd consumed my dreams last night, my body lingering over the memory of our mouths fused together, of her soft curves and sexy scent. I'd woken up eager to see her, ready to pick up where we'd left off. I'd missed every part of her and now I was greedy for the pieces she doled out to me.

"Do we have a shot?"

I waited to see how she'd react to my offer, if she'd open the door another inch to let me in.

"Maybe."

It was the same answer she'd given me last night, but for a guy who deserved to have the door slammed in his face, "maybe" felt like a hell of an opportunity.

I stood up, not wanting to push her, needing this chance to make things up to her, even in this ridiculously small way.

"Do you want soup or something?" I asked. "Tea?"

"Tea sounds good."

I handed her the box of tissues. "Okay. Got it. Peppermint?"

She hesitated for a beat, a flash of surprise crossing her face. It might have been a decade, but I remembered every little detail, all her likes and dislikes, knew all her favorites.

"That would be great, thanks."

I walked into the kitchen. She'd turned her apartment into a cozy space, the decor welcoming shades of blue that reminded me of the apartment we'd shared in college. We'd been so poor, both of us working as much as we could while taking a full-time course load, but even then Becca had been determined to give us a home.

I hadn't appreciated it when I was younger. Not like I should have. I'd taken that side of her for granted, not realizing how lucky I'd been to have someone give me that, not realizing at the time how much I'd miss it when it was gone. I'd been young, stupid, and arrogant, accepting all she gave as standard because she loved giving it, not realizing how much of a bastard I'd been.

I fixed the tea and walked back into the living room, setting the mug on her coffee table.

"Thanks."

If things had been different between us, I would have taken her to bed, wrapping my arms around her and holding her while she slept. Instead I hovered there, my hands in my pockets, waiting for her to dismiss me.

"Is there anything else that you need?"

"No thanks. You can go. I'll be okay."

"I don't mind sticking around for a while." I reached out and squeezed her hand. "I want to take care of you. You shouldn't be getting up when you're sick."

Two spots of color appeared on her cheeks. "You don't have to."

"I know. But I want to."

She hesitated. "Okay." She nodded toward the TV. "Do you want to watch something?"

I couldn't have cared less, could've spent the entire day just sitting with her and not even speaking, but today wasn't about me.

"Whatever you want."

I handed her the remote and she flipped channels for a bit before settling on a movie we'd seen together when it came out and both liked.

I shifted on the couch, sitting on the end near her feet, lifting her blanket-covered legs onto my lap. She flinched at the contact, and I wondered if she'd pull away, but she didn't. Slowly her body relaxed against mine, until she lay there with my hand on her ankles, stroking her legs through the blanket.

An hour later she was asleep on the couch, soft sighs and snores escaping from her lips, her face scrunched up as she dreamed. My heart clenched at the sight of her and the memories it evoked. It was strange to have the remnants of an intimacy that had died long ago. Some things felt so natural, and yet I had to remind myself that I'd lost the right to those parts of her.

I lifted her feet off my lap and stood, scooping her up in my arms and carrying her toward the bedroom. Her eyes fluttered as she stirred.

"Did I fall asleep?"

I nodded, my mouth dry at the feel of her in my arms, at the familiar scent that filled my nostrils.

"What?" Becca mumbled between yawns, still clearly half-asleep.

"Shh. I'm putting you to bed. I'll leave some medicine and juice on the nightstand, okay?"

She didn't answer me, but she turned in my arms, her body burrowing deeper into the curve of mine, her lips resting just above my hammering heart.

She felt amazing. So fucking amazing.

I carried her over the threshold, through the open doorway into her bedroom, my heart thudding at the sight of her big bed, covered with pillows and floral sheets. It was so feminine, so Becca.

I adjusted the covers over her, tucking her in, another pang filling my chest as she buried her cheeks against the pillow, her hands tucked under her chin, a soft smile playing at her lips.

"Thank you."

I bent down, brushing my lips against her forehead. Once. Twice.

"You're welcome. I'm sorry, but I have to go; I have my friend's wedding in Sumter in a few hours."

I hesitated for a minute, wanting to stay with her, some

twisted-up, aching part inside me wanting to watch her sleep. I shook it off, forcing myself to put one foot in front of the other and carry myself away from her. Today felt like another step in the right direction, and no matter how badly I wanted more, I told myself this was enough for now.

Tomorrow I'd take the next step.

ELEVEN

THOR

The wedding went well. Reign and his wife, Sarah, spent the whole evening laughing and dancing. Easy went home with a bridesmaid. I went home alone.

I sent Becca a text the next day to see how she was feeling. On Monday, I ran into her picking up her morning coffee at Casey's.

Okay, fine, maybe "ran into her" was misleading. More like "spent an hour waiting for her at Casey's."

She walked into the diner dressed in a black suit, looking much better than she had Saturday, her gaze sweeping the crowd. And then she settled on me and I felt that familiar piercing sensation in my heart as a smile took over my lips.

I waved and she returned the gesture, her lip slipping between her teeth, indecision covering her features. She adjusted the bag on her arm and then she walked toward me, her long brown hair falling around her shoulders.

She stopped at my table.

"Hi."

I grinned, not bothering to hide how my gaze lingered over her in the suit. The skirt was snug over her hips, showing a tantalizing amount of leg tucked into black heels. She looked hot. Fantasy hot. Bend-you-over-a-desk-and-fuck-you hot.

"Hi. Are you feeling better?"

She nodded, a pink flush settling over her cheeks. "Thanks for taking care of me, by the way. I was kind of out of it, and I don't remember if I thanked you, but I really appreciate it. You didn't have to, and it was really nice that you did."

"No worries. It was my pleasure."

And it was. Everything about her was.

"You look beautiful."

The flush deepened. "Thanks."

"Are you in court today?"

"No, it's a pretty quiet day in the office. My secretary rearranged my schedule just in case I wasn't feeling better."

"But you are feeling better?"

She smiled. "Yeah, I am. I think it was one of those twenty-four-hour things. Nothing that some Vitamin C and rest couldn't cure."

"Good. I'm glad you're better. I was worried about you." I gestured toward the seat in front of me. "Why don't you join me?"

She hesitated. "I don't want to bother you. I can just get coffee to go or something."

"Please."

She sighed, her lip popping between her teeth again, and then she was sliding into the seat across from me, removing her jacket to reveal a pale pink silk top that left her shoulders bare and just the smallest amount of cleavage visible.

There was something about that color—all that pink—

that had me adjusting myself in my seat, trying to calm my growing erection.

"So what did you do this weekend?" she asked after we'd ordered.

"I went to my friend Reign's wedding. He's a buddy from pilot training, and he's stationed at Shaw."

"How was it?"

"It was good. I got to see a bunch of guys I'd known from prior assignments. A big group of us went golfing yesterday."

She laughed. "You golf now?"

"Yeah. Crazy, I know. It's big in the Air Force, so I took it up during pilot training. I pretty much suck, though."

"Please tell me you wear matching plaid shorts and a hat."

"Only on special occasions."

"Hmm. I'd like to see that."

"I'll take you golfing sometime."

She made a face. "I definitely don't golf."

"Okay, no golf. Go on a picnic with me instead."

"I don't think so."

"Come on."

"Are you trying to hit on me?"

"I'm not trying. I am hitting on you. It's just a picnic. Just for a few hours."

"I don't know."

"I'm asking for two hours. Maybe three if you like it. When's the last time you took a break during the day and did something fun?"

"Why am I getting déjà vu of high school and you trying to get me to skip? I have a job, you know."

"And I bet you never take a day off. Besides you said your secretary cleared your calendar, yes?"

She nodded reluctantly.

"So it's already a light day. Come on, you know we only have a few more weeks before it starts to get too cold to enjoy being outside."

"Where is this picnic?"

"Where else would it be?"

We'd spent more days and nights than I could count hanging out in the fields on Mr. Eggers's property—making out and talking about our future, dreaming dreams that never came true.

"I don't know—"

I grinned, feeling like I had a fifty-pound weight on my chest as I reached for her, praying I didn't come up empty. "I promise you'll enjoy it."

I took her hand in mine, leaning across the table until she was inches away, swallowing the sigh that escaped from her lips like it was air and I was desperate to keep breathing. My thumb rubbed over her knuckles, back and forth, savoring the feel of her soft skin beneath me, her lips parting as I touched her.

She made a little noise, somewhere between a hum and a sigh, the faintest glimmer of interest flashing in her eyes.

"Fine. A few hours."

Victory.

BECCA

I was as nervous as I'd been the first time he brought me here, when I was just sixteen and he was the guy all the girls wanted, but few had had. He'd done his own thing in high school, was one of those guys who could have been cool if he'd wanted to be, but hadn't seemed like he cared enough to bother.

There had been something mysterious about him back then, a joke in his eyes and the curve of his lips that you wanted to be in on, the feeling that if he shared his secrets with you, you'd be the luckiest girl in the world.

And he'd chosen me.

Eric drove his rental car—a Mustang convertible—down the highway, slowing as we reached the edge of the Eggers farm.

I'd always loved it here, nostalgia hitting me every time I made this drive. My parents' property had bordered Mr. Eggers's land, and while I hadn't been back to the house I'd grown up in since they died, the drive always made me feel like I was going home. When we were younger, I used to daydream about me and Eric buying the house from the family who'd moved in after my parents died, imagined raising our kids there one day, building new memories and clutching the ones I'd had to me tightly.

Eric turned on a dusty dirt road, one we'd traversed so many times when we wanted to be alone, kicking up gravel as the wind blew my hair.

He was right about the weather. It was the second week in October, and even though this year had been warmer than usual, you could feel the bite of fall lingering behind the sun. Soon the leaves would change, the weather cool, and we'd slide into my favorite season.

And he would be gone.

Eric cut the engine, getting out of the car and walking around to my side, opening the door and holding out his hand to me.

The gesture took me by surprise, a small reminder of

how he'd changed, gone from boy to man. He'd been a thoughtful boyfriend and fiancé, but he'd never had someone to teach him those moves; somewhere along the way he'd acquired them, transforming him into something unexpected.

I placed my hand in his, the touch of his palm against mine, his fingers curled around my fingers, feeling like the beginning of a new start for us. One I wasn't sure I was ready for, but took just the same.

Somewhere between the kiss and him stopping by my apartment and taking care of me while I was sick, I'd thrown my rules out the window. He was only here for a few weeks, and it had been a long ten years of missing him and attempting to fill the void with pale substitutes. So fuck it, as long as my heart stayed out of the equation, I didn't see why I couldn't have a little fun.

With his free hand, Eric grabbed a blanket and picnic basket out of the backseat of the car, and I shamelessly ogled the impressive forearms exposed by the rolled sleeve of his cotton button-down. My heart might have known he was off-limits, but my body was definitely ready to play.

Eric hopped the fence first, using the rails to climb over the top. His feet hit the ground, a boyish grin on his face, and I knew he remembered how many times we'd done this.

My hands met the wooden planks, the memory tugging at me, and then I hoisted myself up, my sandals slipping slightly on the boards. I straddled the fence, careful to keep my dress from billowing in the wind, and Eric reached up, his hands resting on either side of my hips as he pulled me down to the ground.

His body pressed against mine as he settled me on the squishy grass, my back brushing his chest, his lips and breath tickling my neck as he held me to him, his hard length pressing into my ass.

Neither one of us moved.

A line of goose bumps puckered my skin. My breath caught in my throat as I struggled to keep from rubbing myself against him. His hands came up to wrap around my waist and chest, inches away from my breasts, his chest rising and falling rapidly against my body. We stayed like that for another beat, and then he released me with a sigh, reaching down and picking up the basket and blanket he'd discarded, holding his hand out to me again.

At least I wasn't the only one affected. If I was going to lose control, then I wanted him right there with me. My body felt like it was on fire, the breeze doing nothing to combat the heat building beneath my skin. Maybe I still had a fever.

I placed my hand in his, the electricity between us crackling like a live wire. We walked through the field together, the tall grass tickling my bare legs, more memories flooding me, as though we'd traveled back in time.

My gaze swept the open field, the colors bursting—red, purple, yellow flowers, the green grass, blue sky, white fluffy clouds that looked like someone had stretched out pieces of cotton into shapes and sent them up to the heavens. It was beautiful. So painfully beautiful. And so familiar.

I hadn't been here since Eric. Had told myself I'd outgrown dates like this in favor of fancy restaurants, candlelight, and wine. But coming back felt right in a way nothing else had.

Something would happen here; the tension between us was too great to ignore. I wanted it, but I couldn't deny the fears running through my head. It had been ten years. I didn't have a twenty-one-year-old's body anymore. Would he notice? Care? Would things still be as good between us as they used to be?

Eric tugged on my hand, bringing me to a stop next to him. "What about here?"

I nodded, emotions clogging my throat. "This is perfect."

I waited while he spread the blanket down over the ground, while he unloaded the picnic basket, pouring wine into two plastic cups.

My heart skipped a beat.

He'd brought a hamper from Casey's Diner along with a bottle of white wine, in a move that surprised me. The boy I'd known hadn't necessarily been romantic—sweet, yes— but not necessarily smooth. Apparently he'd upped his game.

Eric sat down, patting a space next to him, and I sank to the ground on shaky legs, spreading the full skirt of my dress around me, as if the fabric could keep him temporarily at bay and give me the buffer I needed while I got my heart and pulse under control.

He offered me a cup of wine and I took it, our fingers brushing against each other and undoing that moment of calm. I felt like a teenager again, like the virgin I'd been when we'd first started dating. And at the same time, my body definitely did not.

I knew what was coming and I wanted it—badly.

WELVE

BECCA

I took a sip of the wine and then I set it on the ground and lay back on the blanket, staring up at the sky. The sun beat down on my skin, the smell of dirt and grass around me, the barest of breezes lifting the hem of my dress.

How many times had we done this growing up?

I'd always been reluctant to skip school, too concerned with the prospect of getting in trouble to want to court Mr. Eggers's potential wrath if we were caught sneaking onto his property. But Eric had always been there with a smile and an extended hand, and I'd never been able to resist the urge to wrap my fingers around his and let him pull me wherever he wanted to go. I'd been hopeless at saying "no" to Eric Jansen when I was a kid, and given where I'd ended up—next to him on the faded plaid blanket, our bodies so close we nearly touched—apparently that wasn't a habit I'd been able to break.

"What are you thinking?" he asked, lying down next to me, folding his arms behind his head.

"Just looking at the clouds."

This, too, had been a tradition.

"Cow, three o'clock."

My eyes narrowed as I considered the shape. "It looks like a cat."

"How does that look like a cat?"

I pointed to the sky. "See, those are its ears. And that's its little cat face."

"Nope. That's its cow face."

I grinned. "You always were terrible at this."

"Hey, you were the one who lacked imagination. It used to take you ages to come up with shapes."

I rolled my eyes. "Some of us like to be deliberate. Like to make sure we're getting it right."

"And sometimes you spend so much time trying not to mess up that you miss it entirely."

Touché.

"Do you remember that time we went to the air show at Shaw?"

I did. That had been a rare good day near the end. I'd never been to an air show before, and he'd been so excited to go see the planes. We'd found a spot to set up a blanket and we'd lain down on the ground, my head in his lap as we watched the planes fly overhead, as he pointed out the different airframes. It had been the moment when I'd realized how serious he was about flying.

"Sometimes when I'm up in the air, I'll see a cloud and think of you. Remember the days we spent just looking up at the sky."

I turned my head, staring into his blue eyes. Our gazes locked, a hint of a flush beneath his cheeks. I couldn't fight the smile. He'd always hated those blushes, unable to fight the curse of red hair and pale skin. Of course, it wasn't fair that he also had a warrior's body and a face that broke hearts—my heart.

"Don't," he said.

"Don't what?"

"Don't shut down on me. Not yet. Not this afternoon anyway. Just enjoy this."

That was the problem—it was so easy to enjoy it, to lie here and pretend we were young and in love again. The same nerves that had lived inside me then flooded me now, the same questions running through my head:

Would he touch me? Kiss me? Was it even a question or had we come here for this, the need lingering unspoken between us?

"Do you want something to eat? More wine?" he asked, his voice soft.

For all the nerves pinging through me, I'd come here because I wanted to be alone with him, because he'd kissed me and the promise of it had fueled a fire within me, because even though I shouldn't want it, I *wanted* him to press my back down into the grass. I wanted what this place had represented for us, what my body recognized now, even as my mind protested.

I swallowed, the bodice of my dress suddenly feeling tight, my skin electric. "I didn't come here for the wine."

His eyes darkened and he shifted, his bare arm brushing against mine, his skin warm from the sun.

Hadn't we been building our way toward this all along? Did it matter that it was just temporary? That it was likely just sex? That I didn't know where this was going? That I didn't care?

His pinkie brushed my finger, the soft touch sending a tremor down my spine, my nipples tightening, a flash of heat building just under my skin.

More.

His finger hooked around mine, the breath leaving my body with a soft *whoosh*.

We lay there, staring up at the sky, holding hands, but not really holding hands, rewinding time.

His finger stroked my palm, sending another wave of want through me, a steady throb building between my legs as anticipation built inside me. He shifted beside me, turning onto his side, squeezing my fingers, his gaze raking over me with an intensity that might as well have been his hands shaping, molding, imprinting themselves onto my flesh.

He started at my face, my eyes, my lips, before moving lower, his gaze hot on my breasts in a move that had me arching my back a little, giving in to vanity, to the desire burning inside me to make him want this as badly as I did. To shatter his control.

His gaze dipped lower and I swore I could feel his touch on my stomach as clearly as though he'd dragged the pads of his fingers down my skin, dipping into my belly button, goose bumps rising on my flesh, and then lower still, until I *did* feel him—

His finger grazing my bare knee with such aching gentleness that for a moment I wondered if he'd touched me at all, if it had all been a figment of my imagination—my filthy imagination that was currently running wild with all the things I wanted him to do to me beneath the sky—or if I'd merely confused the breeze on my skin with Eric's hands.

He answered the unspoken question in my head with a soft caress to the hollow spot behind my knee, tickling the sensitive skin there in a move that had me biting down on my lip.

Fuck me, this is happening.

It had been a while. More than a while. So independent of the fact that this was Eric, that he'd forever been the yardstick against which I measured all other men, I wanted this, needed it, had to have it. For once in my life, my brain could shut up. I wasn't interested in hearing all the reasons why this was likely a stupid idea; I knew them all. I just wanted to come, and considering Eric was the Picasso of orgasms, I wanted to come with his mouth on me, his hands stroking me, his cock inside me.

A girl had only so much willpower. It was time for me to get mine.

His hand trailed up my leg lazily, each caress unraveling me inch by inch. I stared up at the clouds, the breeze tickling my face, his magic hands releasing the tension that had been inside me for so long. I stretched out on the blanket, my body languid as he turned me into a boneless heap.

He played with the hem of my dress, his fingers dipping under the fabric and stealing the air from my lungs as he stroked my inner thigh, drifting higher, higher . . .

I turned my head, staring into his blue eyes, the lust there sending another tremor between my legs. I reached out, my fingers tracing his full mouth, and then I watched, arousal flooding me, as he sucked my fingers between his lips, his tongue joining the party and sending a message that had my clit tingling in anticipation.

Yes. So much, yes.

I pulled away, my hand falling to my side, my fingers clutched in a wet fist.

With his free hand he lifted my dress, the warm sun hitting my bare skin. I spread open, any shyness that might have reared its ugly head taking a backseat to how *fucking good* it felt to have him touch me. He lay there, propped up on his arm, his gaze on me as he lifted my dress to my waist, baring the white scrap of lace that, if I were totally honest with myself, I'd definitely worn for him.

His breath grew ragged, and for a moment I thought he'd speak, but then it passed, as if he'd realized that, in this case, words would break the connection between us. I didn't want to be reminded of reality, didn't want anything to spoil this. If this was wrong, I didn't want to be right.

He stroked me through the lace; if there had been any doubts in his mind about how badly I wanted him, they'd just been answered. My eyes closed, my head falling back on the blanket as I gave myself over to the only sensation I wanted to feel—his hand between my legs bringing me closer and closer to ecstasy.

His knuckles grazed me as his fingers hooked under the band of my thong. I lifted my hips and he pulled the lace from me, his big hand resting on my hipbone, the warmth of his touch a brand on my flesh, his fingers inches from where I wanted them to be. And then I felt it—his breath on the inside of my thigh, tickling my skin, sending another shiver down my spine, and then another as he teased me, those little releases of breath nothing and everything at the same time.

I wanted, needed, *more*.

His breath hovered over my skin, the little puff of air blowing directly onto my clit, my body aching and tight, needing relief, grasping for pleasure even as it slid through my fingers like sand.

"What do you want?"

The words sounded rough falling from his lips, as though his control hung by a thread just like mine.

My eyes fluttered open and I stared up at him, looming over me, his mouth a harsh slant across his too-handsome face. Holy hell, in this moment, his call sign seemed totally apropos. He looked like the god of thunder and lightning, like a warrior who commanded and men followed. If I hadn't been close to coming before, the look in his eyes and the sheer beauty of his fucking face propelled me to the edge. The arrogance in his voice had me teetering there.

He didn't ask the question for anything other than to make me answer, because there was no way he could have any doubts about what I wanted. But he was definitely going to make me say it.

Fine.

"Your mouth on me."

No shame. No point.

"You want to come," he drawled, his lazy tone another silken caress.

I managed an eye roll, no easy feat when you were strung as tightly as I was. "Gee, what gave you that idea?"

He rewarded me with a grin, his dimple making an appearance that had me squirming beneath his gaze. I'd forgotten how playful he was in bed.

"I thought you hated me," he teased.

Holy hell. I was *thisfreakingclose . . .*

"Can we not talk? Maybe there are *other things* your mouth could do right now."

His smile deepened, a chuckle escaping those beautiful want-them-on-my-body lips. His answer was to dip his head down, his mouth closing down around my clit—

I bit back a moan, and then his tongue dragged across my swollen flesh, and I gave up all pretense of silence.

He didn't play around, didn't tease me; instead, he feasted on my body like I was a banquet laid before him, sating himself with the arousal that flowed through me, the sighs that escaped my lips, the way my body quivered and shook as he took me closer and closer, that familiar sensation building in my body, except this time there was a sharpness and an intensity that hadn't been there before with him and all the guys in between.

I reached down between us, my fingers threading through his hair, holding on to him even as my world shifted and I lost control. I came hard, my hips bucking beneath his body while he held me down, his mouth swallowing every tremor, his tongue laving my swollen, aching, dripping flesh.

As quickly as it had come on, the orgasm slid out of me, leaving me hollowed out and spent, way too smug with pleasure to make room for doubt or regret.

Maybe we sucked at love, but we definitely knocked this out of the freaking park.

Eric stared down at me, a lazy smile on his face.

I reached out, touching my fingers to his lips again, feeling myself on his skin. Our gazes locked, a conversation passing between us without the need for words. His fingers closed around my wrist, pulling my hand away and bringing our hands together until we were joined palm to palm.

He lay back down on the blanket and hooked his arm around me until my head came to rest on his chest, my cheek above his heart, the steady beat lulling me to sleep beneath the cloudy—*cat*-filled—sky.

$\mathscr{T}$HIRTEEN

BECCA

"You did what?" Lizzie screeched, her eyes wide as she stared at me across the couch.

I flushed. "Come on, have you seen him lately? Tell me you wouldn't have done the same thing."

"I saw him running yesterday. I would climb him like a jungle gym, but that's beside the point."

I snorted, taking another sip of wine. The alcohol was definitely getting to Lizzie. Girls' nights were few and far between since she'd had her son, but we still managed to get together every once in a while, even on a Tuesday. This was one of those nights when I needed my best friend.

"So how was it? Scale of one to ten."

"Four hundred and twenty-two."

"Damn. Have you talked to him since?"

"He texted."

"And?"

"And he wants to go out on Friday night."

"What did you say?"

"I told him I'd think about it."

"Why? You don't think about a four hundred and twenty-two."

"You do if he broke your heart."

"True. It's a shame you can't just enjoy his body without all the emotional stuff getting in the way."

"Amen, sister."

"Wait. Can you?"

"Can I what?"

"Just enjoy his body without all the emotional stuff getting in the way?"

That was the million-dollar question.

"I don't know. I want to. It's so good with him. I mean, better than I remembered, and he was always the best I'd ever had." I took another sip of wine. "But the problem is, just as easy as it is to imagine falling back into bed with him, it's just as easy to imagine slipping back into our old habit patterns. Into the relationship we had."

"Have you guys talked about what he wants? I mean, he's back. He's never been back before. Surely that means something."

I wanted to tell myself that. I wanted to believe it. But unfortunately, I didn't know how much I trusted him anymore. Or my own instincts.

"He's going through a rough time. I get it. And I feel badly for him; I do. But I don't want him to use me like I'm some kind of Band-Aid. To come back here because he can, or because it's safe. To have me fix him and then leave again."

I wanted the upper hand here, wanted him to feel the way I felt—

"What do you want?" Lizzie asked, echoing my thoughts.

"I want him to want me so badly that he's desperate for it. Begging for it."

Maybe not actually begging, but close enough. For once, I didn't want him to sweep me off my feet. I wanted to bring him to his knees.

"So you want to have sex with him?"

So badly. The idea of stripping Eric naked and getting him between my legs had burned itself in my mind and refused to leave. I just didn't know how to get him there on *my* terms. I knew he wanted me, that whatever burned between us burned fiery hot, knew he found me attractive, and still, I'd never been that girl.

For one night, I wanted to be a fantasy. His fantasy. I wanted to grasp the power in my palm, right alongside his dick and his heart.

"Yeah."

"Like hate sex?" Lizzie asked, the expression on her face a mask of confusion.

Maybe I sounded like a crazy person. I didn't know how to explain it to someone who'd only been with one guy, who'd treated her like a princess their entire relationship.

"I don't hate him. I just want to break him." I winced. "Not the way it sounds."

It was official; I was a horrible person. Poor Lizzie—married-for-a-dozen-years Lizzie—looked at me like I'd started the slippery slide into insanity.

"And have sex with him?"

"Yes." I sighed. "I want to give him a night that he can't forget, a memory that will haunt him every single time he's with someone else. I want to feel good, to make him feel so good his mind is blown, and then when it comes time to say good-bye, I want him to stand there, watching me walk away, feeling like I've left a void in his life that he can't fill."

"Because that's what he did to you?" she asked, her voice soft, eyes sad.

"He didn't—"

"Didn't what?"

"It wasn't like that. We were together for over five years; it's not like it was wham-bam-thank-you-ma'am."

"But he left."

"Yeah."

"And you're angry."

So much, yes. I kept trying to move past the anger, to let go, to *forgive*, and I just couldn't. So now I'd given up on letting go of those feelings; instead I wanted to harness them for something else. I wanted to fuck my heartbreak away.

I took a long gulp of my wine, draining the glass dry.

"Maybe he regrets it," Lizzie suggested. "Maybe he wishes he could do things differently, go back in time and make another choice."

Maybe. But it truly was too little too late. I didn't tell her the saddest part, how I'd had that same stupid fantasy for years after he'd left. That there had been a part of me that hadn't been able to believe he was really gone, that we were really over, and had waited, convinced he'd come back.

"I don't think so. He's just visiting; he's only here for another week or so and then he'll be back in Oklahoma. He made his choice and he has the life he always wanted. I don't think anything is going to change."

"Then maybe you shouldn't get involved with him. I'm worried you're going to have sex with him and history will repeat itself. It seems like you still have a lot of feelings about all of this. I'm not sure sex is your best play here."

All good points, but our trip to the Eggers farm had changed everything.

"I'm not twenty-one anymore, and I know who he is now. I thought our relationship was the most important thing for him, never imagined he would dump me for a fucking plane. I now know differently.

"Have you ever looked back on a part of your life with regret? Like if you could have a do-over, would you take it?" I asked, struggling to explain it.

Lizzie grinned. "Sure. I would have gone out with Matt Adams when he asked me to the eighth grade dance."

"You did have a huge crush on him."

"It's not like I would have wanted for it to go anywhere past eighth grade, but I guess it would have been nice to have that moment, you know?"

"I do. This is my Matt Adams moment."

Lizzie laughed. "Somehow I don't think you wanting to screw your ex blind is the same thing as me wanting to have a few awkward dances with my eighth grade crush."

"Potato, po-tah-toe."

"For the record, I think it's a terrible idea."

I poured myself more wine. "So you'll help me?"

Her eyes gleamed. "Hell yes."

On Wednesday we met at Shh!, a store that catered to seduction. From the outside, you never would have known the store was an erotic treasure trove. It had a fairly industrial look to it, the red lipstick kiss logo on the sign out front the only thing that hinted at a naughtier side.

Inside was a different story entirely.

Lizzie clutched my arm, her eyes wide as we walked into

dildo-ville. I wasn't a prude by any stretch of the imagination, but a giant foot-long phallus was a little startling. Especially on my lunch hour. Buy a girl a drink first.

"You are definitely buying something. No way am I doing this alone."

Lizzie grinned. "That's one way to make it up to Adam for having to get a babysitter."

"Sorry about that."

"Please. You need your best friend for moral support."

I laughed. "I definitely do." I took a deep breath, already feeling sensory overload at the bright, flashing lights and the thumping music that gave the feel that we were in a porno film. "Okay, I only have an hour. Let's do this."

We perused the shelves, cracking up a bit over the various implements they had for sale. Some of it was sexy, but most of it was just . . . a little *too* out there. Like the giant blowup doll. And the male thong with a pouch that resembled a barnyard animal. How having a pig over your cock was supposed to be sexy, I'd never know.

We hit the lingerie section, and I attacked with the intensity of a general planning a military campaign. Judging by the enormous bouquet of flowers that had arrived at my office this morning, keeping him on his toes was going better than I'd anticipated.

"What about this?" Lizzie held up a sexy schoolgirl outfit.

I wrinkled my nose. "I feel as if that's more like letting him have all the power. I want to feel in charge."

Her next selection was black leather and chains.

I laughed. "Maybe a step too far. I don't want him licking my boot or anything."

"Just on his knees."

I grinned. "Exactly."

We grabbed different outfits, discarding a naughty nurse ensemble that, while hot, was probably a little too costumey for me to pull off. I worried that if I felt silly rather than sexy, the whole thing would fall apart, since I clung to sexy by a thread that threatened to disintegrate under the weight of my nerves.

I made Lizzie grab a few outfits to try on, figuring she and Adam deserved a freaky-naughty night. I promised to watch Dylan so they could have some privacy.

We tried on outfits, exchanging giggles as each one was more ridiculous than the last. And then I got to the final piece of lingerie, slipped it on, and felt that inaudible click.

Oh yeah.

This was the one.

"Did you find something?" Lizzie asked, calling to me from the other side of the curtain.

"I did."

I couldn't take my gaze off my reflection in the mirror. I felt sexy in this one, like I was still me, but a more wicked version of me. A girl who wasn't afraid to go after what she wanted. A girl who could have the man she craved, any way she wanted him.

"Is the plan still for you guys to meet on Friday for dinner?" Lizzie asked.

"We actually don't have a plan. Yet."

"What do you mean? I thought he texted and asked you out yesterday."

"He did. I haven't responded."

And then inspiration struck.

I peeked out from behind the curtain, the fabric hiding my body.

"Question. I want to be clear with him that this is just

sex. And I want the upper hand." I wanted this to be fun. Not sad exes reconnecting or anything like that. "Up until now, all of the moves have been his. How bad is it if I send him a picture? Hot or desperate?"

Lizzie grinned. "Well, first off, you guys were together for like forever. Second, I was there Friday night and he looked at you like he was gagging for it. And finally, he went down on you in a field on Monday. I'm thinking a Wednesday sext is well timed."

And that was why she was my best friend.

I disappeared behind the curtain, my heart hammering. I'd never actually sent a guy a naked picture of myself. Given my job, anything with my face in it, anything that made me recognizable, was totally and completely out of the question. But a cleavage shot?

I wanted him off balance when I saw him. And I didn't want to wait until Friday.

I pulled my phone out of my purse, my fingers trembling slightly as I turned on the camera. I played around with the angle a bit, taking a few test shots, gaining a whole new appreciation for people who took selfies. Finding a good angle was no joke. Finally, I found one I liked, not bothering to feel guilty about the fact that I adjusted the filter—after all, the push-up magic of the bra was already false advertising. Besides, all was fair in love and war—or in our case, sex and war.

I composed the message, giving him the four things he needed:

A picture of my breasts, popped up to impressive heights, heavy and full in black lace. And then the message—

My place. Tonight. Seven p.m.

THOR

The cold shower didn't do a damned thing to help. Ever since Monday, ever since I'd found myself between Becca's legs, my tongue on her clit, my lips on her pussy, my cock had been hard and aching, begging for release. I couldn't forget the sound of her moans, or the way her nails had scored my skin, or the taste of her in my mouth.

I was high on her, and by the way my dick tented my towel, I wasn't coming down anytime soon. I was a junkie who needed my next fix, and the pisser of it all was that after I'd texted her and asked her out, even after I'd made her come so hard her body shook, she hadn't responded.

I'd checked my phone approximately two hundred and sixty-eight times in the last twenty-four hours.

Crickets.

I removed the towel from my waist, drying my torso, balls, cock, gripping the base, stroking up, over the tip, figuring this was the only way I'd find relief anytime soon.

After our picnic there was no doubt in my mind that she wanted me, but at the same time, I didn't know if it was enough for her to give us a shot, to let me in. Didn't know if I was enough.

I'd sent her flowers. Big, fat roses. Nothing.

I sat on the bed, leaning back against the pillows, my hand between my thighs, eyes closed, imagining it was Becca's mouth on me—hot, wet—her tongue licking me from base to tip, her lips closing down around me, sucking me deep—

My phone beeped. I froze. It beeped again.

I abandoned my cock, lunging for the nightstand, my heart lurching as I felt a mix of hope and dread—that it was

Becca, that she wanted to go out with me, that she didn't want to go out with me, that it wasn't her at all and I was stuck in limbo still.

I grabbed my phone, closing my eyes as I whispered a silent prayer. I opened them and my mouth went dry, dick rock hard, and my heart fucking stopped.

For an instant I was convinced I'd gotten the text by mistake, that it was meant for someone else. But then I saw her name, and the message, and really, I deserved a medal for being able to read and focus on anything at all in the face of that picture.

I was momentarily speechless, the image of her full, perky tits, pushed up like an offering, rosy, red nipples peaked and ready for my mouth and hands, encased in black lace. Seeing her tits pushed together like that . . .

I wanted to fuck her there. Wanted to drag my cock between them, surrounding myself in her silky skin, watching my cock, wet from her pussy and mouth, slide in and out, wanting to come on her tits, to mark her up.

I groaned, my hand sliding down my body, cupping my balls, squeezing gently before sliding up and fisting my dick. I'd been close before, but the sight of her tits, her nipples, the knowledge that she wanted me as much as I wanted her, simply broke me.

I squeezed and stroked myself, hard and fast, gazing the entire time at the picture she'd sent, imagining all the things I wanted to do to her tonight. All the things I *would* do to her tonight.

I felt it, building up inside me, my balls tightening, cock hard to the point of pain as I increased my motions, pumping harder, faster, and then I was coming, my body shuddering and quaking as my release wore me out.

I fell back against the pillow, my hand at my side, my chest heaving and falling like I'd run a marathon.

If it was like that after my hand and a photograph, I could only imagine how fucking fantastic it would be when I had *her*.

I cleaned myself off with the towel and grabbed the phone, shooting off a quick text.

I can't wait to fuck you all night.

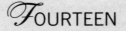

FOURTEEN

BECCA

I stared at my reflection in the mirror, attempting to channel my inner man-eater.

You are sexy. This is the best you've ever looked. You can do this. Do not get awkward. Do not babble. Do not freak the fuck out.

I felt about as nervous as I had my first day in court, except this time I had the added benefit of being sans clothes.

I took a sip of the champagne I'd poured, steadying my nerves.

I'd forgone dinner, figuring there was no point in making this something that it wasn't; the sext said it all—this was physical, nothing else.

Heart, do not engage.

I heard the knock at the front door, my gaze flying to the clock on the nightstand. Seven on the dot. I shouldn't be surprised that he was punctual given his military background, but it was a change from the boy who'd been perpetually late for everything.

Equal parts nerves and anticipation filled me, and I wasn't sure if his promptness was something to be cursed or praised. I could have used another few minutes or hours to get my shit together.

Now or never.

I took a deep breath, steadying myself, noticing how the motion made my breasts bounce. Seriously, this corset was better than a freaking boob job.

I walked to the front door on the ridiculously high stiletto heels I'd bought at the sex shop. I'd never owned anything quite like them, but in for a penny, in for a pound.

I unlocked the door, taking a quick sweep of the room—low lighting, candles, seduction music that was more sexy than romantic. Perfect.

I opened the door with the flourish of pulling back a curtain and stared up into Eric's eyes. Even in the heels, he still had a few inches on me, but by the time my gaze met his, the full punch of lust had settled there. And I basked in it. Drank it up like fine wine.

I stepped back on shaky legs, opening the door for him to step over the threshold, hoping I wasn't giving my neighbors a hell of a show in the process.

He swallowed, his Adam's apple bobbing. He didn't speak as I closed the door behind him.

He looked hot tonight—really hot.

Dark jeans. Another button-down with the sleeves rolled—this one navy, complementing the blue in his eyes. He smelled good, he looked amazing, and whatever nerves lingered inside me converted themselves to desire by the time my perusal reached his fine ass.

Eric turned and stared at me, his gaze piercing me again, lingering on my breasts, sliding down to the scrap of lace between my legs, a flush rising on my skin under his scrutiny before he lowered his attention to my bare legs and the strappy sex heels covering my feet.

He grinned, his gaze sparkling with mischief. "Please tell me you don't always answer the door like that."

I opened my mouth to respond with something normal, and then I remembered my mantra and the fact that I was supposed to be some kind of sex-vixen or whatever. Man-eaters didn't explain themselves. Right.

I took a step closer to him, and then another one, until the tips of my breasts—my already-pebbling-in-anticipation nipples—brushed against his pecs.

He groaned, reaching for me, his hands cupping my bare ass, squeezing, kneading the flesh there.

Get control. You need the upper hand.

I tilted my head up, inhaling his scent, my lips grazing the curve of his neck, reveling in the shudder against my mouth.

Oh, yeah. I could get used to this.

My lips found his ear, sucking gently on the lobe, nipping the soft flesh with my teeth, my body tingling as another groan fell from his lips, his fingers digging into my ass.

"How badly do you want me?" I whispered, trying for the throaty sex voice I'd spent some time practicing earlier this afternoon. The fact that I was getting over a cold had definitely helped.

His cock hardened against me and I purposefully shifted my body, drawing him closer to the throbbing point between my legs.

Eric buried his face in the curve of my neck, mouthing the skin there, his breath wet and warm. Moisture pooled between my legs.

"You sent me that picture and I was already hard, wanting you. Already aching, remembering how sweet you tasted on my tongue, what it felt like to have your pussy quivering beneath my mouth. When I saw your tits like that, all I could think about was fucking you there, sliding my cock between them while I cupped you, pushing them together so they swallowed me, jacking myself off over all of that creamy white skin."

Cannot breathe. Need air. Legs giving out.

I dug deep to withstand the impact of his words without completely dissolving into a writhing, needy mess.

"I ended up fisting myself, getting myself off to the picture of your tits, just like this, and the image of what I'd do to them later," he growled.

Ahh hell.

A tremor slid down my body, then another one. Tension slammed into me, and for a moment I couldn't do anything but stand there like a rabbit caught in his snare, my heart pounding in my chest as lust hit me wave after wave and I fought the desire to throw caution to the wind and give myself over to pleasure.

This mattered. It mattered to me. I wanted to be the one left standing when he walked away and I wasn't so naive as to think sex wasn't a big part of this. Right now boundaries were my best friend and I wanted the power that surged through me at the idea that I'd turned him inside out. I wanted to do it all night long.

I slipped out of his grasp, taking a step back, putting the distance I needed between us to give my body a chance to get this raging need under control.

I tilted my head up so my gaze locked on to his, holding myself steady in the face of the arousal I saw there.

"If you want me, you have to do what I say." His gaze sharpened as the words left my lips, and I felt it then, that familiar ping of power.

He'd always been older, always been the more experienced one, and I'd always been happy to follow his lead.

Not anymore.

His mouth quirked into a smile that was a couple notches above his usual mischief, as though he were channeling the devil himself.

That did things to me, too.

I kept my voice firm, using the tone I adopted when faced with a difficult judge or pain-in-the-ass opposing counsel. No way was I going to let him charm me. If he wanted in, he was going to have to earn it.

As soon as I rolled my tongue back into my mouth.

He took a step closer to me, that fucking smirk in his eyes that I recognized all too well. Then another step.

"Just what are you going to do with me?" he whispered, his hand trailing down my arm, leaving a flash of goose bumps in its wake. I fought the tremor.

"First off, you have to ask permission to touch me."

Oh, his smile turned wicked at that, warming me from the inside out like molten lava sliding through my veins. He pulled his hand back slowly, letting it dangle at his side.

"Can I touch you?" he whispered, his voice teasing me, slithering inside and curling around my heart.

I barely resisted the urge to fan myself.

Get a freaking grip.

"Take off your shirt first."

There. That was good. Commanding. Plus it gave me the added advantage of eye candy, and if I was going to have all of my naked bits hanging out, then he should have the same.

He started at the top button of his shirt, undoing it and exposing the skin at the bottom of his throat, and then the next one, and then the next, those clever fingers baring his beautiful body before me and sucking all the air from the room. Eric shrugged out of the shirt, the fabric hitting the floor.

I looked my fill and he let me, standing there as though he knew exactly the effect his body had on me, and he loved every minute of it.

To be fair, though, he deserved the adulation.

He clearly worked at it and it showed. He was all smooth planes and sculpted muscles, light hair sprinkling across his chest. And then my gaze dipped lower, to the trail of hair disappearing below the waistband of his jeans, and suddenly, I wanted more.

"Pants next."

His eyes gleamed and a dimple popped out. Yeah, he was definitely enjoying this.

"How about boxers?" he asked, his voice husky, raising the stakes as his hands rested on his belt buckle.

"Boxers, too."

It felt like all the noise had disappeared from the room but for the sound of the metal buckle clanging together, then the soft whoosh of the leather leaving the loops, the belt hitting the floor with a thunk. Then came his zipper, dragging down slowly in a move I was pretty sure was designed to be my own private fighter pilot striptease.

I ate it up like an ice cream sundae.

Then the jeans slid down his hips, exposing a pair of black boxers, a defined vee like an arrow pointing down to a spot I desperately wanted to go, and the even more impressive erection I'd felt against me.

Maybe I should sit down.

Eric bent, his body rippling with the movement, and removed his shoes, kicking his pants off. And then he hooked his thumbs into the waistband of his boxers, dragging the fabric down until his cock popped free.

He was thick, long, and really fucking perfect.

And damn him, he knew it.

"Can I touch you now?"

Seriously, how did he do it? He was standing naked in my living room, I was in charge, and yet his questions sounded suspiciously like commands cloaked in a veil of faux deference.

And yeah, at this point, I didn't really care all that much who ended up on top, as long as I came. But that didn't mean I wasn't going to try my damnedest to get there first.

I nodded, figuring that seemed more imposing and authoritative. Plus words weren't really coming in the face of the fact that he looked like a more well-endowed version of the statue of David. Or like the god his call sign proclaimed him to be.

"Where?"

Oh, he really was the devil.

I swallowed, looking into his eyes and seeing the challenge there, hearing the unspoken dare to commit to what I'd started.

I couldn't say "tits"—I tried for like a second, but my mouth just wouldn't form the words—so I settled for "breasts" instead. So what if I sounded like a sex-ed lecture, I figured the lace, cleavage, and tight nipples more than made up for it.

He took another step toward me, invading my space, his hand reaching out and cupping my breast, squeezing, testing the heavy weight. I bit down on my lip to keep from groaning, unable to resist the urge to arch forward, wanting more than just his hand on me. I waited for him to move, but he didn't. He just stood there, my breast in his hand, until finally I couldn't take it anymore.

"What are you waiting for?"

I tried—and failed—to keep the tremor from my voice.

I was so wet now, so beyond aroused, and I needed more than just the scraps he'd given me—nothing at all, really.

"I'm waiting for you to tell me how I can touch you. Where. Waiting to make sure I don't do something I'm not supposed to do."

I stifled the growl that rose in my throat. He was totally fucking with me and not in the fun orgasm-inducing way, but in a teasing, arrogant sort of way, which made me want to make him beg for it all that much more and also ratcheted up my attraction another notch or ten.

Was it rude to ask him to stop talking? I couldn't handle the talking.

"For example," he purred, his voice bathing me in silk. "If I wanted to lift those pretty tits out from your bra and run my thumbs over your nipples, tugging on them until they got hard"—he broke off, his gaze lowering to my breasts, that fucking dimple popping out again—"*harder,*" he corrected, as I blushed. "Would you let me do that?" he whispered. "What if I wanted to suck on them, take those nipples between my lips, feasting on those gorgeous fucking tits?"

My head went back, pleasure, sharp and sweet, surging through my body. I swallowed, gathered my courage, and looked him dead in the eye. Two could play this game.

"I want your hands on me. And then I want your mouth. Now."

THOR

If she hadn't ruined me for other women before—which I was pretty sure she fucking *had*—then she'd definitely accomplished it in one afternoon and evening.

I didn't know what had gotten into her or what I'd done to deserve it, but she'd taken sexy to a whole new level and I was more than happy to reap the rewards, especially if it got me more of what I'd found when I'd laid her down on the blanket in the field and teased her orgasm out of her, when she'd shattered against my lips until I swallowed every drop.

I reached out, feeling the tremor in my hands, the twitch in my cock, as I grazed the lace cup of her corset, my finger inches away from her nipple.

Her eyes fluttered closed, her lips parting.

Fucking gorgeous.

I trailed my finger up until I found the spot where the swell of her breast met lace, stroking her there—*so soft*—before I did what I'd promised—sliding my fingers under the lace, and lifting her gorgeous tits from the fabric so that they were exposed to my gaze, the corset pushing them up even higher in a pose that was so hot, it was obscene.

It took a moment for me to get my body under control, a moment when all I could do was stare at her, and then I had to move, my hands cupping her breasts, fingers teasing her nipples, until I found heaven.

"What do you want?" I whispered, getting off on this demanding thing she had going on more than I ever imagined I would.

When she answered me, her voice shook. "Just keep doing what you're doing."

I fought the need thundering through my veins, telling myself I had to go slow, had to make this perfect for her. I worshipped her breasts with my hands, everything I had focused on giving her the best night of her life.

When her voice threaded through the moans and sighs coming from both of us, when she told me she wanted my mouth, I was already so far past my breaking point, it wasn't funny. When my lips closed down around her nipple— sucking the tight bud into my mouth—I swear I saw stars. She tasted so fucking sweet, her body so responsive as I laved her flesh with my tongue, tugging on the tip with my teeth, switching from one to the next, all while she ran her hands along my back, her body bowing as I supported her, as I ravaged her skin until she was the prettiest shades of pink I'd ever seen. Until I leaned back and admired my work, the way her nipples popped like two berries, red and shiny from my mouth.

"Do you have any idea of how badly I want you?" I ground the words out, my heart racing, dick aching. "Any idea of how you look right now and how you just make me want to do all kinds of filthy things to you?"

Her nails dug even deeper into my skin.

I reached behind her, my fingers unhooking the corset, trembling with the movement until I finally reached the last one and the fabric hit the floor, baring her torso to me. I slid my hand down her stomach, reveling in how soft she felt, my fingers hovering above the top of her thong.

My gaze met hers. "Can I touch you? Lick you? I want to make you come."

Her eyelashes fluttered, the look in her eyes somewhere past dazed, her skin flushed. She nodded like a fucking queen addressing a peasant.

I sank to my knees, finesse going out the window as I gripped the waistband of the lace covering her, pulling it down her hips, down her legs, and then she was naked before me.

I didn't wait, didn't take the time to admire the view; I just put my mouth on her, wanting more of the taste I'd already had of her, the taste I'd been craving since I'd gone down on her in the field.

She was so wet, so warm, her body shaking beneath my touch, and I lost a bit of my sanity. It didn't take long before I felt her shattering, her orgasm on my tongue as I gripped her ass, as the carpet dug into my knees. I held her up after, swallowing the aftershocks that quaked her body, and then I was sweeping her up and carrying her into the bedroom, needing to get inside her.

I set her down on the giant bed, kissing the inside of her thigh.

"I have condoms in the nightstand," she said.

I opened the drawer, my fingers shaking with anticipation, grabbing one of the foil packets like it was buried treasure, tearing it open and sliding the condom over my cock.

I moved on top of her, only to be surprised when she gripped my arms, hooking her leg over my hip and changing positions, pushing me onto my back so she straddled me.

My heart clenched as I reached out and grabbed her hand, lacing my fingers with hers.

Her orgasm seemed to have taken the edge off her need, because suddenly she was back in control again and I was the one on my proverbial knees, begging her to give me what I wanted, craved—

She fisted my cock, lifting her body up, positioning herself just over me, hovering there, our flesh barely touching, the heat and wetness spilling from her body, coating the tip. She braced herself, her body sliding down over me, her neck thrown back as she impaled herself on my cock, her back arched, tits thrust forward.

I groaned, going into sensory overload at the feel and sight of her. It didn't get better than this.

I released her hand, gripping either side of her hips, pulling her down onto me, needing to feel all of her. I began to move, setting the pace, but in that, too, I lost control.

I was helpless beneath her as she began riding me, her hands braced on the iron headboard above me, her tits hovering inches away from my mouth. I couldn't resist the urge to capture her nipples between my lips as she rocked over me, her tits bouncing and swaying as she gripped my cock in a tight, wet glove.

I slipped my hand between us, my thumb finding her swollen clit, needing to feel her come again, wanting to watch her lose the last vestiges of control. I felt her clench down around me, drank in the moans falling from her lips as she gripped my cock, as she came.

And then I felt it, the orgasm building at the base of my spine, my balls tightening, as I came hard and fast, until we both sprawled out on the sheets, sated and spent, and she had my heart and body in the palm of her hand.

FIFTEEN

BECCA

I might have given myself more credit than I deserved.

As far as the whole taking-control thing went, I figured I got an eight for effort, although the Russian judge would likely knock me down for the fact that, by the end of it, I was so far gone I could barely remember my own name. Considering Eric had appeared to suffer in the same way, I figured the whole thing was a wash.

What I had failed to account for, and what barely earned me a freaking three, was how good it would feel to have his arms wrapped around me again, or how easy it would be to sink into sleep when I was riding the wave of two of the best orgasms I'd ever had. Or that I would wake up to him in the morning and, stupidly, curl into his warmth again, because it felt so good to have him next to me that my brain apparently switched off and forgot that this was supposed to just be physical.

"I can hear you thinking," Eric murmured, his lips brushing my hair as he pulled me tighter against his naked body.

"I should go take a shower. I need to go to work."

I tried to keep my voice hard, as if the force of my words could push him away. I figured I would have been more successful if my arms didn't wrap themselves around him, my lips seeking out the curve where his neck met his shoulder, my fingers brushing against the light hair covering his chest.

He looked over at the alarm clock, cradling the back of my head in his big hand.

"It's five thirty."

"I have a busy day."

We were cuddling. Spooning. It would be one thing if we were having morning sex, but this? This was bad. This was on the list of not-a-good-idea. Hell, it was at the top, right after me telling him I still loved him.

He wanted me as badly as I wanted him. I could feel him hard and heavy against my hip, and yet neither one of us made a sexual move. It was as though we *preferred* to cuddle.

Fuck me.

Did he just nuzzle me?

His hand curled around my breast in a move that was more possessive and sleepy than sexual, and I felt a bit of my resolve flee.

"You feel good like this," he whispered.

He did, too.

I stifled a groan, figuring Cupid had a sense of humor, because it was so not fair that I'd somehow careened back to where I'd started. I was smart; I should have known better, and still, I courted trouble, giving myself over to the pleasure of holding him in the palm of my hand, even as I knew it wouldn't last.

He turned me in his arms until we were facing each other, pressing soft kisses to my face, my neck, my lips. Death by a thousand kisses. I couldn't fight the laughter that rose, the brush of his lips against my skin tickling me and setting off a whole other host of sensations.

And just like that, I threw in the towel.

I could spend the next week freaking out every time we were together, trying to put a wall up just for him to knock it down, but I was a big girl, and I wanted this, without guilt or fear, wanted to bask in this moment for as long as I could.

So here we were—

This wasn't forever. It wasn't even necessarily tomorrow. But we had today and who knew how many days after that, and I was going to enjoy the ride until it was time to get off.

A smile slid over my lips as I pulled back to look at him, my fingers tracing his cheekbones, stroking down his skin until they found his mouth, my thumb rubbing over his bottom lip—

I hissed as he sucked my thumb inside, nipping at the pad.

"I might have a couple hours before I have to go to work."

His lips curved into a beautiful grin. "Then you're lucky that I can get a lot done in a couple of hours."

He rolled me over so my back sank down into the mattress, his body hovering over mine, and then his lips were at my neck, his hand between my legs, as he got to work and showed me just how productive he could be.

THOR

I took my time getting dressed, too caught up in the sight of Becca to rush.

I'd never been all that into business suits, but something

about the way she rocked them went straight to my dick. Or maybe it was the black heels she slid her feet into, the black-rimmed glasses she slipped on. She didn't wear them all of the time, but when she did, it was like she put on a mask, giving me a different version of herself, one I wanted just as much as all of the other versions she gave me.

Becca walked over to where I sat on the edge of the bed buttoning my shirt, a gleam in her eyes. I dropped the fabric, finding her hips, wrapping my arms around her, unable to resist the urge to lay my cheek against her stomach, loving the way her fingers stroked through my hair, how she held me to her like she didn't want to let me go.

Something had changed between us this morning. Last night had been mind-blowing, but I'd still felt that wall between us, and even sex hadn't been able to erase the feeling that she held me at bay.

And then she'd woken up and wrapped her body around me, and I felt like I'd died and gone to heaven. The wall was down and while I had no idea how it happened—or why—I couldn't be more grateful.

I'd never felt this way about anyone before. Wasn't sure I'd even felt this way about her before. Maybe it took losing her to realize just how much I needed her, the contrast between my life with Becca and my life without never clearer than in this moment.

"Have dinner with me tonight."

She grinned. "Okay."

I'd graduated from "maybes" to "okays," and I felt like a fucking king.

"We can go to Columbia. Go to your favorite Mexican place if you want. Do you still love chips and salsa?"

The smile she gave me nearly took my breath away. I hadn't seen her smile since I'd been back—not like this. Not the kind of smile that transformed her face, that made it impossible for me not to smile in return.

"Yeah, I do."

"What time do you finish up work?"

"I can probably be ready to leave about six thirty. Does that work for you?"

"Sounds perfect."

She moved out of my grasp, grabbing her purse and shoving her keys and cell inside. Her glasses slid down the bridge of her nose and she pushed them back up. My dick twitched.

"What do you have planned today?" she asked.

"Probably go to the gym and lift. Maybe go for a run. My grandmother wants to paint her kitchen so I told her I'd go pick up some paint and get started on that." I grinned. "I'm sort of a gentleman of leisure right now."

My vacation back home had been pretty low-key, but given how much I'd been working, low-key was exactly what I needed. I spent time with my grandmother every day, worked out for a few hours. I'd run into a few people I'd grown up with and caught up with them, surprised to see that nearly everyone was married with kids. The whole thing made me feel old and out of place, as though I'd missed a crucial stage in life somewhere along the way.

I stood up, fastening the last buttons of my shirt, sliding my feet into my shoes as I followed her out of the apartment. I walked her to her car, admiring the view as I went. One day I was going to have her like that, bent over a desk, her skirt hauled up, ass bare.

Becca stopped in front of her car and I wrapped my arms around her waist, pulling her close, nuzzling her neck, inhaling the scent of her perfume. I kissed her and she made that little noise in her throat that she did when she was turned on, kissing me back, her arms sliding around my neck.

"Have a good day at work," I whispered against her lips.

She grinned. "I'll see you tonight."

I stood in the parking lot watching her drive away, and then I opened the door and slid into the Mustang.

My cell rang as I put the key in the ignition. I stared down at the screen, surprised by the strange country code.

"Hello?"

"Hey, man, it's Burn."

Burn and I had been stationed together in the Wild Aces before he PCSed to a squadron in South Korea with his now-wife, Jordan, a few months ago. We still talked occasionally, but we hadn't caught up in a couple of months. I always felt better when I talked to Burn; he had his shit together more than most, and he'd been in the formation the night that Joker died so he got it in a way that no one else besides Easy did.

"Hey, how's it going? How's Korea?"

"Complicated."

"What's wrong?"

"The amazing thing is that Jordan's pregnant."

"That's awesome, dude. Congrats."

"Thanks."

He and Jordan had one of those relationships that seemed completely rock solid. I'd known him before he met her, had been there in Vegas the weekend they'd gotten together, and I'd never seen him as happy as he was with her. I didn't doubt they'd both be great parents or that Burn was thrilled.

"So what's the bad thing?"

"She's fine and the baby's fine, but it's looking like the pregnancy might be bumpy. The medical situation here isn't great and I'd really feel more comfortable if she was back home to have the baby. The Air Force won't move her to Florida and she feels weird about staying at her parents', so she's planning on going back to my house in Oklahoma. I already talked to Easy and he's moving out so she'll just stay there, and I'll take my mid-tour so I can be with her when the baby's born."

I felt bad for the guy. No man wanted to be separated from his wife, especially when she was pregnant and a newlywed, but I also didn't blame him for his concerns about her staying overseas.

"Can I do anything to help?"

"Yeah, can you pick her up from the airport? I'd ask Easy, but he's going TDY to Hill."

"I'm in South Carolina right now, but I'll be back in Oklahoma soon. When will she be flying in?"

"We haven't booked it yet, but two weeks should work. We're trying to finalize everything before she goes back."

He sounded tired and beyond stressed.

"You know if there's anything I can do to help while she's in Oklahoma, I'm happy to."

Burn and Easy had been roommates before he left for Korea, and Easy and Jordan had a friendship of sorts, but it had to be hard for Burn to know his wife would be so far away and it would be easier if she had a big support network in place.

"Thanks, man. I really appreciate it. Her family and her best friend are planning to come out and visit her, and I'll be there for my mid-tour, but it'll be nice to have the guys in the squadron to look after her. I really appreciate it."

"No problem."

This is what we all did for one another—we stepped up and filled the gaps when it was needed. That was one of the things that had drawn me to military life in the beginning; for a guy who hadn't grown up with much of a family, having a group of people who always had my back meant the world.

"Did you hear about Dani?" Burn asked.

I felt a twinge at the sound of her name. Even though Dani, Joker's widow, was around my age, she had been the unofficial "mom" to our rowdy group. I'd spent several holidays at their home; when she'd found out that people in the squadron didn't have anywhere to go, she'd opened the doors to all of us, making us feel like we really were a part of their family.

She'd sent care packages on deployments, made cupcakes on birthdays, basically did everything she could to make our lives better and our jobs just a little bit easier. Joker had been one of the best guys I'd known and he'd been like an older brother to me; his wife was equally beloved.

When he died, we all stepped up as best we could to help out Dani. She went home to Georgia to spend time with her family, but we still occasionally traded e-mails. I didn't know what to say to her, didn't know how you helped someone through the magnitude of her loss, but I did the best I could to be there for her.

"Is she okay?"

"Yeah, she is. She and Jordan talked the other day and she mentioned that she's coming back to Oklahoma."

"Seriously?"

It had been several months since Joker died and she'd left right after the memorial service we'd had for him at Bryer.

"Yeah. She wants to get their house ready to go on the market and figure out her next step. She's planning on arriving right before Thanksgiving."

It would be good to see her again, and at the same time, there was always a tightness in my chest that appeared when I saw Dani, a guilt I couldn't help but feel that I'd come home when her husband hadn't. But whatever feelings I had about

Dani's return paled in comparison to the ones Easy would have.

"Does he know?"

There was no point in saying who "he" was. Easy had done a decent job of covering his feelings for Dani when Joker was alive, but considering everything we'd been through together, I could read Easy pretty fucking well.

"I haven't told him." Burn was silent for a beat. "How is he?"

"I don't know. The same, I guess? We don't talk about it or anything."

"How are you?"

We were fighter pilots; we typically did not talk about emotional shit. So I had a pretty good feeling that someone had told him about my freak-out in the air.

"Let me guess, you talked to Loco?"

"He's worried."

"I have it under control."

"Do you?"

No.

"Do *you*?" I countered.

He sighed. "I miss him. I still occasionally have dreams. But when I'm in the air, I keep that shit out. I have a wife, a baby on the way. I can't risk getting fucked when I'm in the jet. It's too dangerous for me and every single person in my formation."

That was the worst part. It wasn't just that my PTSD, or whatever the hell it was, was dangerous to me. It was the fact that I was putting the guys in my formation in danger, too.

"You going to talk to someone?" he asked.

"Come on. How well do you think that's going to go over for my career?"

It was hard enough to get to the top; once you were there, you had to bust your ass to stay there, to keep a fighter spot, a Viper spot, when more guys were getting pulled out of the cockpit and sent to bullshit assignments. Something like this was an easy way to weed me out.

"I know, but think about how much worse it could be. You have to get your shit straight on your own or else you have to get help. You can't just leave it and hope it'll go away. It won't."

"I know."

"How is it being back home?"

I grimaced. "Is there anything you and Loco didn't talk about?"

"He didn't know about the girl you left behind there."

I'd totally forgotten about the night I'd told Burn about Becca. I'd been drunk and missing her, and it had all just tumbled out.

"Have you seen her yet?"

I groaned. "Are you trying to play matchmaker now that you're married?"

He laughed. "Maybe. I'm just saying—it's a hell of a lot easier to fight when you have something you're fighting for."

"Let's just say I'm working on it, although I'm not sure how this one is going to play out. She hates my job and there's a fuckload of baggage there."

"Trust me, Jordan wasn't wild about it, either, but you find a way to make it work."

If only it were that easy.

"I gotta go, early brief, but if you ever need to talk, I'm here."

"Thanks, man."

He was one of those guys who'd definitely been tapped early on by the Air Force brass to go far. He was a patch—a graduate of the prestigious USAF Weapons School—and I didn't doubt that he'd be a squadron commander someday in the not too distant future. He was also one of the best guys I knew.

"Thanks for the help with Jord. I'll let you know when I have her flight info."

"Sounds good."

Burn was quiet for a beat.

"You're there. I'm not. How badly is he going to take this Dani business?"

He and Easy had always been more brothers than friends.

"I honestly don't know. He doesn't talk about what happened—about her—at all really. He's up to his usual routine; I've been out with him three times and he went home with two different girls. He could be totally fine and over it, or he could freak the fuck out."

Burn sighed. "If he goes off the rails, let me know."

"Copy."

"Sometimes I feel like everyone's fucking dad," he grumbled.

I grinned. "It's good practice. Stay safe."

The call disconnected, but the smile lingered on my face, and I realized that as much as I'd enjoyed being home, as amazing as it had been to be with Becca, there had been a part of me that missed this, missed talking to my bros, to the guys I would give my life to protect. Ours was a small brotherhood, the bonds forged through a life spent on the edge, but more than anything, it was a family.

SIXTEEN

BECCA

We drove to the restaurant with the top down, Eric's hand on my thigh, "Jack & Diane" blaring from the stereo speakers. When we were younger, little more than kids, we'd done this drive so many times in Eric's beaten-up car, eager to escape the quiet of Bradbury. By most people's standards, Columbia probably wasn't considered a big city or anything, but to us it had been a whole other world, full of limitless possibilities.

Neither one of us had the greatest home lives, both of us ending up feeling more than a little alone, and Columbia had represented a fresh start for us, that first step toward building lives of our own.

I didn't know if it was how much all of this felt like déjà vu or the fact that I'd grown up a bit, but it hit me, really hit me, how young we'd been back then. It hadn't seemed like it—I'd been on my own for all intents and purposes for a long time at that point, but I'd still been figuring out who I was, what I wanted out of life. I'd thought otherwise, been so sure of my path, but now? Looking back, I realized how little I'd known about myself and life. And as much as it had hurt me at the time, a part of me couldn't help wondering if I'd found a part of myself somewhere along the way when I lost Eric, a part I never would have found without that loss.

Eric's hand drifted a little higher on my leg. "You okay tonight? You're quiet."

I turned and smiled at him, studying his face in profile. "Just enjoying the ride." I hesitated, not wanting to spoil the mood with bringing up our past but, at the same time, failing at pretending with him. "I was remembering all the times we did this drive when we were younger."

His lips curved, his attention turning from the traffic to look at me.

"We made this drive on our first date."

I couldn't believe he remembered that.

"You're right, we did."

I'd been so nervous that night. We'd officially met when I started tutoring him in English, although I'd known who he was before then. Everyone had. Our high school was small and we'd all grown up together, but Eric had been a year ahead of me. He was held back at the beginning of high school when his parents divorced and he started skipping school, so we ended up in the same grade.

After a couple weeks of sitting at a cramped table in the library, hunched together, he asked me out, which had been a pretty good thing considering I'd had a massive crush on him by that point and *Middlemarch* had been the last thing on my mind.

"You wore a blue dress with flowers and your hair was down."

Shock filled me. I totally had. I still remembered going shopping for the dress with Lizzie after school, remembered when I'd nearly called the date off because I'd hated my hair and had so badly wanted everything to be perfect. I just couldn't believe *he* remembered. It had been fifteen years.

"How do you remember that?"

"I remember everything about you."

God, I didn't know if I was ready for this. It hurt and yet his words tempted me until I wanted to cloak myself in them. In him.

"What else do you remember?"

"I remember that you take your coffee with skim milk, no sugar. That your favorite breakfast food is pancakes. You hate scary movies. Your favorite color is blue. If you could go anywhere in the world, you would go to Venice. You like bananas, but not banana-flavored things. Bizarrely enough, you like strawberry-flavored things, but not strawberries, because it's a texture thing."

I was either going to laugh or cry.

"You hate waking up in the morning. You love to read, especially romance novels because you're always looking for a happy ending. You love your job because justice is its own form of happy ending. You're not a big fan of cats, but you're a sucker for dogs, the fluffier the better." He shot me a smile I couldn't quite read. "Do you want me to go on?"

I couldn't have answered him if I wanted to; my words were frozen in my throat.

"You're the most loyal person I've ever met, and when you do something, you don't believe it's worth doing unless you give it your all. You love fiercely, would die for the people you love, but the flip side is that you don't forgive easily, and once someone breaks that bond, it's tough to get back in.

"But if someone is lucky enough to be one of those people that you love, if they're lucky enough to get just a moment of what you give, then they'd have to be a fucking idiot to do anything to jeopardize that. And if they were stupid enough, then they'll do everything they can to get back what they lost because once someone's had it, life without it is unimaginable."

I couldn't breathe.

"Pull over."

"What?"

"Pull over," I repeated, my voice and heart tight.

"Becca—"

"Just pull over."

He slowed the car, and then he pulled over to the shoulder of the highway. The road between Bradbury and Columbia was mostly rural and there wasn't a ton of traffic at this time of day—it was past rush hour and most people were home with their families.

I didn't care.

I took off my seat belt.

"I didn't mean to upset you. I'm sorry—"

His words were cut off by my mouth, my lips, my tongue. I didn't so much kiss him as I attacked him, every single word that had fallen from his lips building an ache inside me that had been a low-level hum since I'd left him this morning.

Getting dumped, especially getting dumped when *you were engaged*, made you question everything you thought you knew about your relationship. You wondered how you could be so stupid as to think you were in love, to imagine your relationship was one thing when it turned out it was actually very different. I'd run the gamut of self-doubt, analyzing so many moments of our past, wondering where I'd gone wrong and what mistakes I'd made.

So to hear things from Eric's perspective—not just that he was sorry, but the fact that I hadn't been just a phase in his life, that what we'd had together had meant something to him—well, it affected me. A lot.

And while I wasn't sure I was ready for a big emotional discussion, while there was still a part of me that felt the need to keep my heart under lock and key, my lips didn't get the memo.

So I kissed the hell out of him.

His lips parted beneath mine instantly, his hands gripping my hips, pulling my body closer to his. We couldn't have sex—it wasn't *that* remote—but I figured tongue was totally fine.

My fingers threaded through his hair, tugging his head toward me. I sucked on his lower lip, capturing it between my teeth, before moving down, kissing the line of his jaw, inhaling that masculine, woodsy scent that was as familiar to me as breathing.

Eric groaned. "You know we can't have sex here, right?"

I grinned, pulling back to look into those gorgeous blue eyes. *Gah.* He really had an embarrassment of riches in the looks department.

"I know. Sorry, I couldn't resist," I said, not sorry at all.

I climbed off his lap, settling myself back in the passenger seat, rebuckling my seat belt with shaky hands.

His hands clutched the steering wheel, a pained expression on his face that I was pretty sure could be attributed to the impressive bulge in his pants.

Yep, not even a little bit sorry.

"I'm guessing a blowjob is out of the question?" he asked.

I laughed. "While you're driving?"

He gave me a hopeful look.

"Sorry." I patted his leg inches away from where he wanted me to be. "But if you're good, I'll go down on you when we get home."

He groaned. "You can't give me that mental image and expect me to get through the night."

"I don't. I want you to be horny and miserable." I grinned. "Kidding." I reached out and ruffled his hair, unable to resist screwing with him a bit. He could be so cocky that it was difficult to turn down the opportunity to steal the upper hand on the rare times it presented itself.

"Well, now tonight definitely has something in common with our first date."

I snorted. "Seriously?"

He grinned at me, that boyish charm taking another swipe at my resolve.

"Hey, like I said, I remember that blue dress *very* well. I spent half the night wondering if you were going to let me get under that short skirt."

I made a face. "I definitely wasn't going to put out on our first date."

"I knew you weren't. But I was a seventeen-year-old boy. I hate to break it to you, but ninety-nine point nine percent of the time my thoughts involved sex."

"And now?"

He laughed. "I've grown up since then. Much better control."

"Ninety-three percent?"

"More like ninety-five." He gave me a wolfish grin. "In that dress? One hundred percent."

"Just wait until you see what I'm wearing underneath," I teased.

His head jerked toward me so quickly, I worried he'd have whiplash.

My lips curved. "Let's just say I bought a few things at the sex shop."

He groaned, his hands gripping the steering wheel more tightly. "Jesus, Becca."

I leaned back in my seat, looking up at the sky, loving the rush of power, the knowledge that he would be thinking about us all night long.

And then I felt his free hand gliding up my inner thigh, teasing the hem of my dress. My legs parted and a sigh escaped my lips. He slipped under the fabric, walking his fingers up, higher and higher, until he reached between my legs, strumming my clit through the silky fabric, rubbing against the wetness already gathering there.

"What color are they?" he asked, his voice husky, vibrating with need.

"Red." I struggled over the word, struggled to breathe.

"Describe them."

My voice shook. "They're soft. Sensitive against my skin."

He continued stroking me, his gaze intense. We were on the side of the road, and while there wasn't much traffic, anyone could drive by and see. My dress was down, but if anyone looked at his hands, at my face . . .

"Keep going."

"They're . . ." *Ohmigod*. He was going to get me off, somewhere between Bradbury and Columbia. I was so close, so . . .

"You're so wet. So slippery. So warm. I bet I could just slide my fingers inside you."

"Yes."

"You want to come, don't you?"

I bit down on my lip, feeling panicky and aroused, and *sofreakingclose*.

"Yes. Please."

His thumb stayed on my clit, his fingers hooking under the silk and thrusting inside with one smooth glide.

"Fuck," he hissed, a groan escaping his lips. "I can't wait to get inside you."

Me, either. Did we really need to do dinner? We could eat later. Much later.

The force of his thrusts increased, his thumb playing me expertly, and then I was coming, gripping the seat, my body bucking beneath his touch. When I'd finally come down from the high, he slid out of me, his gaze on me as he sucked me off his fingers, his eyes dark.

I died. Again.

We just sat there for a minute, neither one of us talking, the sound of our harsh breaths filling the car.

Finally he took a deep breath, gathering himself and maneuvering the car back onto the highway. I went someplace else, my head reduced to colors, sounds, the feel of the wind on my face, the lingering pulse between my legs. Nothing and everything. The music playing on the stereo filled the silence between us until Eric spoke again, his voice stripped of its usual cockiness, as though he'd been sanded down.

"You didn't ask me what I was doing the other half of the night."

I couldn't follow the conversation we'd just had, couldn't gather my own thoughts.

"What?"

"On our first date. I told you I spent half the night fantasizing about you. You didn't ask me what I was doing the other half."

I grinned, feeling a little drunk on him. "Do I really want to know?"

Whatever I'd imagined, his answer definitely wasn't what I'd expected.

"I was falling in love with you."

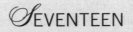

SEVENTEEN

THOR

It was, hands down, the best date I'd ever been on. It wasn't just that she was hot, the way she leaned over the table, thrusting her tits forward, inspiring quite a few fantasies that kept me turned on and fighting an erection throughout the night. Or how good it had felt to make her come in the car earlier. More than anything, it was the simple fact that I'd never been able to talk to anyone the way I could talk to her. Never felt as comfortable with anyone as I did with her.

I'd forgotten that. Or maybe not forgotten it, but forgotten how much I'd counted on it, how much she'd been an integral part of my life, like a limb I'd been missing all this time. Forgotten what it felt like to be with someone who knew you better than anyone.

I'd been nervous to talk to her about my job, worried that it was the white elephant between us considering how much of a wedge it had created in our relationship, but surprisingly I found myself telling her how I felt when I flew, about the deployments, and the friends I'd made, letting her in on the parts of my life I never thought we could share.

We didn't talk about the future, didn't talk about the fact that I'd be returning to Oklahoma in a week. But I gave her the most important parts of the last decade of my life.

"So what's your favorite part of the job?" she asked in between bites of chips and salsa.

I thought about that one for a beat. "Probably the flying. It's amazing up there."

A smile played at her lips. "You always did love pushing the limits."

"Yeah, I guess a thing like that doesn't really go away." I shrugged, taking another bite of my burrito. "I like the challenge of it. In the beginning when I was going through pilot training, it was such a fucking struggle. Your first flight you're absolutely clueless. It's like watching a baby learn how to walk. But little by little you get more comfortable, learn more. Every step is a new challenge—just learning how to fly, then learning how to fly like a fighter pilot, then an F-16, then how to be good enough in an F-16 to keep progressing, to start having the experience and knowledge to teach other guys how to fly.

"We're constantly adapting to new threats, new mission sets. And even when you get used to it, there's always the chance that weird shit can happen in the air and suddenly you're back to feeling like a newbie again, just trying to stay alive." I swallowed, taking a sip of my margarita. "I told you that I had an issue flying before I came here."

She nodded, her mouth tightening. "It sounded dangerous."

"It was. I was flying, and all of a sudden, it was like I was back there on the night he died."

I remembered my conversation with Burn, and while I

wasn't sure I was ready to talk to a shrink or anything, part of me did want to talk to someone. Needed to talk to someone.

And my "someone" had always been Becca.

"What happened when he died?"

I took another deep breath, feeling like a lead weight pressed down on my chest. "We were TDY in Alaska. It was a night sortie and we were finishing up, on our way home. Everything was fine, or so we thought. I was on Joker's wing." The familiar guilt came rushing back. "He made a radio call; we were doing low-level strafing as a four-ship." She looked confused. "Basically, shooting the gun at targets on the ground while we were flying low. It's one of those things we do in combat a lot and we practice it all the time. Completely routine." She nodded. "Apparently, he spatial D'ed. Spatial disorientation. You get confused on where the jet is, think you're in a different position than you are, and by the time you realize it or when you try to correct yourself, it's too late. Joker didn't realize how low he was flying and he crashed into a mountain."

Becca's jaw dropped. "Oh my God."

"The whole thing happened so fucking fast. He was fine and then he was just gone."

"Oh my God. I'm so sorry. I can't imagine what that must have been like for all of you. I can't imagine how hard it must be to fly after something like that."

"It spooked me. And I can't seem to move past it."

She took a sip of her margarita, fear in her eyes. "Does that kind of stuff happen a lot?"

"Spatial D? Yeah. Most of the time you recover, no big deal." I ran a hand through my hair, my voice cracking. "It happened to me on my last flight before I took leave. The flight that made me realize that I needed to figure out what the hell was going on. It was the same kind of situation as what happened with Joker. And I just . . . I freaked. I've probably spatial D'ed dozens of times in my career, and I've always recovered, always been lucky. But this time, it was like I was back in that night, and I couldn't shake it. The worst thing you can do in the cockpit is lose your shit. We're trained to stay calm always. And I couldn't get control. And that scares me more than anything, because a spooked pilot is a dead one.

"There was an upgrade to the jet, a new system that sets off an alarm if you get too close to the ground to keep what happened to Joker from happening again. It saved my life. I keep thinking that a few months would have made the difference between saving his. If he'd only had the upgrade . . ."

"I'm so sorry." She reached out and took my hand, squeezing my fingers as though she could infuse me with some of her strength.

"I know. I'm sorry, I don't mean to ruin things by getting so heavy, I just . . ." My voice trailed off again and I played with my food. "I haven't been able to talk about it. It's hard."

"You can always talk to me."

She knew all my secrets, had been there for all of the rocky times in my life when I was younger.

"I know. It means a lot."

"Do you think you can move past it when you fly? Find a way to deal with it?"

"I don't know. I want to. I know I need to, that it's too fucking dangerous for me to be up in the air if I'm going to lose it again."

"Can you talk to a professional or something?"

"I mean, yeah, I can, but I'm worried about how it could affect my career."

"Why? That's bullshit."

I shrugged. "I'm not much of a fighter pilot if I'm cracking in the jet."

"Yeah, but what about you? Just as a person. How are you supposed to deal with this if you can't talk about it, if you can't get the help you need?"

"There's not a lot of coddling or hand-holding in my job. They don't really give a shit about that stuff as long as we get the mission accomplished."

She opened her mouth and closed it again, and I could tell her sense of justice was deeply offended.

I grinned despite the depressing conversation. It was reassuring to see that some things never changed. For all of her shyness when we were younger, she'd always been the first person to sign up for a protest, to volunteer when help was needed, to speak out against a wrong that had been committed. She was fierce about the things she believed in, and it had always been one of the qualities I admired most about her.

"Has being back helped at all?"

I made a face and she laughed. "I'm not talking about your orgasms; get your mind out of the gutter."

"It's definitely been worth it for the orgasms alone," I teased.

"You know what I mean."

"I do." I sobered. "Honestly, I'm not sure. A little bit maybe? I guess it recharged my batteries. I've been so fucking tired for so long, and it feels good just to have the time off to process everything.

"I went from a series of TDYs and then Joker's death, and things have been pretty intense lately as we've ramped up for our next deployment. There hasn't been a lot of time to breathe." I brought our joined hands to my lips and pressed a kiss over her knuckles. "And I promise, I'm not just saying this because I want to see what you're wearing under that sexy dress, but seeing you again, having you in my life again, has definitely helped. I've never been able to talk to anyone the way I can talk to you. I've missed this."

She didn't answer me, not audibly anyway, but I saw her answer in the emotion lingering in her eyes, felt it in the way she held on to me and didn't let go.

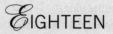

EIGHTEEN

BECCA

It was a fantastic date. One of those dates when you could feel the chemistry just sparking, when you finished each other's sentences, the conversation flowed freely, and you had to fight to keep a smile off your lips.

Danger zone.

I unlocked my front door, Eric at my back. I stiffened as he lifted my hair off of my neck, pulling it to the front so my nape was bare. I went a little weak in the knees when he pressed his lips to my flesh, when his teeth grazed my skin, when he wrapped an arm around my waist and pulled me back so I could feel his cock, hard and heavy against my ass.

"I had a great time tonight," he whispered, his lips grazing my ear.

A shiver ripped through me.

His hands fumbled at my hip, trying to peel back layers and layers of dress.

"How does this thing open?" he mumbled, his voice frustrated.

I grinned. "It's a wrap dress."

"What?"

"There's a tie on the side."

His fingers struggled with the knot just above my left hip, a few curse words tumbling from his lips. Patience had never exactly been one of his virtues.

I batted his hands away. "Here, let me do it."

I turned in the circle of his arms, my fingers shaking slightly as I undid the knot, pulling the fabric from my body until I was naked but for the silky red bra and thong I'd bought on the Great Sex Store Expedition. His eyes widened.

"Whoa."

A flush crept up my cheeks and I tossed him a flirty wink.

"Glad you like it."

"Babe."

I figured that one word contained a whole lot of meaning.

He reached for me but I evaded his grasp, wanting to prolong this moment, to bask in the gleam in his eyes. I'd never been big on sexy lingerie, my style tended to be way more conservative, but seeing how much he obviously enjoyed it . . . let's just say I had a feeling another trip to the sex store might be in order.

His smile dipped. "Are you going to take charge again this time?"

Heat spread across my body. "Did you like it?"

"I like anything that involves you naked, so yeah." He hooked an arm around my waist. "Scratch that. I like anything that involves you, period."

God, it was really hard to keep my heart disengaged when he said things like that.

He stroked my back, leaning into me so his face was buried in my neck, pressing gentle kisses to the curve of my shoulder.

I groaned. "I don't think I can wait much longer."

"Sorry, you'll find no sympathy here. I had hours of torture sitting across the table, wishing I could have my way with you, wanting to slip my hand under your dress to see if you were as turned on as I was. You can wait a few minutes."

"Is this payback?"

He pulled back, his finger trailing down the edge of my bra, a wolfish smile on his face. "Nah, this is just fun."

He dragged the pad of his finger down the curve of my breast and back again, his smile deepening as we both watched a line of goose bumps flare up on my skin, as I arched my back forward, pressing more of myself into his hands.

I had a feeling he was getting off on tormenting me as much as I'd felt the same way about him last night. It was a weighty thing to watch someone unravel before you because they were desperate for you.

And I was desperate. My arousal burned me from the inside out, a fire blazing below my skin. I needed more than these featherlight touches, more than the way he teased me, each barely there touch ratcheting my arousal up another notch until I couldn't stand it anymore and I wrapped my arm around his neck, pulling his head down until his lips were mine.

He might have been pretending to go slowly, might have acted like he could drag this night out, but the second our mouths touched, pretense went out the window.

He kissed me like he was dying for my lips, my mouth, my tongue. Like the same madness that coursed through my veins was inside of him, too, pushing to get out. Finesse went out the window and taking it slow became a pipe dream.

He was so good when he was being oh, so bad.

Eric tugged at my hair as he kissed me, as he pulled me toward him, inch by inch, kiss by kiss, until it felt like we were one. Our hands and bodies became extensions of each other as we reconnected, as we came together once again with an inaudible click, as though the rightness of it all overshadowed everything else.

We fumbled for each other's clothes, laughter filling the room when he struggled with my bra, when it caught on my elbow, when he tripped on his pants. And then the laughter disappeared when we were both naked, standing in my living room once again.

Eric picked me up, wrapping my legs around him, carrying me into the bedroom while I straddled his waist, my nipples rubbing against the hard planes of his chest, my hands exploring his back. We walked toward the bed and I waited for him to lay me down on the mattress, but he didn't. Instead, he carried me into the bathroom, setting me down on my feet.

I blinked, surprised by the turn of events.

Eric smiled, his mouth swollen from our kisses, red marks already forming along his neck and shoulders from where I'd raked my nails across his body and sucked on his skin.

"I get to play tonight. Let me take care of you."

The breath whooshed out of me and it was an effort not to sway on my feet. There was something about having sex when I could feel like I was in control, or when we both lost our minds. It felt safe. Like I wasn't the only one engaging in this madness, and if I lost myself, it would be okay because he would have lost a bit of himself, too. Letting him take control was another thing entirely, and I could tell by the way he watched me, gauging my response, that he knew it.

I had feelings for him, still loved him. I probably would always love him. And I was obviously attracted to him. But that didn't mean that I ever wanted him to see me vulnerable again. Not after what we'd been through. Not after I'd laid myself bare before him and begged him not to leave, not to end our engagement, and he'd walked away anyway.

It might have just been sex, but I wasn't sure I was ready.

"Let's go into the bedroom." I gave him a forced smile, trailing my hand up his torso.

He caught my hand, unfurling my fingers and linking his with mine until our palms connected.

I fought the urge to jerk back.

I knew what he was doing. He wanted more than casual sex, and he was pulling out all the stops to get back to the couple we'd been before, when there had been no barriers between us, nothing off-limits. I just didn't know how to go there. Not after everything.

"Becca."

I heard the plea in his voice, felt a rush of pleasure at the sound of my name said with such aching gentleness. Once again, my head warred with my heart.

"Trust me. Please."

It was a small thing—a concession to make in the bedroom—and yet, we both knew what he was really asking had nothing to do with sex. He kept sneaking his way past my defenses, and I kept letting him, because no matter how hard I fought to deny it, he had always been my weak spot.

I waited for him to touch me again, to use his body to tempt me. I was so close, so turned on, that I didn't doubt that it would take little encouragement for me to break down my walls in order to get off. But he didn't. He didn't touch me except for the point where our hands met, didn't speak except for those three words—

Trust me. Please.

And then I remembered why I'd never hidden myself from him, why he'd had every single part of me years ago. Because he was a good guy. He was honest and he was fair, and for all of his flaws, he had never lied to me. Ever. As much as I'd been angry with him for the fights we'd had, for the way we'd broken up, he'd been honest with me there, too. He could have told me things would be okay, could have lied about the demands of military life, and I would have probably believed him considering how little I knew about the Air Force. But he hadn't. He'd given me the facts, answered my questions, even when the truth had made a future together seem insurmountable. And he hadn't once tried to convince me to give up my dreams of being a lawyer. If anything, he'd supported me, wanted me to follow my dreams, even when it put us on opposite paths. He wasn't a player. He wasn't an asshole. He might have been wild when he was younger, but he'd never been a bad guy. So I gave him this part of me, too, because in the end it had always been his.

"Okay."

"Thank you," he whispered, his voice thick with emotion.

I nodded, a lump in my throat, a flutter in my stomach, and a pounding in my heart.

He walked over to the big whirlpool tub and I admired the view before me, anticipation running through my veins. He bent down and turned on the water, filling up the bathtub.

He gestured for me to step in and I did, feeling simultaneously turned on and a little self-conscious. I didn't know why, but for some reason this felt as intimate as sex, or maybe more intimate in a different way. We were both naked, but I felt like I was even more exposed, like I was giving him a sneak peek into my daily routine, giving him a part of myself, even as it was something as little as this.

I sat down, sinking back until the water spilled over me.

"Is it too hot?"

I shook my head. It felt so good. I'd had a crazy day at work and I hadn't had much downtime between coming home and our date, so this was the first chance I'd had to really relax.

"Close your eyes."

And with that husky, sexy tone, there went relaxing.

My pulse raced and I opened my mouth to protest, but something in his gaze, the sheer force of how much he wanted me, of how much he was enjoying this—and how badly I wanted the release he offered—had my mouth and eyes closing instead.

"Good girl."

Who was I kidding? At this point he could tie me to the bed and I'd be down with it.

I sat there, the jets pulsing around me, the warm water lapping at my skin, my muscles relaxing. I couldn't hear Eric anymore, didn't know if he was standing there staring at my naked body, if the sight of me was getting him even harder. And something about that, the idea that I was just spread out before him, waiting, had my nipples tightening and another pull of arousal pulsing between my legs. And then I heard the low strands of music coming from the radio on my nightstand—"Heart Skipped a Beat" by The xx.

The scent of vanilla filled the room next—the oils and bath salts that I kept on the edge of my bathtub. A little hum of pleasure slipped from my lips. Between the music, the warmth of the water, and the aroma wafting around me, I'd somehow surpassed relaxed and gone straight to a meditative state.

He gave good bath.

Minutes passed and I waited for Eric to touch me, waited for him to speak, wondered if he was even in the room. I could have opened my eyes, but I was a rule follower to the extreme, and somehow it felt like cheating.

And then I felt something brush against my breast. At first I wondered if it was the water from the jets, but then I felt it again, a stroke down the side and back again. I bit down on my lip.

He'd always had big hands, but I'd never really appreciated how large they were until I was reduced to the feel of him touching me. With each stroke his movements grew bolder, his touch firmer, but still, he avoided my nipples. He cupped my breasts in his hands, testing the weight of them, squeezing, pressing them together. The water caressed me, both soothing and tormenting my aching nipples.

He groaned, another flash of heat filling me at the sound falling from his lips.

"You look so gorgeous like this. So fucking beautiful."

His thumbs tweaked my nipples, and my head rolled back as a little spasm of pleasure filled me.

Holy hell, he really was fan-fucking-tastic with his hands. He played with me, over and over again, until whimpers escaped my lips, until I was moaning and thrashing, water spilling over the edge of the tub, hitting the tile floor.

He didn't stop.

His hands glided down my stomach, stealing the breath from my body, and then his fingers found my clit, and the beginnings of my orgasm roared.

He wasn't gentle and it wasn't slow. He touched me as

though he knew how close I was and he was determined to take me there.

When it started, when my body began trembling under his touch, his fingers slipped inside me, filling me as I clenched around him. When my orgasm subsided, he lifted me in his arms. My eyes flickered open and I stared at the wall of chest, pressing my lips to his heart, feeling soothed and relaxed, and falling maybe just a little bit deeper in love as he laid me down on the bed.

I waited for him to pounce, but instead he just stared down at me, a crooked smile on his face and so much emotion in his eyes. He reached out, his hand on my knee, holding me steady, and then he spread my legs before him until I was sprawled out on my comforter.

I couldn't look away.

Eric leaned forward, covering me with his big body, burrowing his head in my neck again, inhaling, his breathing ragged as he pressed a line of kisses down my throat. I felt him against me, the head of his cock brushing against my clit, and then lower until he was pushing inside me with a groan. He went slowly, his muscles tense, sliding in deeper, inch by inch, until he was fully seated inside me.

We'd had the condom discussion and I was on the pill, so as much as this was just another thing that bound me to him, another way my guard went down, I welcomed it, loved feeling him like this, knowing there was nothing between us.

I wrapped my arms and legs around Eric, holding him against me. Our gazes locked, and his mouth opened as though he wanted to speak, and I *knew*, simply *knew*, the three words that would tumble from his lips if I let him. I didn't know if he saw the answer in my eyes, understood that I wasn't ready to hear them, wasn't sure I would ever be ready to hear them again, even as they blasted through me, but he shut it down.

And then he began to move.

My eyes slammed closed as he thrust in and out, as he took me closer and closer to my second orgasm of the night. I held on to him, our bodies one. I came, and then a minute later, his body tensed inside me and his orgasm followed.

We collapsed on our sides, our limbs entwined, and the combination of a long day, alcohol at dinner, and two mind-numbingly good orgasms had me losing the fight against sleep. Just before I drifted off, it occurred to me that my heart was wide-fucking-open, but at the moment, I just didn't have it in me to care.

THOR

I watched her sleep, my fingers clutched tightly in her fist, my heart in her palm.

I still loved her. No question about it. I'd never felt this way about anyone else, would never feel this way again. Becca was it for me, and even as I watched her fight it, I damned well knew I was it for her.

You couldn't fake what we had. Couldn't duplicate it. We were so fucking lucky to have found each other once, and even as I'd always suspected it, I knew without a shadow of a doubt that letting her go was the biggest mistake of my life.

Now I needed to fix it.

I'd started thinking about my options, trying to figure out what I wanted to do next. I had a year left on my Air Force commitment, but that would probably get extended a bit due to our deployment to Afghanistan. The squadron needed bodies, and I had the experience they would rely upon. Technically they couldn't force me to extend past a year if I decided to get out of the military, but I owed the Wild Aces and the guys I flew with, and if I could fix my problems in the cockpit, then I wanted to have their backs in combat.

I was about to pin on major in the next month and I should be getting my next assignment. All of my choices had been Viper combat squadrons, and at the time, location hadn't mattered much to me.

Now it did.

Even if I got Shaw, even if I had three years close to Becca, I would still finish out the rest of my time until retirement going through normal PCS moves. That would mean seven years of the same problems we'd fought about when we were together. Neither one of us was getting any younger; she wanted a family, and given the way she'd grown up without parents, I was sure she would object to having kids only for me to be gone and miss the important events in their lives—first steps, first words, birthdays, holidays.

Then there were the Guard and the Reserve, which had the benefit of keeping me in the Viper, but they were a crapshoot in terms of availability. They were a pretty sweet gig considering they gave you all the perks of being a fighter pilot without the hassle of moving all the fucking time, so they were as competitive as hell and you had to hope the stars aligned and a spot opened up when you needed it. I couldn't make that promise to her because even if I made the decision, there was no guarantee that there would be an available spot for me to take.

Rock, meet hard place.

I could get out completely, but I was still left feeling like my skills were pretty fucking limited—*can blow things up with a missile* looked pretty useless on a résumé—and considering how much time I'd spent advancing in my career, I wasn't sure I wanted to start all over again.

But if anything would convince me otherwise, it was the girl sleeping next to me.

NINETEEN

BECCA

"I don't want to interrupt your bang-fest."

I laughed at Lizzie's not-incorrect characterization of the past two days with Eric. "I promised to babysit. You know I love Dylan. It's no big deal. Honestly. Besides, you and Adam need a bang-fest of your own. Get a hotel room and show your husband the lingerie you bought."

Lizzie sighed. "I'll give you one last chance to back out, because as much as I feel like an asshole taking you up on your offer, I haven't gotten laid in three weeks. Dylan's taken to sleeping in our bed again, and Adam is starting to get growly and not in a good way."

I grinned, shifting the phone to my other ear as I flipped through the file for an upcoming case. "I'm there. Does six o'clock work? That should give you guys plenty of time."

"Bless you. That's perfect."

"Good. Tell Dylan that I'll make his favorite dinner and we can watch a movie."

"By his 'favorite dinner,' do you mean animal-shaped pancakes?"

I winced. "Yeah. Sorry about that. I didn't realize sugar at night was kind of a no-go for a six-year-old, but he got so excited that I didn't have the heart to tell him no. What can I say? I'm a sucker."

Lizzie snorted. "Hey, you're the one who has to deal with the fallout. Have fun."

We said good-bye, and I hung up, dialing Eric's cell next. We'd had tentative plans to hang out and I felt bad for canceling, but I also thought it might be a good thing to have a night apart. We'd spent the past two nights and mornings together, and I was already growing way too used to seeing him when I came home every day, to him sleeping next to me, supplying me with orgasms, and then being there when I woke up in the morning. We hadn't talked about the fact that he was leaving soon, but it was only a matter of days, a week at the most, and I needed to slowly start weaning myself off him, because the withdrawal symptoms would be a bitch if I went cold turkey.

He answered right away, sounding out of breath. "Hey, babe, what's up?"

"Are you okay?"

"Yeah, just painting my grandmother's house."

I grinned. "I thought it was just the kitchen."

"It was just the kitchen. Now it's the whole house."

Okay, that was a little cute.

"She says 'hi,' by the way."

"Tell her I said 'hi' back."

I'd always had a soft spot for his grandmother, and she'd continued to treat me like I was a part of the family even after we'd broken up.

"Wait . . ." Silence filled the line. "Okay, we're invited to Sunday brunch."

I froze. Sunday brunch was kind of a tradition. She had it after church and always hosted a big crowd in her tiny house. We'd gone when we were dating and engaged, but I hadn't had the heart to go in the years after, always making up an excuse when she invited me. It felt too weird to be back in that house without Eric beside me.

"And I promised that we'd go to church with her," he added, his voice cheery.

Oh, hell no.

Church in Bradbury was an *event*. Everyone went. If I showed up with Eric and his grandmother, the gossip would spread throughout the town before the service ended.

No freaking way.

"Sorry, I think I have plans. You should totally go, though."

"Come on, don't be a heathen," he teased.

I snorted because I was pretty sure there was a snowball's chance in hell that Eric had seen the inside of a church unless he'd done so at his grandmother's insistence. I had no problem with going; I just didn't want to go with him.

"I have to cancel our date tonight," I said, ignoring his invitation.

"Why?"

"I promised Lizzie I'd babysit. She and Adam really need a night out."

"They have a kid?"

Sometimes I forgot how much he'd missed.

"Yeah, Dylan is six. He's my godson, and a holy terror, and he's relying on me to make him animal-shaped pancakes for dinner."

He chuckled. "I would never stand in the way of a cat-shaped pancake."

"Actually, Dylan likes zoo animal–shaped pancakes. He's discerning that way."

"I see. And you can make these?"

I heard the skepticism in his voice, and considering he'd seen my artistic and culinary skills—or lack thereof—I didn't blame him.

"I use a mold," I admitted reluctantly. "But seriously, he thinks it's magic and I can't lose my godmother street cred. Competition is fierce. Adam's sister has a pool in her apartment complex."

Eric burst into laughter. "God, I forgot how competitive you could be."

Valid.

"Okay, I'll make you a deal. I'll forgive you for canceling our date if you agree to come to church and brunch on Sunday."

I groaned. "No."

"Come on, babe."

"Don't call me 'babe' at your grandmother's."

"Pretty sure I called you 'babe' before."

"Yes, but that wasn't using sex voice," I hissed.

He cracked up again. "Sex voice?"

"DO NOT SAY IT OUT LOUD."

It took him a minute to get his laughter under control enough to speak.

"Well, now you have to come; she'll be too worried about your immortal soul if you don't."

His grandmother was one of the nicest, least judgmental people I'd ever met, so he only said it to appeal to my sense of guilt—of course, it worked.

"Fine. But no hand-holding. No kissing. No mentions of our sex life."

He snorted.

"No one can think we're anything other than friends."

"I was worried we were just fuck buddies, so friends is a vast improvement—"

"DO NOT SAY 'FUCK BUDDIES' AT YOUR GRAND-MOTHER'S HOUSE."

My cheeks flamed as horror flooded me. I buried my head in my hands as he burst out into more laughter. When the laughs had finally subsided, it hit me.

"She's not anywhere near you, is she?"

"Nope," he answered cheerfully. "She went outside to garden after I asked you about church."

"I hate you," I muttered.

"You wound me."

I rolled my eyes. "I'm hanging up now."

"Wait."

"What?"

"Go to the Harvest Dance with me."

Jesus. What was up with him today?

"No way."

The Harvest Dance was pretty much *the* event in Bradbury. They held it at an old farm on the outskirts of town with hayrides, dancing under white lights, and marshmallow roasts. It was a huge tradition that I'd experienced every single year Eric and I were together.

You didn't go to the Harvest Dance with someone you were just sleeping with. It was so sweet, it was saccharine, and while I secretly loved the rustic romance, there was no way we could go to something like that and keep things casual. When Eric eventually left, I'd be the one stuck here with the questions, and the pitying looks, and the whispered conversations about how I couldn't find a man no matter how hard I tried.

"You owe me a date."

"Dinner followed by dessert. If you're lucky, I'll put a blowjob on the table. No Harvest Dance."

"You love the Harvest Dance."

"Correction. I *loved* the Harvest Dance. I haven't been in a while. It's not the kind of thing you go to single."

His voice went a little funny. "But you said you'd dated."

"In a decade? Yeah, I wasn't sitting at home knitting."

"But no Harvest Dance dates?"

"It just never worked out."

Because the Harvest Dance was ours. Because all of my memories were inextricably tied to him, and the one year I had tried to go, I'd ended up freaking out before I even saw the white lights and wound up on a date at a fast-food restaurant.

"Come with me."

I put my head in my hands. "Did you just decide to call me to be annoying today?"

"Um, you called me."

Shit. So I did.

"Becca?"

I groaned. "You're not going to let this go, are you?"

"Not a chance."

"Why? Why is this so important to you? It's just a stupid dance."

"It was never a stupid dance."

No, it wasn't.

I sighed, already feeling exhausted. "Fine. I'll go."

I hung up the phone before he could get the last word in. Somehow it still felt like he already had.

* * *

Oh God, I should have just gone with a mix. I was wearing more flour than had made it into the stupid bowl, Dylan was jumping around playing with some kind of faux-medieval sword, the TV blaring in the background, I had the migraine to end all migraines, and I was about to cry.

I'd forgotten how exhausting these babysitting nights could be, and honestly, considering I only had to watch him for five hours and then I could hand him back to his parents, I had no clue how Lizzie did it. I was getting her a spa day for her birthday along with a giant bottle of wine. She was my freaking hero.

"Dylan, buddy, can you sit down for a second?" I called out. "Do you want to watch me make the pancakes?"

I figured "watching" was better than "helping," considering he was definitely responsible for a solid third of the flour caked on me. The other two-thirds were the result of my own ineptitude with cooking, which somehow made it worse.

"Can't. I have to kill the dragon."

God, he was a bloodthirsty kid. He was smart as a whip, but definitely a handful.

The doorbell rang, mixing with the cacophony of the blaring TV, and I looked down at my clothes again—thanks to the flour, I'd channeled either a zombie or a ghost—wondering if the neighbors had finally given in and called the cops to report the chaos. And then another thought hit me—I really hoped it wasn't Lizzie saying she'd forgotten something, because I was pretty sure she would freak if she saw the destruction I'd wrought to her normally clean kitchen. I figured I had four hours to somehow get it back to the state I'd found it in.

I padded through the living room, wincing slightly at the

sight of flour falling onto Lizzie's pristine carpet. I was definitely going to have to vacuum later.

Shit.

The doorbell rang again.

"Coming," I shouted, rounding the corner and colliding with Dylan, sword in hand.

"I got you!" he yelled.

"Am I the dragon?" I was strangely hurt by that.

He shook his head emphatically. "Nope."

Okay, I gave up. I had no idea what game we were playing, but I went with it.

"You did. You're the fiercest knight." I really needed to get that sword away from him before dinner. It was plastic, but it could do some serious damage to Lizzie's house.

"Does your mom usually let you play with that inside, buddy?"

He shook his head again. "No. Last time I did, I broke something and Mommy got mad."

Fuck.

I scooped him up on my hip, my knees buckling a little at his weight—he'd definitely grown since the last time I'd done this—and tried to pry the sword out of his hand before he could realize what I was up to.

The doorbell rang again.

I groaned. "I'm coming!"

Dylan laughed. "You're getting mad like Mommy."

I couldn't help grinning. "Sort of. Yeah."

He cuddled into me, and something inside me melted. I forgot about the stupid flour, and the sword, and the headache, and the blaring cartoon.

I opened the door, a smile on my lips, and my gaze connected with Eric, standing on the other side of Lizzie's doorstep, a bag in one hand and a bouquet of flowers in the other.

TWENTY

THOR

I'd never seen Becca look more beautiful than she did now, covered in flour, a little boy trying to hit her with a plastic sword with fake jewels on the hilt, a goofy smile on her face.

"Bad time?"

"Are you a dragon?" the little boy asked at the same time.

I grinned. "Sometimes."

He cocked his head to the side, considering, likely assessing whether or not I'd make a worthy opponent. Finally, he nodded.

"I'll chase you with my sword."

I laughed. "Best offer I've had." I leaned forward, pressing a swift kiss to Becca's cheek, her expression still stunned.

"What are you doing here?" she sputtered.

I shrugged. "I talked to Lizzie. She said it was cool. Besides, I heard a rumor that this was the best place to get zoo animal pancakes."

"It is," Dylan interjected, wiggling around in Becca's arms before she set him down and he took off running, sword in hand.

She faced off against me, her hands on her hips, the movement leaving a cloud of white powder in its wake.

"What is that?" I asked, not bothering to hide the smile.

"Flour. I was trying to make the pancakes from scratch, which was a terrible idea."

"I bet."

We'd both been hopeless cooks, topping each other with inedible concoction after inedible concoction.

"Why don't you get back to the pancakes and I'll hang out with Dylan? You're channeling ghost more than dragon right now anyway."

Her eyes narrowed into slits. "How about now?"

I grinned. "Well, you got the fire-breathing part down. Nicely done."

I hooked an arm around her waist, bringing her against me for a quick hug that left a trace of powder in its wake, and then I released her, going in search of the knight who wanted to slay me.

I died twice before we all sat down at the big dining room table, animal-shaped pancakes stacked in front of us. Something tightened in my chest at the sight before me, at the realization that this—or a variation of it, at least—could have been my future.

Dylan talked the whole time we ate, in between shoveling forkfuls of animal-shaped pancakes, shifting topics with a lightning speed and randomness I couldn't even begin to follow. I'd thought the dragon game was exhausting, but I hadn't known exhausting until now. Becca kept shooting me tired little smiles and I had a strong feeling she was pretty used to this.

He began to slowly wind down as the evening wore on, after Becca read him a story in bed, changing her tone to do funny voices for each of the characters. I couldn't remember the last time I'd laughed so much.

We closed the door softly behind us after many protests from Dylan saying he wasn't sleepy, he needed a glass of water, he wanted to stay up longer, until finally his eyes closed and dreams overtook him.

Becca sagged against the wall in the hallway. "I could sleep for a year."

I laughed. "How does one kid have so much energy?"

"No idea." Her voice softened. "He's adorable, though, isn't he? And I'm not just biased because he's my godson."

I grinned. "Boys don't like being called 'adorable' as a rule, but he is pretty cute." I surveyed the living room. "So what do you usually do now?"

"Collapse on the couch with a glass of wine until Adam and Lizzie come home. They're usually back around eleven."

"Sounds like a plan to me." I nudged her toward the sofa. "I'll bring the wine. Sit. You made like twenty pancakes tonight."

She didn't fight me, walking to the living room while I went to the kitchen and poured us two glasses of the moscato Lizzie had in her fridge with a Post-it Note that said, "Drink Me."

I walked back to Becca, handing her the glass and taking a seat next to her on the couch. She looked exhausted, her body bundled up in one of the blankets Lizzie had strewn over the arm.

"Do you want to watch TV?"

I shrugged. "Sure, if you want. I'll probably just stare at it with a catatonic expression for a while."

She laughed. "Me, too. He saps me of my energy."

"He'd sap anyone of their energy. How do Adam and Lizzie do it all the time?"

Becca took a sip of her wine, making that little sound she made in the back of her throat when she thought something was good. "Hell if I know. They're so good with him, though." She hesitated for a second before continuing. "Lizzie was so nervous when she found out she was pregnant. They'd been trying, but I think the reality of an actual kid hit her hard. But the second he was born, it was like something just clicked inside her. She's an amazing mom."

I swallowed a big gulp of wine, wondering if I was picking at an old wound, but curious just the same. "Do you still want to be a mom?"

"Yeah, I do." She sighed. "I've actually started thinking about having a kid on my own, or adopting, or something. It's exhausting, but it also feels really rewarding. And I want to have that experience." She gave an embarrassed laugh. "It's stupid, but I want to do the little things—bedtimes and doctor's appointments. I want my ankles to swell up and I want my belly to get bigger. I want all of it, and for the longest time I thought I had to have the right guy to have it, but I have a good job and benefits, and even though I work a lot, I'm starting to think it might just be something I end up doing alone. I mean, think of how many two-parent households fuck up a kid. I figure my odds are decent. I think—hope—that I'd be a good mom."

"You'd be an amazing mom." A knot formed in my chest, born of guilt and regret over the decisions I'd made years ago. Would she have had the family she wanted? Would *we* have had that if I'd stayed? It was so easy to imagine that it was our son sleeping in the next room, our son filling dinner-time with stories about his day.

I took her hand, entwining our fingers, holding on to her now to make up for the fact that I'd been so fucking stupid to let her go.

"I fucked up with you. Spectacularly so. I hurt you and I hurt myself, and if I could undo all of the wreckage I caused, I would."

"Do you regret it?" Her voice was so quiet, I barely heard the words. Or maybe they just sounded quiet in comparison to the pounding in my chest.

"Yes."

She exhaled, her fingers curling around the stem of her glass, staring into the crystal as though it contained some answer that eluded her. I didn't want to screw with her. Didn't want to lead her on. All I had to give right now was the truth, and I'd be lying if I didn't admit the breadth of my regrets.

She tilted her chin to face me, her eyes wary. "I don't know what I want here. I don't even know what you're offering."

"Me, either."

"When we ended things before . . ." Her voice trailed off again as she looked down at her hands. "I'm not sure I'm okay with going through that again. Even the possibility of it. I'm thirty-one. I feel like I only have so many fresh starts left in me. It took me years to get over you and I don't want to do that again."

I nodded, even as the lump in my throat grew boulder-sized. "I get that."

"I threw the ring in Cranberry Lake."

"What?"

Her lips twitched, her eyes watery, looking like she was somewhere between laughing and crying. "I was so angry when you broke off the engagement that I threw the ring in the lake. Not right away, but later when I realized you weren't coming back. I got drunk and made Lizzie drive me out to the dock and I just chucked it."

I didn't blame her.

"We're a disaster," Becca muttered, taking another big gulp of her wine.

I draped an arm around her shoulders, pulling her closer to me so she rested in the curve of my body.

"Do you regret this? Us starting up again?"

She met my gaze this time, her voice even. "In the moment, this always feels like the best decision I've ever made. It's the after that's the problem.

"One of my first cases was a kid who stole a car and took it for a joyride through some fields. He wasn't even legal, but he drove that car all over until he was caught. When I talked to him afterward, he was so scared, his skin pale, his voice trembling. I asked him why he took the car and he said that he just wanted to feel free. Just for a moment. He had prior offenses, and he ended up in juvie for a bit, and it always stuck with me that he'd had his hour or so of freedom, just to spend months essentially locked up."

"Are you comparing me to a prison sentence?" I asked, not sure if I should be offended or acknowledge the fact that she'd hit pretty fucking close to home.

"No," she answered after a long moment. "A joyride."

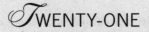

TWENTY-ONE

BECCA

Eric held my hand as we got out of the car and walked toward the old metal barn where they held the dance. He held my hand while my palms grew clammy, butterflies in my stomach, a lump in my throat, my knees weak. I told myself this shouldn't feel like such a big deal, that it shouldn't matter so much, but I would have been lying if I attempted to deny how much it did mean.

Before, I could convince myself that we were a secret, that whatever happened between us could exist in the cracks and crevices where you hid the most vulnerable parts of yourself. But now, Eric had scooped those parts out of me and put them on display, illuminated with twinkling white fairy lights and the giant harvest moon that shone down on us.

You couldn't make this stuff up. The night was just . . . magical. And I wasn't necessarily a romantic person by nature, but the simple beauty of a night like tonight could make even the toughest cynic a believer.

Eric squeezed my fingers, dipping his head to smile at me, and my heart lurched for what felt like the millionth time tonight.

He wore a slate blue cotton button-down shirt, the sleeves rolled, and a pair of worn denim jeans with equally worn brown leather cowboy boots. He'd clearly stopped shaving at some point in the week, because he now had a nice buildup of scruff that made a girl go *rawr*, and there was definitely some kind of sorcery going on with his cologne because he smelled amazing. I'd spent the car ride over taking discreet whiffs and hoping he hadn't noticed that I might just be a little crazy.

There was something about Eric, something beyond the obvious physical characteristics, that drew me to him. I didn't know if it was the pheromones or something less scientific—the feeling that he was mine on some primal level. Whatever it was, I felt the rightness of this, even as nerves filled me the more steps we took.

It was an exaggeration to say the entire town of Bradbury had come out tonight, but it definitely felt like they had, and all of their eyes were trained on the point where my flesh met Eric's, our palms pressed together. I tried to jerk my hand away, but he held steady as if he'd anticipated it, his lips quirking slightly before bringing my fingers up to his mouth and kissing them softly, his breath tickling my skin, sending a whole other host of sensations through my body.

Aww hell.

"This was a bad idea," I hissed, no easy feat while forcing a smile for the crowd at large. "Everyone is staring at us."

"Everyone's staring at you," he countered, his voice going oh-so-sweet, "because you're stunning tonight."

He didn't say it like a line, like he was trying to flatter.

No, he said it like I was beautiful to *him*, and that made all the difference.

"But if it makes you feel better," he added, his voice going lower, his words for me alone, "pretend they aren't even here. Tonight's just for us. To hell with everyone else. If people want to speculate about what's going on here, let them. We're the only ones that matter."

I didn't answer him; instead, I leaned up on my toes, fusing my mouth to his, wrapping my arms around his neck and pulling him closer to me, the harvest moon a spotlight over us, the twinkling lights flashing a giant I-told-you-so, and I didn't care who saw. So yeah, I guess I gave him an answer after all.

I just hoped it was the right one.

THOR

"Want to dance?"

Becca pulled back a few inches and nodded, her lips puffy from my mouth and her cheeks pink from the cold.

I led her out to the dance floor, the familiar strands of a country song playing over the speakers. I was a pretty shit dancer, but we'd been to enough high school dances and clubs and parties in college for Becca to be fully aware of my skills or lack thereof. I didn't step on her feet or anything, but my signature move was my arms wrapped around her body, her cheek on my chest, our feet shuffling next to each other.

Then again, it wasn't a bad move to have.

When we were younger, before things had grown serious between us, I'd lived for the school dances she wanted me to take her to, the ones I never would have attended if not for her on my arm. Those excuses to touch her had been like air to me.

In the beginning, our relationship had progressed slowly. She'd never had a boyfriend, had been shy at first, but the more we'd talked, the more time we'd spent together, the farther I'd fallen. It had just been so easy to talk to her; she always seemed to get it the way other people in my life didn't. Or maybe it was the fact that I trusted her in a way that I didn't trust anyone else.

We stopped on the edge of the dance floor and I looped my arm around her waist as she stepped into me, our movements rote. I didn't know if it was muscle memory or what, but it was like my body knew instinctively how to adjust to hers, as though we operated on a frequency no one else knew. Even with the ten-year absence.

The height difference between us was enough that she fit under my chin, my lips brushing against her silky hair as I held her as tightly as I could, swaying along to the music, completely caught up in Becca.

In the distance the bonfire kicked up, that familiar smell of burning wood reminding me of the last one I'd been to—the night we'd burned a piano after Joker's memorial service.

My grip around Becca tightened.

I hadn't thought about him in days. I'd been playing knights and dragons, flirting with Becca, painting my grandmother's kitchen, covering major ground as I ran all over Bradbury. I hadn't thought about flying much, either, besides that one call with Burn. Early in my career when I'd just been a young wingman, days spent not flying were wasted days. I'd volunteered every time a sortie opened up, chasing hours, convinced that flying defined me. It wasn't just that the novelty had worn off—

I didn't miss it. Not as much as I'd expected to, at least.

Sure, my time in Bradbury wasn't completely real. I wasn't working, this was more like a mental health vacation, but it felt good for once not to be chasing the next adrenaline high, not to be constantly on edge, stressed out, and utterly consumed by my job. It felt good just to dance with the girl who meant more to me than anyone ever had. To laugh and just be me. Not fighter-pilot-me, but the other guy who wasn't defined by rank, call sign, and patch.

I needed to sort my shit out when I went back to Oklahoma, needed to figure out where my future was headed. Right now I couldn't imagine my future not including Becca.

One dance bled into another, and then another, both of us content to stay like we were, somewhere between where we'd been and where we could be.

Finally, Becca pulled back.

"I'm getting chilly. Do you want to go stand near the bonfire?"

"Sounds like a plan to me."

I took her hand as we walked through the crowd gathering near the flames, standing close to the edge. My gaze locked with a couple a few feet away, and I grinned as I saw Katy from the grocery store, her husband and my old high school buddy, John, next to her. They waved us over.

Katy and Becca exchanged hugs while John and I caught up. I hadn't had a chance to make it to their place for dinner, and the longer we talked, the more I regretted it.

I didn't have any friends outside of the guys in the squadron. The Air Force was both personal life and job, and as much as I loved talking about flying, it was nice to chill and talk about other things.

Becca and Katy went off to say hi to Megan. John barely waited before they were out of earshot before he asked—

"Are you guys back together?"

I grinned. I couldn't help it. Maybe the answer wasn't exactly a "yes," but I was closer and closer to "yes" the more time we spent together. Getting her to come with me tonight was a huge step, her agreeing to go to church and my grandmother's tomorrow an even bigger one.

"Let's just say I'm working on it."

"It took you long enough."

"I know." I hesitated, not sure why I was asking, not sure what answer I wanted him to give. "We haven't talked a lot about the past, but every time we have, she's made it seem like there wasn't anyone serious . . ."

"And you want to know what I've seen and heard through the rumor mill?"

"Kind of? I just don't . . . I can't imagine a girl like her being single. And it's fucked up, because it's not like I want her to have been with another guy or something, but at the same time, I hate the idea of her being miserable and alone."

"I don't think she was miserable. She seemed okay for the most part. She dated a few guys. Daniel Perkins. Brad Marshall. Toby Dryer."

I recognized all the names. Daniel and Brad had been in our high school class; Toby was a few years older. They were all okay guys—which didn't surprise me because Becca was way too smart to date a guy who was an ass—but . . . Maybe it was unfair, but I couldn't quite imagine her being happy with any of them. They were kind of boring, and as much as Becca said she wanted stable, she loved the rush.

"How much longer do you have here?" John asked.

"Less than a week."

"You coming back?"

I started to say, *If she'll have me*, but I caught myself. Part of staying away from Bradbury had been fear; part had been a desire to keep from hurting Becca. I wasn't sure how things would play out between us, but my self-imposed exile was over. I still had my grandmother, still had ties and memories here, and even though those ties had felt like chains pulling me down when I was younger, now they felt like roots keeping me grounded when the wind shook the fuck out of my branches.

"Yeah. I am."

He gave me a slap on the shoulder and a smile. "Good. Missed you, man."

"You, too."

We talked for a few more minutes and then our conversation trailed off as Katy and Becca walked back toward us, the glow of the bonfire adding to the punch of their beauty. My chest tightened as I watched Becca, her brown hair down and tangled from the wind, her cheeks pink, her lips curved.

I took a step away from John and then another, hooking my arm around Becca's waist and hauling her toward me. I put my mouth on hers, catching her off guard as her lips parted beneath mine in surprise. I kissed her hard and deep, my hands holding her hips, tucking her against my body.

I love you. I love you. I love you.

The words pushed at me, clawing their way out. Ten years ago I would have just said them, wouldn't have held anything back. Now I understood what I'd taken from her when I broke up with her, when I told her I no longer wanted the life we'd planned together, when I'd taken the love she gave me and threw it in her face. I'd been the one constant in her life, the only person who had always been there, and for a girl who had lost her family in a crunch of glass and metal, losing us hadn't just been a breakup. I'd shaken her foundation, taken everything she knew to be true, and made her question it. I couldn't do that again.

So I held the words in, reeling them back until I could give her the certainty she needed and the future she deserved. My hands were still tied by the strings attached to my military commitments, and I couldn't offer her a future until I untangled myself, until I could offer those hands to her.

We slid under the covers, Becca burrowing against my side in a move that had become habit. She was a maximum contact sleeper, and if I moved, she would reach for me in the middle of the night, in sleep.

Some things hadn't changed.

"I had fun tonight," I whispered in the dark, reaching out and tracing the curve of her cheek. "Thanks for coming."

She threw her leg over mine, kissing my pec.

"I had fun, too. Thanks for making me go. I forgot how much I enjoyed it."

I grinned. "Yeah, me, too. It was good to catch up with everyone. To be with you."

"Sorry Lizzie was a little fierce," Becca mumbled between yawns. "She's protective."

We'd run into Lizzie and Adam later in the evening. She'd pulled me aside and mock threatened me that if I screwed Becca over, she'd sic Dylan after me, which considering how bloodthirsty the kid was, probably wasn't an idle threat.

I was glad that after everything Becca had been through after I'd left, she had someone like Lizzie in her corner, someone who had her back when she needed it.

"Shh. Don't apologize. She loves you."

I love you.

Becca's hand trailed down my stomach, sleepily caressing my abs, and my cock sprung to life.

"I thought you were tired," I murmured.

She yawned again. "I am. We can still have sex, though."

I squeezed her shoulder. "It's okay. You're falling asleep. There's always tomorrow morning."

"We came back here."

We'd ended up at my hotel room since it was closer than Becca's apartment.

"Yeah. But that doesn't mean we have to have sex. We can just sleep."

"So I guess we're definitely not just fuck buddies, huh?"

I laughed at her tone. I couldn't tell if she was happy, annoyed, or amused about that fact. Maybe a combination of all three.

"Babe."

She yawned again. "Have I ever told you it's kind of sexy when you call me 'babe'?"

I grinned. "Nope."

"It is. It's weird, because if any other guy said it, it would probably annoy me, but it's kind of cute on you."

"Good to know."

I reached out and stroked her hair, listening to the sounds of her breathing, until I realized she'd fallen asleep.

I stared up at the ceiling, my arms and heart full of Becca.

I whispered her name. "Are you awake?"

Silence. She'd always been a heavy sleeper; apparently that hadn't changed, either.

"I love you," I whispered, needing to say the words even if it wasn't time for her to hear them, my arms around her tightening.

This time I wasn't letting go.

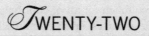

TWENTY-TWO

BECCA

The crowd at Eric's grandmother's place was huge, spilling out of the tiny house onto the porch, into the yard. I knew everyone here so I shouldn't have felt uncomfortable, but I couldn't escape the feeling that I was an impostor, living on borrowed time. We looked like a couple, acted like a couple, and yet we weren't really a couple. It all felt like a lie or a fantasy, and while part of me wanted to indulge it and enjoy the moment, another part of me had alarm bells going off, warning me I was headed for heartbreak.

I carried some plates into the kitchen, setting them down on the countertop, taking a deep breath and basking in the moment of silence. We'd been here for almost two hours and it felt like not a minute went by without someone coming up to us, either alluding to the fact that we were here together or asking outright. I'd finally left Eric with the minister, excusing myself from the conversation by saying that I needed to help his grandmother clean up a bit. I was pretty sure the minister was talking to him about marital counseling, and a girl had to draw the line somewhere.

"Thank you so much for all of your help."

I turned at the sound of Eric's grandmother entering the kitchen, a tired smile on her face.

"I love having everyone over, but these things just keep getting bigger and bigger." She winked. "When everyone leaves, I'm going to put my feet up on the sofa and have some tea."

I grinned. "You deserve it. I don't know how you do it every weekend. People come because it's the best party in town and your chicken is amazing."

She squeezed my hand. "I'll have to give you the recipe. It's been in my family for generations."

"I'd like that," I replied softly.

Her gaze swept past me. "He did a good job with the kitchen, didn't he?"

I grinned. "He did a good job with the whole house. I love the color you chose."

"Thank you. He's a good boy."

I nodded. "He is."

"It's been nice having him back, seeing him in town again."

I nodded again, not sure where the conversation was headed or if I was ready to go there.

"He loves you." Her gaze turned shrewd, searching, and she squeezed my hand. I was pretty sure I'd gone pale, because with those three words she'd taken the conversation somewhere I definitely wasn't prepared for.

"I hated seeing the two of you break up," she continued. "I always loved you like the granddaughter I never had, always was so proud of both of you, so happy to see you together."

I bit down on the inside of my cheek, trying to control it, but I couldn't. Tears welled up in my eyes.

"Oh, honey."

She wrapped her arms around me and held on, and my eyes closed as I relaxed in the comfort of her embrace. I hadn't had a lot of hugs in my life. Not like this. There had always been Eric, and occasionally Lizzie, but I'd missed out on having a mom I could talk to, who hugged me when I needed it. My grandmother hadn't been physically affectionate, so for a moment I just let Eric's hold me.

"It wasn't you. He wasn't ready. He was young and still figuring out who he was, how to grow into the man he needed to be. He loved you so much. Always. But you wanted different things, needed different things."

I pulled back, wiping at my eyes. "I know. I'm sorry." I shook my head. "I guess I just thought that if he loved me, I would be enough to give him what he needed."

"I know you did, but he wouldn't have found himself here. He needed to grow, needed to challenge himself, become someone he could be proud of, someone who could be secure enough to be a husband and father someday. It was different for you—you were always so mature—you had to be with what you'd been through. I know it's hard to understand, but I think he needed what the military gave him so he could become the man he is today.

"You always loved him, always saw the best in him back then, but he wasn't quite there yet. Now he is. You both are. It's not an accident that you found your way back to each other."

She was right. The man before me was more settled than the boy had ever been. And I could see now that, on some level, I'd been so desperate for a family that I'd put a heap of responsibility and pressure on Eric at a young age, not realizing that even though I was ready for those things, he wasn't. But I still wasn't sure he was ready, that the future I wanted was even on the table.

"I don't think he knows what he wants."

"Have faith."

I wasn't sure I had much faith left to give.

"I know why you stayed away all these years, and I understand, but I want you to know that I'm always here for you. I love you, too."

God, apparently today was my day for crying.

My vision turned blurry, and I leaned forward, giving her a quick hug.

"Thank you."

THOR

Becca didn't speak for most of the drive back to my hotel and I couldn't tell if she was upset or just pensive.

I was still reeling from the afternoon. I'd figured she was exaggerating when she'd protested my invitation to the Harvest Dance and my grandmother's brunch. Bradbury was a small town, but I hadn't quite realized how interested everyone would be in our relationship or the questions that would dog us all day.

No one was rude and there wasn't any malice, just . . . aggressive curiosity. About my job. About Becca. About me and Becca.

If that was what it had been like for her after we broke up . . .

"Are you okay?" I asked, glancing her way when we hit a stoplight.

"Yeah. Just tired."

I didn't blame her. I'd had a pounding headache for the last hour.

"That was a big crowd. I had no idea it had grown that much. When I was a kid, it was like ten people. Now I feel like the whole damned town is there. I'm not sure how she still does it; I swear she has more energy than I do."

My grandmother was seventy-five and showed little signs of slowing down. She still worked part-time at the library, supervising a small staff manned mostly by volunteers who adored her. She took two trips a year, both with her church group, and managed to make it down to Florida every few years to visit my mother.

"I need to come back more often. I shouldn't have let it go as long as I did."

Becca didn't respond.

I frowned, turning down the road toward the hotel. "Are you sure you're okay? Did someone say something to you?"

She laughed. "Seriously?"

I grinned despite the worry filtering through me. "Fair enough. Did anyone *not* say something to you?"

"Nope."

"Is it always like that? Always so intense?"

"You mean people being nosy about us?"

I nodded.

"In the beginning, it was worse." Her voice tightened and my stomach lurched. "Everyone had an opinion on where we went wrong, a suggestion on what I needed to do to win you back."

Fuck.

"You didn't need to do anything—"

"I know. Now. Twenty-one-year-old me spent more time than I should have wondering if they were right."

I let out an oath. I never wanted her to think the problem had been her. It was my restlessness that had driven me away, and if anything, she'd kept me here far longer than I would have stayed if not for her presence in my life.

"It's okay. They all meant well, thought they were helping. It wasn't their fault that it was basically like pouring acid into a wound."

It was anything but okay.

"God, I'm sorry, Becca. I honestly had no idea it was like that for you."

"Hazards of small town life, I guess."

"I'm surprised you didn't stay in Columbia. Get a job there."

I was, but then again, I wasn't. She'd always said this was her dream, and she was loyal. When she committed to something, she was all in.

"I thought about it," she admitted. "But I do love it here. Bradbury has always been home, and I couldn't imagine living anywhere else. My roots are here, my memories of my parents. I always imagined raising my kids here, telling them stories about the grandparents they'll never get to meet."

"I'm sure they'd be so proud of you."

She smiled softly. "Thanks. I hope so." She reached out and took hold of my free hand, linking our fingers. "You know, your grandmother's proud of you. Her face lights up when she talks about you. I used to hear about you through the grapevine because she was constantly telling the patrons who would come into the library about your accomplishments."

I felt my cheeks heat.

"I was proud of you, too. Even when I didn't want to be. She said something to me earlier—"

"I'm sorry—"

"No. It's okay. She was right. She told me that when we were younger, when we were together, you were still trying to figure out who you were. I guess that while I was trying so hard to push for an 'us,' I didn't appreciate the fact that you never really got to be your own person or figure out what you wanted independent of me."

"You weren't—" I cleared my throat. "I don't ever want you to think that you held me back or that you were a burden. I know what I said about Bradbury, but I didn't see you that way. I loved you; I just didn't know who I was yet."

"I know that now. I just didn't then. We were both young and we made mistakes. Forever's hard to navigate when you're still in college, when you have no clue what your future will look like."

We needed to talk about what was next for us; we'd certainly volleyed the question enough today. I figured I'd lay my options out for her and see what she wanted, prayed she was willing to give us a shot. It was a lot to ask. Nothing about this life would be easy on her. I'd seen the other wives struggle, watched guys get divorced over the weight of deployments and TDYs, all the shit that got piled on us. My job was dangerous, and for someone like Becca, who'd lost her family in an accident, I figured it would be tough to live with the uncertainty and the fear that she'd get a call in the middle of the night saying I wouldn't be coming home.

The part of me that was completely in love with her wanted to throw caution to the wind and take the next step, but we had to go slowly. Not only were we reentering each other's lives after a decade, but this was going to be a huge adjustment from two college kids in love. The military could put stress on the most solid relationship, not to mention a new one filled with lingering resentment from all that we'd been through.

It wasn't in my nature to take things slowly, to be anything other than balls-to-the-wall, but I told myself this wasn't the time to rush, that if I wanted a future with Becca, I was going to have to ease her into it and slip past her defenses into her heart.

I followed her into my hotel room, lying back on what had somehow become "my" side of the bed, enjoying the view as Becca stripped out of the pretty flowered dress she'd worn to church and my grandmother's. I reached out and caught her hand, tugging her toward me.

She grinned. "Again?"

We'd definitely burned off some calories before brunch at my grandmother's.

"Maybe."

She sank down on the edge of the bed, her lips twitching. "You're incorrigible."

"Maybe I just can't resist you. And I definitely don't want to."

I leaned forward, resting my forehead against hers, closing my eyes.

"Eric . . ."

I loved hearing my name fall from her lips.

My nose grazed hers, my lips finding her cheek, pressing a soft kiss there, and then another one at the corner of her mouth.

I love you. I love you. I love you.

Her hands went for my shirt, tugging at the material, an urgency to her actions that always seemed to be there between us. I helped her, shrugging out of the sleeves. When I was naked from the waist up, I lifted her in my arms, rolling and twisting so she was beneath me.

I reached between us, gathering her hair in my hand and spreading it out over the pillow. For a moment I just stared, a lump in my throat as I asked myself how I'd ever gotten so lucky—then or now—to have someone like her in my life. To have someone who looked at me the way she did, because for all that she was cautious, she looked at me now with so much love in her eyes that I ached from it.

She humbled me. Constantly.

When I was younger, it had terrified me, the responsibility of living up to the kind of expectation that lingered behind that love overwhelming me. It wasn't intentional, but I still felt the pressure there, the need to be more, better, enough. But now, instead of scaring the shit out of me, it drove me.

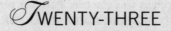

TWENTY-THREE

THOR

I shifted, spreading Becca's legs beneath me, and then I settled between her hips, my arms wrapping around her again, arching her forward so her breasts brushed my pecs, her hands running over my back.

I told myself to go slow, tried to temper my movements to drag out her pleasure, but I just fucking couldn't. I was strung out on her, on the feel of her under me, the taste of her on my lips. I slid my hand between us, rubbing her clit over her silk underwear, her wetness seeping through the fabric, coating my fingers.

We both hovered on the edge.

I pulled back, reaching between us and tugging on the waistband of her thong, ducking and pressing kisses to her stomach that had her twisting her hips in response.

She gripped my back even more tightly, her nails raking the skin there in a move that had my dick tightening in anticipation.

Words fell from our lips but I had no clue what was said,

my mind gibberish, my heart already gone. There were other times when I mastered foreplay, other times when the buildup between us was electric. This was not one of those times. The only thing that mattered was sliding inside her, some primal part of me needing to feel like we were one, grasping the connection between our bodies even as I felt as though life pulled us apart.

When her underwear hit the floor, I spread her even wider, opening her, my gaze drifting down to admire the view before me. I positioned myself at her entrance, her wetness seeping out onto my cock, and then I slid inside in one smooth stroke, a groan torn from my lips as she clenched down around me, all of that wet heat drawing me deeper into her body. My lips found hers as I held myself still inside her body, as she throbbed around me. I gripped her hair, looking into her eyes, needing to see the arousal there, needing to feel that connection as well.

Nothing beat this feeling. Nothing came close.

We didn't speak when we were finished, our limbs entwined on the bed. I could feel the crash coming, knew we both thought of the moment we didn't dare speak of, hovered on the precipice of what came next.

It fucking terrified me.

BECCA

Eric rose, walking toward the bathroom, giving me one hell of a visual. I turned onto my side, gathering the sheets around my body, unable to take my gaze off him.

We had to talk about the fact that he was leaving soon.

The longer we left things unsaid, the more they settled around us like a miasma.

A lump formed in my throat.

Do not get emotional. Do not cry.

Eric walked back into the bedroom, gloriously naked, a smile on his lips and something that looked a hell of a lot like love in his eyes.

"Do you want to order some dinner?" His smile deepened. "I worked up an appetite earlier."

I shrugged. "Sure, if you want. We can do pizza or something."

There was too much tension rolling around in my stomach for me to be hungry. I needed to rip off the Band-Aid, needed to face our dwindling time together. I took a deep breath and went for it, trying my best to sound casual.

"So when do you go back to Oklahoma?"

His body stiffened, the lazy smile falling from his lips. Something flickered in his gaze—remorse, regret? When he spoke, his voice was devoid of the husky tone I loved.

"My flight leaves Wednesday morning. I have to be back at work on Thursday."

I'd known he was leaving soon, but now, having the date . . . it just felt so final. Like we were hurtling to an inevitability we couldn't escape.

Hell, maybe I was the only one who wanted to escape it. For all I knew, he missed flying, was eager to go home. For all I knew, I was the only one feeling like my heart was shattering into pieces.

I swallowed, trying to beat back the emotions, the hurt, the loss of him that I began to feel even though he wasn't gone yet. I'd been here before, though, had become an expert at getting over Eric Jansen—trying to, at least.

"You know what? I'll take a rain check on food. I should get dressed and head back home. I have to be in court tomorrow morning."

I leaned forward, the sheets pooling at my waist, and Eric reached out, leaning over me, his fingers walking down my spine, stroking me until I had to fight the urge to lie back and go for round two.

"You could stay a little longer," he murmured, his lips brushing the skin below my nape.

I wanted to, but I wasn't the one who was leaving. If it were up to me, I'd choose us. Even now there was a part of me that was like, *Screw it, give up your job*. I'd had a good run. I didn't need to keep practicing law.

Except I did.

Because I believed in the work I did, in helping people. Because it mattered to me, and even if he mattered more—which, yes, he probably did—the part that I couldn't get past was that even if I chose him and left everything to follow him around the world, he *didn't* choose me. In fact, twice, he'd chosen a plane over me, over us. And I didn't want to give up everything so I could play second fiddle to his job. I wanted him to love me, to put me first, to put any children we might have together first. And nothing in our history together had told me he would do that, that he could do that. He loved me. The last couple weeks together had answered that question with finality. But it wasn't good enough. I couldn't give up my future, all I'd worked for, the things I loved, knowing he wouldn't do the same.

I loved him, but I still had to be able to look myself in the mirror at the end of the day and hold my head up. And I couldn't. Not like this.

His grandmother was right—he'd needed the time to figure out who he was, what he wanted. But I'd taken the decade we were apart to do the same and knew exactly what I wanted—I wanted the career and the family. I didn't want to give up one to have the other.

"I really should go."

I'd told myself I wouldn't lose it, that I wouldn't indulge in some kind of binge-eating-ice-cream-cue-the-emotional-breakup-music scene since I'd gone into this with open eyes and he hadn't made any promises. And I wasn't planning on it. But I definitely needed to get the hell out of here so that if I did lose it, even just a little bit, I did it in the privacy of my own home.

I slipped out of his grasp, grabbing my clothes from the hotel room floor.

"Becca."

I kept my head ducked as I slid my underwear on, reaching for my dress.

"Are we going to talk about this?" he asked.

I fastened my bra then slipped the fabric over my head and turned to face him.

"What is there to talk about? You're leaving; we knew it was coming. It's fine."

"That's not what I'm talking about and you know it. What about us?"

"What do you mean, what about us?" I kept my cool, even though that word, "us," sliced me to ribbons. "We'll still keep in touch." It hurt, but I'd sort of given up on the idea of me having a life that didn't include him in it. We could be friends, just as soon as I found a way to kill the feelings inside of me that wanted so much more.

"That's it?"

I took a deep breath, struggling to keep my voice even.

"Yeah, pretty much. I don't know what you want me to say here. We knew this would happen. There's something between us, there always has been. And I'm not going to lie to you and say that the last decade apart hasn't shown me that what we have isn't easy to find. But none of the other things between us have changed. These past few weeks have been amazing, but they were more like a vacation than our normal life."

"It could be more."

The first spark of anger filled me. "How? Please tell me how it could be more."

"We could date. Long distance. We could talk on the phone and fly out and visit each other." He made a frustrated noise. "It's really not that weird. People have complicated relationships all the time. My friend Burn and his wife, Jordan, got together that way."

"Okay. So let's say we do long distance. Then what?"

He blinked.

"We were together for five years before we broke up. We know each other. There is no getting-to-know-you period for us. Even with the time apart, we caught up in what, a few days? So where do we go after dating?

"I'm thirty-one years old. I've been ready to have a family for over ten years. We were *engaged*. We've done the get-to-know-each-other thing. We've been to the next step. So this idea that we're just going to screw around isn't really appealing to me. It was one thing when we were talking about a couple weeks, but I'm not going to live my life perpetually on the hook.

"I know what I want. I want a husband and kids. I want a home. I want to put down roots. And you don't want that. So don't tell me we should just see where this is going. It's been a decade. I don't have it in me to wait anymore."

"Do you think I don't want a family?" Eric asked. "That

I don't want kids? That I don't want to put down roots? That I don't want you?"

I couldn't do this. This was the exact opposite of what we were supposed to be about this time—fun, sex, maybe friendship, because there was simply too much history between us to ignore.

"I've changed," he said.

Had he? Or was he just hurting, and confused, and back here because it was easy? Because he knew that even after all we'd been through, I'd always be the constant in his life. Would always welcome him with open arms.

"I don't believe you."

And that was the problem. Trust was the missing ingredient here, the biggest casualty of our breakup, and I feared it was lost for good.

"What would it take for you to believe me? To take a chance on us?" He took a step closer to me. "What would it take for you to come with me?"

I froze. "To move to Oklahoma?"

He nodded, his jaw clenched, his gaze intent.

Ten years ago we'd fought and fought, stuck between my dream and his, and I'd offered to give up my dreams, to give up on law school, to follow him to Texas where he was undergoing pilot training. It had hurt, and there had been doubts, but I'd loved him so much that I'd been willing to give up my dreams in exchange for his. Had been ready to throw away the dream of finally having the home I'd craved since my parents died.

And he still hadn't wanted me.

"I offered you that."

Guilt flashed in his eyes. "I know. And I made a huge mistake."

That was the part I couldn't get over, that no matter how hard I tried, I couldn't let go. I'd offered to change my life for him, and instead he'd walked away. It wasn't quite the same; he'd been young and unsure of himself then, but I didn't know how to trust that it would be different this time. Maybe we'd hurt each other too much; maybe he'd hurt *me* too much.

"I didn't want that for you. I don't want that for you now. You love what you do and you're great at it, and I never want to be the cause of you losing it. But there has to be another way. I can't believe that we found each other after all of this time just to have it slip away again. Please. Think about it. Give us a chance."

"What about you? Would you give up flying for me? You said your commitment was almost up. You talked about your frustrations with your job. How unhappy you've been. Have you considered a different path?"

He looked stricken, and so torn, and I figured that brief flash of panic was a better answer than anything he could give me.

"It's all I've ever known. All I've ever done. It's the only thing I've ever been good at in my entire life. I'm a fighter pilot. It's who I am. I don't know how to be anything else."

"So that's it. If we're going to be together, then I'm supposed to give up my career and choose you. Even though you wouldn't do the same for me."

He looked pained. "I can't."

"You can. You just don't want to." I grabbed my bag, evading him as he reached out, trying to hold on to me.

I hesitated before turning back to face him. "Do you have any idea what it feels like to love someone with everything you have, only to know that you play second fiddle to his job? To a fucking plane? To know that I will always be second to you, to worry that if we have children, you won't love them as much as your job?

"Maybe it makes me selfish. Maybe I should be the kind of person who doesn't care. Who's just content with the scraps you throw my way. But I'm not. I haven't had a family since I lost my parents. That's my dream.

"I want a home. Christmas mornings watching my kids open presents. I want to fall asleep and wake up staring at your face. I want to sit at the dinner table each night and talk about our days. I want those little moments that you flung in my face a decade ago, that weren't good enough for you then. I'm not going to give that up for someone who doesn't really want me."

"I love you," he whispered, the pain in his voice nearly enough to call me back.

"Not enough."

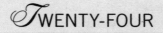

TWENTY-FOUR

BECCA

I got into the car, my hands shaking, restless energy pouring through me. I needed to get out of here. Now. My chest felt too tight, like each breath was a chore, anger and panic washing over me.

I wrapped my hands around the steering wheel, leaning forward and letting my forehead rest against the leather. I took deep breaths, trying to steady myself, and maybe, if I was really being honest with myself, waiting to see if Eric would come after me.

He didn't.

Motherfucker.

How was it possible that I was just as fucking stupid at thirty-one as I'd been at twenty-one?

I placed the key in the ignition, turning the car on, and pulled out of the parking lot, not sure where I was going, but determined to get the hell out of here.

I put the windows down, the air cooling me, the breeze doing the trick and releasing some of the tension from my chest. I turned on the radio, flipping around until I found a song I loved, turning it up to blaring, letting the air dry the tears on my cheeks.

I was fine. I would be fine.

I'd survived this once. I'd do it again, no problem.

I hit the highway, torn between driving somewhere and just heading home. And then it hit me, and I was turning off onto the narrow gravel road, not sure if I was trying to ease the wound inside me or making it worse by opening it up and pouring salt inside.

The drive was familiar, another spot like the farm, where we'd spent so much of our youth.

Cranberry Lake was a popular spot for teens to hang out. It was gorgeous, private, and the kind of place you took a date when you wanted to get busy and had nowhere else to go. I'd lost my virginity to Eric on a blanket underneath the stars, had gone skinny-dipping and swimming there with him more times than I could count, and when he'd proposed to me on Valentine's Day during our junior year of college, it had been on the dock of Cranberry Lake.

I'd avoided this place for ten years. Avoided the memory of what it had been for me. Of what he had been for me. Tried to do everything I could to forget the moment he'd gotten down on one knee and asked me to be his wife, and then the moment that felt like its counterpoint after he left— when I'd come here for the last time and tossed my diamond into the lake.

I got out of the car, walking down the dock, not sure where I was headed, but hoping I'd figure it out when I got there. I'd nearly reached the end when I heard the sound of a car engine, of tires over gravel, and then the engine cut off, a door slammed, and I didn't have to turn around to know that it was Eric's footsteps heading toward me. He knew all my moves, even before I did.

"What do you want?" I asked, not bothering to turn and face him, knowing that looking at him would make everything so much worse.

His voice scraped over my skin like sandpaper.

"I don't know."

"Well, I don't know what to do with that."

I stared out at the water, trying to fight the anger bubbling up inside me. Why did this have to be so hard? Why did he keep doing this? Why did I keep letting him?

"It's been my life for over a decade."

"Yeah, I'm aware of that. Thanks."

He made a frustrated noise. "I know you're pissed at me. I'm sorry. I'm not trying to hurt you. I don't want to keep repeating the same mistakes."

I turned, my heart clenching at the sight of him standing there before me, six-feet-Prince-Harry-hair-blue-eyes of everything I ever wanted and could never quite hold on to, no matter how hard I tried.

"Really? You're doing a pretty good job of it."

"I don't know what I want, okay? I thought flying was what I was meant to do. I loved it. Love it. When I'm in the air, everything makes sense in a way it only ever has when I'm with you. And yeah, I'm confused. My life seems like it's spiraling out of control, and I'm trying to hold on, but I'm afraid I'm holding on to the wrong things. I love my job, but I love you, too."

God.

I'd thought I'd hardened my heart to him, thought I'd prepared myself for this, and now that it was here, I couldn't keep him out. Those four words did stupid, stupid things to me, making me hope, making me *feel*. I was angry at him, but this wasn't his fault; it was mine. I should have known better from the beginning. I should have listened to my instincts and stayed away from him. He'd broken my heart once, and against my better judgment, I'd let him do it again.

"This was a mistake."

His hand caught mine, holding me in place. "Don't say that."

I shook my head, tugging away. "It was. I knew better than to get involved with you again. I *knew* this would happen, but I thought I was older now, wiser, thought I could somehow survive you again, and you know what? I can't."

His voice broke. "I'm not trying to hurt you."

"You keep saying that, but it doesn't mean anything. You might not be trying to hurt me, but you *are*. So just let me go. We keep trying, but maybe we need to stop and realize this is never going to happen between us. We're going around in circles and hurting each other in the process." I took a deep breath, steadying myself, trying to get a handle on my traitorous heart. "You need to leave. You need to go back to Oklahoma and move on with your life. You need to let go."

I need to let go.

His jaw clenched. "So that's what you want? You want me to leave. You don't ever want to hear from me again."

I wanted him to pick me. I wanted him to *want* to pick me. I felt like the girl I'd been before, heart in my hands, waiting to see if he'd make the right choice, if he'd pick us, and *fuck that*. I was done waiting for him to wake up and see what was right in front of him. Done waiting for him to see *me*. If this wasn't what he wanted, then it was time for both of us to move on.

"I'm asking for more time." He ran a hand through his hair, his face pale. "I just need to figure everything out."

"You had ten years to figure it out. And what? Would you have ever come back here if we hadn't run into each other? Or would another ten years have passed?" My voice rose, the truth behind my words hitting me like a slap in the face. "Your friend died. And I'm sorry you lost him. Sorry you feel responsible. It's not your fault, but you don't see that, and you know what, I can't change your mind if you don't want to change it.

"You came back here broken and gave me the pieces, and like the idiot that I am, I put them back together for you. Because I'm stupid enough to love you no matter how many times you break *my* heart." I shook my head, too worn out and sliced through for tears. "I did what I always do—I put you back together again. So go back to your life. Go home."

He flinched.

"This isn't your home anymore. *I'm* not your home anymore."

"Don't do this—not like this." The plea in his voice might have meant something once upon a time. Now it was just another thing standing between me and gone, and I wanted to get the hell out more than I'd ever wanted anything. "Give me time. Just give me—"

"I gave you everything. There's nothing left to give."

"Becca—"

I stepped toward him and he froze, his big body braced for an invisible blow. I stopped when I was close enough that our clothes brushed against each other, the hem of my skirt flirting with the bottom of his khaki cargo shorts. My hand reached out, my palm connecting with the worn cotton fabric of his T-shirt, the breeze ruffling my hair so it brushed against his arm, grazing the freckles dusted there.

His heart beat beneath my palm, steady and sure, the rhythm of it predictable even as I struggled to understand the *how* and *why* behind how it drove him, as I tried to decipher the language it spoke.

As I gave up trying.

I pressed my lips to his, his chest heaving on a sharp inhale and then back again as the breath flowed from his mouth to mine. My fingers curled around his tee, holding him toward me for an instant before I pulled back, the heel of my palm pushing him away.

I gave in to a moment of weakness, letting myself get a little lost in his blue eyes, the pain there scraping over me.

"Becca—"

"Good-bye, Eric."

I turned, the sounds of my shoes hitting the rickety wooden dock, a series of slaps. I could feel his gaze on me, boring holes into my back, and if I turned around, if I hesitated, if I indulged the feelings raging through me—the hope and pain beating my breast—I wouldn't have the strength to do this. It would be so easy to sink back into his embrace, to give myself over to the power of his touch. It would be so easy and would steal whatever chunk of my heart remained.

So I walked on. And on. Each step taking me farther away, each step leaving Eric firmly in the past whether I wanted him there or not.

They were the hardest steps I'd ever taken.

THOR

I watched her walk away, hands fisted at my sides, panic in my chest. I wanted to go after her; I commanded my feet to fucking move, a voice screaming inside, telling me I was going to lose her, that this was it, this was *good-bye*. I stood there, impotent, confused, drowning, feeling as if I'd been thrown an anchor only to have it ripped from my grasp.

Fuck that.

I wasn't a kid anymore. I wasn't losing her. Not again.

"Becca."

She didn't turn around, her dark hair swinging behind her, her strides angry as she walked down the dock, toward her car.

My footsteps picked up, my long legs eating up the distance between us until I'd broken out into a run, my heart pounding with panic and fear.

I caught up with her quickly and she whirled around as I reached for her arm, her gaze pinning me.

"What?"

"I'm not giving up on us. I'm not choosing the Air Force. I'm telling you I can't make promises right now because I have to sort out my job. I'm sorry, but it's the truth. I need to go back to Bryer and see what my future holds. I'm going to look at options for getting out. I *want* to look at options for getting out.

"I don't want this to be the end. I love you. I'm sorry that doesn't come with a ring right now, that in a way it probably feels like we've gone backwards, but given how crazy my life is, I think the best thing for us is to take things slowly. To see how you feel about being with me in the military. I have a year left on my commitment, but in that year there's a deployment, and I know it's a lot to ask you to deal with."

I pushed past the boulder in my throat, the tremor in my voice filling my ears.

"I know you're scared. I know losing your parents the way you did was hard, and I know you're afraid that something will happen to me. And with everything that's happened lately, I'm scared of that, too. I wish I could promise you that it'll be easy, that I'll always be safe, but I can't. I've already broken too many promises to you; I don't want to break another. But I promise I'll put you first. Put us first. That I will always love you.

"I want to examine my options. Want to figure out the best career move for both of us, so I can be the man you deserve. I want to build a future with you. That's all I want. I want to wake up in the morning with you and go to sleep with you at night. I can't promise I can give you that life any more than you can promise you're going to be okay being with me while I'm in the military, but I want to see where this could go. I want to stay together. I love you."

Tears spilled down her cheeks, but I saw the moment when her expression changed, the flicker in her eyes that told me she'd let me in instead of pushing me out.

"I'm scared," she whispered. "You're right; I don't ever want to lose you. Don't want to get a call in the night saying there's been an accident. I know I hold on too tight, but I'm scared that if I let go, you'll be gone. I'm scared that we aren't kids anymore, that we've built our own lives and that as hard as it was for us to come together ten years ago, it'll be even more difficult now that we're set in our ways."

"I know. Me, too. I've been thinking about the PTSD." It was the first time I'd put a label on this feeling inside me. "I'm going to talk to someone when I get back to Bryer. I need help. And yeah, maybe it'll screw me in the long run, but it's the right thing to do. I want to take care of myself. For you and for me, and for the guys who depend on me when I'm in the air.

"I don't know if this will work. Don't know if it can work. But you're the only woman I've ever loved and that will never change." I reached out, stroking her face, staring into her big brown eyes. "I let you go once; I can't do it again."

"I don't want to let you go, either."

"Then don't. Thanksgiving is in a month. Why don't you come out to Oklahoma and visit? I'll get four days off. You can meet my friends, see what my life is like. It'll give us a chance to see how things are between us outside of Bradbury. Do you already have plans for the holiday?"

"I usually spend it with Lizzie, Adam, and Dylan, but they won't miss me."

"Then come out. We're doing a big Thanksgiving dinner with the guys in the squadron who can't spend the holiday with their families and there'll be lots of wives and girlfriends there. Everyone's dying to meet you."

"You've told your friends about me?"

"Well, yeah. How could I not? You're it for me, Becca. You always were."

She wiped at her eyes, the look there filling me with the kind of hope I'd never dared to feel.

"Okay." She reached for me, her arms wrapping around my neck, pressing her body against mine.

"I love you," she whispered in my ear, so quiet I barely heard it, but loud enough to count.

I held on to her tighter, hoping those three words were strong enough to keep the world at bay.

"I love you, too."

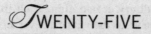

TWENTY-FIVE

BECCA

I stared up at the clear blue sky, my gaze searching, heart pounding.

"Which one is he?"

"He'll be the first plane to come into view," Jordan answered from her spot next to me on the flight line.

Eric hadn't been able to come pick me up from the airport when I flew to Oklahoma the day before Thanksgiving, so he'd sent his friend Noah's wife, Jordan, in his stead.

I liked her from the start; she'd explained that she was new to military life, too, and that she and her husband—who she referred to as Noah rather than the call sign I'd heard from Eric—had been married only six months. Eric had explained they'd been living together in South Korea until Jordan became pregnant, but owing to complications, her doctors had advised she come home. I couldn't imagine spending your first married holiday away from your husband, but she seemed to be taking it in stride. We had a big Thanksgiving dinner planned with eight of Eric's friends,

Jordan included. I was equal parts nervous and excited to meet the rest of the group, to see this side of his life.

Back in Bradbury, it had almost felt like nothing had changed between us, as though he'd never left. But here there was evidence of all the differences between us, of the decade we'd spent apart. None more glaring than the way I stared up at the sky, waiting for his F-16 to land.

When he mentioned that he had to fly when my plane arrived, he'd made this suggestion for me to come see what he did all day, the excitement in his voice impossible to resist. So here I was, trying to envision a future for us even if it looked nothing like the one I'd always imagined.

"It's surreal, isn't it?" Jordan commented, tilting her head to smile at me. "The first time I watched Noah land, I felt like I was having an out-of-body experience."

I grinned. "That sums it up."

Suddenly, a loud roar filled the air around us, cutting off all conversation. It was a shriek unlike any I'd ever heard, heralding something impressive heading toward us.

Easy walked up beside me, staring up at the sky. He'd been nice enough to escort us onto the flight line so we could watch Eric land. He pointed up, his voice rising to be heard over the plane's engine. "There he is."

At first it was just a speck against the few clouds—a *loud* speck—and then the big jet came into view.

It hit me so unexpectedly, but my chest went tight, an enormous feeling swelling inside of me, as though my body couldn't contain the emotions spilling out. So many images of Eric filled my mind—the boy who'd courted trouble with single-minded determination, who'd bitched about having to read *Middlemarch*, who'd picked me up for our first date, given me my first kiss the same night, the boy I'd stayed up late with, talking about our dreams, the memory of the night he'd come home and told me he wanted to join the military, confessed he wanted to be a fighter pilot, a touch of embarrassment in his gaze at how *big* the dream was, his voice full of so much excitement.

And then I saw the man he'd become. Who sat in the cockpit now, living his dream.

I was so proud of him. So, so proud.

And just like that, I knew—no matter how much he loved me or what he was willing to give up for us to be together, I didn't want him to give up this. I didn't know how we were going to work this out, only that we would. Somehow. But not at the expense of his dream, not at the expense of the thing that had turned him into the man he was today. A man I loved with every fiber of my being.

Tears spilled down my cheeks as my emotions overtook me and I was grateful for the sunglasses hiding my eyes, a little embarrassed by how much the sight of Eric in that jet made me feel. Jordan reached out and put an arm around me, her free hand on her stomach, hovering over the tiniest of bumps.

I watched him soar, amazed at the skill it must have taken, at how he could fly the jet with such ease, held my breath as he descended, as the wheels touched down on the runway. And then he was on the ground, safe, and all was right in my world.

"We'll wait until he taxis into his canopy spot and then you can go see him," Easy said.

"I'm allowed to go out there?"

"To the canopy? Yeah." Amusement filled his voice. "I think Thor's going to want the full impact of you seeing him get out of the jet."

Jordan snorted. "You're such an ass." She ducked her head, whispering conspiratorially in my ear. "He's not wrong, though. It is pretty hot."

I couldn't argue with that point. I'd *never* imagined that I'd find his job sexy—especially with our track record— but I'd been really, really wrong. There was something about that roar, seeing the jet soaring in the sky, knowing all the hard work, dedication, sacrifice, and determination that had gone into it, that made it awe-inspiring.

And yeah, really freaking sexy.

Easy nodded as the jet came to a stop under an awning. "Go for it."

I walked toward the F-16 on shaky legs, torn between wanting to run up there and trying to keep my cool. Finally I settled somewhere between the two, waiting until the jet canopy popped open and I got my first full-on view of Eric in all his glory.

Holy hell.

The smile got me first. He looked so happy to see me and so proud, that same expression on his face that he'd always had—the one that suggested he'd take you on the ride of your life if you let him—and I fell even more in love with him.

We'd talked every day in the last month, and I'd known it would be amazing when we finally saw each other again, but nothing compared to this moment and the feeling bubbling up inside me like someone had shaken up a bottle of champagne and let it fly.

I stood there waiting while he took his helmet off, his hands going over his flight suit, unhooking parts of his gear with a self-assured grace that impressed me. He hopped out of the jet, his feet hitting the metal ladder as he climbed down toward me.

He looked . . . there really weren't words. He looked like

flight suits had been designed with him in mind, like he'd been born to this. He seemed even taller, his body encased in a green suit that zipped up the front. The suit was smattered with patches on the shoulder and chest, his call sign prominent.

He wore an impressive pair of boots that might have had something to do with the additional inches he appeared to have gained, his hair mussed from the helmet he'd removed, faint lines on his face from what I assumed was the mask he'd been wearing.

He looked like an all-American fantasy and he walked with an air I'd never seen on him before. He'd always been confident, brushing right up against cocky, but now? He carried himself like he could do anything, as though the remnants of the adrenaline high he must have felt in the jet crackled through his body like electricity.

He looked at me like he wanted to devour me, like those moments up in the sky hadn't been enough and he needed to burn off more steam.

I was definitely up for the job.

I took a step forward, and then another, meeting him halfway so he caught me around the waist, smelling like machine and man.

When we were younger, we hadn't experienced absences in our relationship, so I'd gone into the month apart unprepared for what it would be like to be away from each other, somehow expecting the worst. What I'd gotten instead was four weeks of reconnecting, of sexy video chats and talking about our days. We'd fallen back into our relationship so easily, but this was the best of both worlds, having him here in front of me, strong and steady.

He broke apart first, his gaze running over my face, his hands traversing my body, a smile playing at his lips.

I reached out, my thumb brushing against his lower lip, wiping the hint of lipstick that had gone from my skin to his.

"Hi," he whispered.

I grinned. "Hi."

"I missed you."

"Missed you, too."

He brushed a strand of hair away from my face, hooking his arm around my waist and pulling me toward him.

"God, I love you."

I would never grow tired of hearing him say that. Never grow tired of saying it back.

"I love you, too."

He reached down, grabbing my hand and linking our fingers, waving to Easy and Jordan standing next to each other with matching grins on their faces.

We walked back into the squadron together, my hand in Eric's, his helmet bag dangling from his free hand, a line of gleaming F-16s behind us, and I felt like each step toward the squadron took me away from the life I'd known and into a new adventure, a new world.

THOR

The squadron had emptied out by the time I got through the debrief and went to my office in search of Becca.

I found her sitting in my desk chair, flipping through her phone, and for a moment I just stood in the doorway watching her.

She'd worked in the morning before flying to see me, and she hadn't changed from the knee-length, ass-hugging skirt or the silky black button-down top that hinted at cleavage. She'd draped her coat over the couch in my office, leaving her beautiful body on display.

I closed the door behind me, locking it, before turning back to face her, eternally grateful for the dull, windowless space that now afforded me the privacy I craved.

"Have I ever told you that I sort of have this thing about you all dressed up for work?"

She looked up from her phone, her lips curving into a smile. "A thing?"

"As in, when I see you in those tight little skirts you wear, I want to bend you over a desk, lift your skirt, and fuck you until you're screaming my name."

She grinned. "I could be down for that."

This girl slayed me.

"Stand up."

She rose from the chair, and I closed the distance between us, figuring I'd never look at my office the same way again. I drank in the sight of her, my dick already so fucking hard, the month apart catching up with me.

"You're so beautiful," I whispered, coming to stand behind her, my hands settling on her hips, holding her against me.

Becca trembled as I lifted her hair and kissed her nape, as my hand drifted from her hip, to her stomach, and higher still until I cupped her breast in my hand, my fingers finding her nipple through the fabric.

She moaned.

My other hand slid behind her, between us, cupping her ass, stroking her through her skirt, squeezing, my mind already four steps ahead, consumed with all the things I wanted to do to her.

My teeth grazed the curve of her shoulder, and then I

nipped her there, loving how she squirmed against my dick, the sound of her breaths growing louder, harsher, as though she clung to her control by a thread.

I ground myself against her ass, the zipper of my flight suit digging into my dick to the point of pain, and then I couldn't take it anymore, and I pulled the zipper down until my boxers were exposed, and I'd freed my cock.

I bent her forward over the desk, swiping some papers away, and then I was lifting up her skirt, watching the fabric slide over her ass and the lacy black thong she wore.

I groaned. "You are so fucking gorgeous. Perfect. Absolutely fucking perfect."

I laid my palm on her ass, caressing her there before reaching up and pulling the lace from her body, dragging it down her thighs, loving the visual of her spread open before me. I would never sit at my desk again without seeing her here, just like this.

"Eric . . ."

I leaned forward, my cock brushing against her bare ass, my hands sliding between her body and the desk, cupping her breasts, tweaking her nipples while she rocked against me.

Fuck. She was soaked.

I couldn't take it anymore, couldn't hold back, and my hands left her breasts, gripping her hips, just below her skirt bunched up around her waist.

With one hand I positioned myself at her entrance, rubbing against her clit, her wetness smearing around the head of my cock. My balls tightened, a bead of sweat popping up on my forehead as I slid inside, a slow steady glide, feeling her clench around me.

When I'd pushed all the way inside, I grabbed her hips, holding her steady, stilling, trying to get my shit together, and then I couldn't take it and I *had* to move.

I fucked her hard and fast, biting down on my lip hard enough to draw blood to keep from shouting out when I came, when I felt the beginning of her orgasm pulsing around my dick, when my name fell from her lips.

When we'd finished, she sagged against the desk, and I wrapped my arms around her, pulling her down into my lap, my heart hammering. Minutes passed before we spoke, until Becca broke the silence.

"That was one way to welcome me to Oklahoma." She grinned. "Turns out a month is a really long time."

"Tell me about it."

She kissed my cheek. "Take me home. I have another round in me."

She was definitely going to kill me, but I couldn't think of a better way to go.

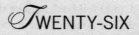

TWENTY-SIX

THOR

Becca straddled me, her naked body calling to me like a homing beacon. I lay beneath her, fully clothed in my flight suit while she . . . explored. It had been quick and desperate between us back in my office, but now that we were in bed, she seemed eager to take her time, and as much as she was slowly killing me, I was only too happy to indulge her.

I groaned as she reached between us, taking advantage of my open zipper and slipping inside the slit of my boxers, her hand fisting my cock.

We'd gotten back to my rental house and she'd pounced. She seemed fascinated by my flight suit, taking her time until I was lying here with an aching cock and an escalating need to get inside of her.

She knew it, too.

She slid down my body . . .

Fuck. Yes.

Becca took me into her mouth, her hand gripping the base, her tongue licking me over and over again, swirling around the tip, sucking me deep, taking the orgasm barreling toward me to a whole other level.

My eyes closed and I fell back against the pillow, losing myself to her lips, her tongue, her hands, the way she moaned around my dick. I reached down, rubbing my thumb over her nipple, cupping her breast, her moans growing louder.

"Babe. I can't. I'm so close. Babe."

Our gazes locked, and then she was straddling me, giving me exactly what I wanted, her hands guiding my cock inside her with agonizing slowness, inch by fucking inch.

I groaned as she contracted around me, her body drawing me deeper and deeper inside until I couldn't take it anymore and I lifted my hips, thrusting deep. Our hands found each other, our palms touching, fingers linking midair as I pumped into her, as her body swayed over mine, all soft curves and sexy lines.

I brought her to the edge, watched her orgasm hover just out of her grasp, and then my thumb found her clit, sliding into the slippery wetness, taking her over the edge so that she came apart, her body quaking over mine, pushing me past the finish line as my balls tightened and I came hard, my gaze on her.

Becca leaned forward, wrapping her arms around me, hugging my body close to hers as we both relaxed into each other. She tipped her face up, her chin resting on my chest, eyes full of mischief.

"Have I ever told you that I sort of have this thing about you all dressed up for work?" she asked, echoing my words from earlier.

I burst into laughter. "Somehow I didn't expect that. I figured you'd be more briefcases and business suits than helmet bags and flight suits."

"I guess you changed my mind." She moved closer to me, her hand stroking down my stomach. "I like your place, by the way."

Considering how eager I'd been to get her naked, I hadn't exactly given her much time to see it.

"Thanks." I shrugged. "It's just temporary. Some guys buy houses when they PCS, but I figured it was more hassle than it was worth."

"That makes sense considering how short your assignments are."

She sat up in bed, the sheets dropping to her waist, her long hair falling down over her breasts.

So fucking beautiful.

"So explain how your assignment process works. When do you find out where you're moving next?"

I would have been lying if I didn't admit that I was nervous to have this conversation with her, afraid she'd freak out the same way she had before. Becca's entire life had been about needing structure, about finding stability after the loss of her parents. The only thing that was guaranteed about my lifestyle was that there were no guarantees, no way to predict what would happen next. You had to be able to go with the flow, and Becca was all about control.

"The active duty service commitment I signed in exchange for the Air Force training me to fly is nearly up. I have a year left. I should find out where I'm moving in the next month or so. When that happens, I'll have about a week to decide if I'm going to accept that assignment or get out.

"If I decide to get out, I'll still have to finish out the year, and I probably will extend it for a few months because the squadron really needs instructor pilots and more experienced guys for this deployment to Afghanistan."

"Have you thought more about your options?" she asked.

"I have. I talked to some guys I know who got out and are in the Guard and the Reserve. Either option would still keep me flying. I'd basically keep my rank and benefits; I just would be assigned to one location and wouldn't have to move every few years.

"I would still deploy, though. Still have to go TDY. And the hours would still be crazy. It's an option, but I don't know that it's going to be one you would be happy with."

"Would you be happy with it? Independent of me?"

There really wasn't an "independent of her" anymore, but I knew what she meant.

"Yeah. I would. The more I think about it, I'm starting to burn out on active duty. I like the flying and the squadron's great, but the higher you get, the more you realize how political everything is. The job becomes less about the kind of pilot you are and more about how well you network.

"You know me. I'm not that guy. I don't care if I'm a general one day; I just want to fly. The other bullshit that comes with it doesn't really matter."

"And the private sector?" she asked, her expression neutral. "Is there anything else you could see yourself doing? Anything else you would be interested in?"

I wanted to tell her that I'd realized my lifelong dream to be a dentist or found a previously undiscovered talent for crunching numbers. Unfortunately, that was not the case. I'd racked my brain thinking of alternative options, only to come up short. I was good at what I did, with a very defined set of skills that didn't necessarily translate to the civilian world.

"I don't know," I hedged. "Maybe? There's always defense contracting. Not exactly the stuff of dreams, but the money's good. The life would be stable—"

"And you would be miserable."

"No. Maybe," I admitted. "It's just never seemed like something I would enjoy. I'm not exactly a suit."

She grinned. "I noticed." She reached out, linking our fingers together and running her lips over my knuckles. "You looked amazing out there today. You looked like you were in your element, happy, confident. Like the world was yours for the taking and you could do anything while you were in the cockpit."

I'd never thought of it that way, but she was right—

Flying made me feel like I could do anything. It made the impossible possible.

I'd been going to weekly sessions, talking through my PTSD with a counselor the military had assigned me. So far it was helping more than I'd anticipated. I hadn't had another freak-out in the jet, and she was right—the last few weeks I'd enjoyed flying more than I had in the last year.

"How do you always do that?" I asked, falling a little more in love with her with each moment that passed.

"Do what?"

"Get me. Know what I'm feeling even before I do."

She ran her hand through my hair, a smile playing at her mouth. "I love you. I've loved you forever. And I see the fire in your eyes when you fly, see the passion there. You wouldn't be happy behind a desk somewhere. Not after the life you've lived. I don't want to be the cause of you waking up every morning and dreading going to work. It's so rare to find a job that you love. Don't throw that away."

"I don't think of it as throwing it away. I want to be with you. Want to make this work."

She leaned forward and kissed me. "I know. And I know I've been reluctant to consider military life, but I think you're right. There can be a compromise here. We should look for something that will let us both do what we love."

"I think the Guard or reserves could be a good option. There are F-16 units around the country. Would you be okay with moving out of South Carolina if we needed to? That would be it—just the one move and then you could set up your practice somewhere. I know it's not exactly what you wanted—"

"It's perfect. If that's what we need to do, we'll do it. I can still be an attorney, still build my career."

"That's the big positive with it. At the same time, I'm going to be honest, Guard and Reserve spots can be tricky. It's a timing thing—you have to hope for an open spot when you need it, and depending on the base, they can be competitive. I don't know for sure that a job will open up, but I'm trying to figure something out. I've put out feelers with a bunch of guys I know in the community. We'll see if anything becomes available."

"Okay." She extended her hand to me, a soft smile playing at her lips. "I'm in."

I took her hand, tugging her back under me.

"Me, too."

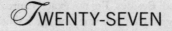TWENTY-SEVEN

BECCA

I spent Thanksgiving morning in bed with Eric, watching the parade on his gigantic TV, and the afternoon cooking with Jordan and her friend, Dani, at the house Jordan and her husband, Noah, owned.

"Why is it that the guys are getting away with watching football and we're in here cooking for ten?" Jordan complained.

I grinned. "Trust me, you don't want to see Eric cook. I tried to teach him when we lived together in college and finally just gave up. Unless he's made some radical changes in the last decade, he's hopeless."

Not that I was much better.

"Hey, I heard that." Eric walked up behind me, wrapping his arm around my waist and snagging a deviled egg off the counter in front of me.

I swatted him with the dishtowel. "You have to wait until everyone gets here."

"Oh, come on. We're waiting on Easy. He doesn't count."

Jordan laughed. "He has a point there. If Easy can't bother to drag his ass here on time, then all bets are off when it comes to food. Besides, I'm not exactly sure he eats things like deviled eggs. Can you imagine the havoc mayonnaise would wreak on his six-pack?"

"Hey, I'll have you know it's an eight-pack, thank you very much," Easy joked, walking into the kitchen with the swagger I'd come to recognize as standard.

His gaze swept the room and then he froze, his gaze settling on Dani standing near the oven, a ladle in her hands.

Eric told me that Joker's widow had returned to Oklahoma after spending the months following her husband's death in Georgia with her family. I hadn't known what to expect when Eric mentioned she'd be joining us, couldn't imagine what she was going through or how difficult it must have been to spend her first holiday without her husband.

She was quieter than Jordan, but just as friendly. Seeing her rocked me in a way I hadn't expected. She was young— my age or even younger—and she was a widow. There was a sadness that cloaked her and made her seem so much older, as though life had worn her down.

For the first time since I'd arrived, I watched as Dani's lips curved into a blinding smile, her eyes lighting up at the sight of Easy, and then in three strides the crowd had parted and she had her arms around him, her tiny frame dwarfed by his.

He stiffened the instant she touched him, his eyes slamming closed, his arms at his sides. It took him a second, but we all watched as he slowly lifted his arms, his hands stroking her hair.

"Hey, Dani."

My jaw dropped.

He said her name like it was the most beautiful thing in the world, as though it cut him up inside to say it, his voice husky and raw.

My gaze darted from Jordan to Eric, expecting to see the same confusion I felt, trying to figure out what I'd missed—

Jordan looked like she was about to cry. Eric looked worried.

What the hell?

They stood there like that for a moment, and then Dani let go, taking a step back, smiling up at him.

"I've missed you. How have you been?"

Easy swallowed, her presence seeming to have sucked the swagger out of him.

"I'm good. How are you? I didn't realize you'd be here." Guilt flashed in his eyes. "Sorry I wasn't there when you flew in."

Last week Eric and the rest of the squadron had gone and greeted Dani at the airport when her flight landed.

She smiled, reaching out and squeezing his hand. "Don't worry about it. I heard you'd just gotten back from a TDY to Hill."

Easy's gaze drifted over her head to Jordan and then Eric, shooting daggers at both of them.

Was it just that she reminded him of the friend he'd lost? Did he share the same guilt that plagued Eric? Or was it something more?

They spoke for another minute, the whole room frozen by their encounter. Jordan tried to look like she was messing with the stuffing, but I could tell her attention was wholly focused on the conversation going on behind her. Eric hovered in the doorway, tense.

I shot him a look, my brows raised.

Easy and Dani finished talking and he grabbed a beer from the fridge before giving Eric a dark look and walking out. Eric grimaced and then turned, heading after him.

THOR

"How the fuck could you not tell me she was going to be here? What the hell were you thinking?"

I closed the door and stepped out onto the deck, facing off against a very pissed off Easy.

"You wouldn't have come if I told you."

"No, I wouldn't have."

"You're being an asshole. She misses you. You were one of her closest friends, one of Joker's closest friends. She asked where you were when we went to the airport. She looked for you."

He let out an oath.

"You can't avoid her forever."

"Leave it alone."

"No. I'm not going to leave it alone. I know you have your shit to work through, and I'm sorry, man, I really am, but you know what? She's lost everything. She needs to have a support network around her right now, needs the people she considers her family to be there for her now that Joker's gone. So whatever you're dealing with, lock it down. She doesn't need your drama."

"You don't think I fucking know that? Why do you think I'm keeping my distance?"

"Honestly? I don't know what you're thinking."

"I love her. I've loved her since the first fucking moment I saw her. Everyone knows. Hell, it took your girlfriend, what, a minute to figure it out? What I don't need—and what Dani definitely doesn't need—is for Dani to figure it out.

"I'm not abandoning her. If she needs me, I'll be there. But I need some time to get this under control."

"You've had seven months," I answered. "She's been gone for seven months."

He gave me a twisted smile. "And there hasn't been a day when I haven't thought of her. When I walked into that kitchen and saw her . . ." He took a deep, ragged breath, raising the beer bottle to his lips. "You should have told me she was going to be here. Don't blindside me like that again."

I nodded, realizing how much I'd underestimated him. I'd never really seen this side of Easy before, had never been as close to him as Burn was. I'd known he was attracted to Dani, but I'd figured it was because Dani was gorgeous and funny, and because she was one of the kindest people I'd ever met. I'd never imagined it ran this deep, had expected out-of-sight, out-of-mind would have tempered the feelings inside Easy.

"Did the time . . . When you saw her . . ."

"Did the time apart help? Did it make this easier? Did I see her and think, 'Oh, there's Joker's wife, glad that crush is over'?" he mocked.

I grimaced.

"What the fuck do you think?"

BECCA

Dani left the kitchen to call her family in Georgia and wish them a happy Thanksgiving. Jordan and I stayed behind, finishing up the last touches on the meal. I'd never cooked for so many people before, never had a big family, but it was nice celebrating the holiday with such a large group. In addition to me, Eric, Jordan, Easy, and Dani, Jordan had invited five single pilots who weren't able to be with their families.

"It's weird not having Noah here," Jordan commented, stirring the gravy. "I feel guilty knowing he won't get much of a Thanksgiving in Korea while I'm here doing all of this."

"I bet. Will they do something like this over there?"

"Yeah, his squadron was planning on doing a dinner, but it won't be quite the same."

"It's gotta be rough, spending your first Thanksgiving apart."

"It is, but I'm sort of getting used to it. Everyone warned me it would be like this." She gave a little laugh. "I guess I'm really an Air Force wife now."

I shook my head, a smile playing at my lips. "The things we do for the men we love."

"Amen, sister."

"Eric mentioned you got married earlier this year."

Her smile widened. "Yeah, we sort of eloped to Vegas in May. We met there, so it seemed appropriate to return to the scene of the crime, so to speak."

"I love that."

"We really needed it. It was rough after Joker died. His death put in perspective what's important. I met Noah when I was in Vegas for my sister's bachelorette weekend, and everything afterward was a whirlwind. I knew embarrassingly little about the military and was overwhelmed by how different everything was, by the challenges of the lifestyle. It wasn't just starting a new relationship; I felt like I was entering a whole new world. And for a long time, I didn't see how I would fit in it. But that night . . . the crash . . . it just changed. And I realized the most important thing was that we loved each other. Everything else didn't matter."

"That makes sense." I sighed. "I'm trying to ease my way into this. I feel like I suck at it, though."

"Then you're definitely in good company. Trust me, we all feel like that at one time or another. Often, more times than not. You have to push through and do your best, as corny as that sounds. And I wouldn't be too hard on yourself. You and Thor seem really happy together."

For some reason, that made me smile even more. I wasn't sure I would ever get used to hearing Eric referred to by his call sign.

"We are. It's a long time coming, obviously, but I'm glad we found our way back to each other. I knew I missed him, but I didn't realize how much until he returned."

"He needed to go home." Jordan's expression sobered. "It's been really rough for the guys since the accident. Noah has dreams sometimes. Thor looked so devastated after it happened. And Easy . . ." She sighed. "Easy's a mess."

I hesitated, not wanting to seem nosy and, at the same time, not wanting to put my foot in my mouth later on.

"Is Easy . . ." I struggled to find the right words. "He just seemed to be a little, uh, uncomfortable around Dani."

"That's one way to put it." She gave me a wry smile. "Yeah. Let's just say there's some stuff there."

I figured "stuff" was the diplomatic way of saying that Easy was definitely into Dani.

"She doesn't know?"

Jordan shook her head. "She's really close with all the guys. Joker was the squadron commander and Dani took her role as his wife seriously. They were an amazing couple. One of those couples that seemed so in love. And they were good to everyone around them.

"She basically adopted the squadron—cooking meals, celebrating birthdays, being their family when they needed it. It's who she is. She's the kind of person who would do anything for you.

"Easy was one of Joker's closest friends and he spent a lot of time with Dani. So yeah, they're really close. But she definitely has no idea that it's anything else for him. Joker was her whole world. I don't think she really sees anyone else. Not like that. I don't think she ever will, either."

That sounded so sad for both of them.

"Did Thor tell you about the lantern release we're doing later?"

I nodded. Eric told me it had been Dani's idea to release sky lanterns as a way of remembering Joker, and Jordan had jumped on the idea, coordinating everything.

"I think it'll be good for her. There were a ton of official events after he died, but she was still so numb from the shock, still processing everything, trying to hold it together for her family, his family, the squadron, for Joker's memory. She didn't really get a chance to grieve, and now, seven months later, I think she's coming to terms with the fact that he's gone, that her life has to go on without him. I'm hoping this will help her feel like she's saying her own good-bye, on her terms, at a time when she's ready to do it."

My eyes welled up with tears, a matching expression on Jordan's face.

She reached out and wrapped her arm around me, giving me a side hug.

"This is a sisterhood of sorts. We're a weird, slightly fucked up family, but we're ride-or-die and we have your back when you need it." She pulled back and gave me a wry smile. "Unfortunately the way this lifestyle goes, you will need it. But at least know you aren't alone, and I promise you, whatever you're feeling, we've all been there and get it. You can always talk to me. I hope we'll become friends."

I grinned, wiping at my eyes. "I'd love that."

"Me, too."

She grabbed our wineglasses off the counter, handing me mine just as Dani walked in.

Jordan wrapped her other arm around her friend's waist, handing her the spare glass.

"I'm making a toast."

Dani smiled. "Okay. What are we toasting?"

"Us."

"That sounds like an excellent toast to me," Dani answered.

We lifted our glasses with a silent toast, and suddenly it hit me that I'd always seen the Air Force as a threat to the family I wanted, imagined it taking Eric away from me and the family I'd been trying to build. But standing here in the kitchen with two women I'd just met yet felt a kinship with, I realized that maybe it would give me a different kind of family instead. One I could lean on when this life rocked me.

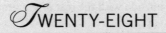

TWENTY-EIGHT

BECCA

It was one of the best Thanksgivings I'd ever had. The food was amazing. I wasn't the greatest cook and Jordan had admitted she wasn't much for domesticity, either, but Dani had just grinned and whipped us into shape in the kitchen.

I revised my initial impression of her. I'd thought she was shy, quiet even, but that wasn't it exactly. She was just understated in a way that reminded me of Southern grace—and at the same time, steel resided beneath the manners and quiet tones. I liked her. A lot.

Dinner went well, the conversation mainly revolving around flying. I quickly realized Easy and Eric were more experienced than the rest of the group, and it was cool to hear the way the other guys looked up to them, asking them questions and seeking their input.

I was so glad I'd come out here to visit Eric. I saw a new side of him now, one I admired and respected in an entirely different way. He'd accomplished so much in the time we'd spent apart, and as much time as we'd lost, more and more

I realized how badly we'd needed it to get us here, to a place where we felt stronger than ever.

We walked outside with the rest of the group, our hands linked.

I took a step forward, but Eric tugged me back, bringing me to his side, his arms wrapping around me as he leaned down and pressed his lips to mine.

He kissed me in the cold, his mouth warming me up, my heart so full of love, I thought it would burst.

"Thank you for coming out here. And for giving me an amazing Thanksgiving."

I grinned. "Thank you for inviting me. I'm having a great time."

I was surprised by how easy it had been to relax around the group, to join the camaraderie and laughter.

"Really?"

"Everyone is so nice. I love Dani and Jordan. And you were right, I get it a bit more now, see the family you've built for yourself here. It's not what I thought it would be, and I understand why you like it so much. How it appeals to you. They make you feel like you're part of something bigger than yourself."

"Yeah. They do." He took my hand again, squeezing my fingers. "Thanks for being here for this, too."

"Of course."

Joker had come up a few times over the course of the dinner and I could see that both Easy and Eric still carried that loss with them. I supposed it was something you never really entirely let go of. That was how it had been with my parents, at least. There wasn't a day I didn't think of them, didn't miss them. But somehow you just kept on going, putting one foot in front of the other and trudging through your life, carrying their memory with you. It didn't get easier as much as it became more bearable, and that was what I hoped for Eric now.

We walked toward the crowd gathering in Jordan and Noah's backyard, where Jordan had set out all the lanterns. I'd been to a wedding once where someone released these lanterns and it had been absolutely gorgeous. Considering how Joker had died and lived his life in the sky, it seemed like the perfect gesture.

We all took our cues from Dani. She opened her mouth to speak, and then she shut it again with a little shake of her head, as though there were no words she could put to a moment like this.

Jordan squeezed her hand, handing her one of the lanterns and a lighter.

My gaze drifted over the group, settling on Easy.

He stood off to the side, watching Dani, his arms crossed in front of his chest, his expression inscrutable. He didn't look away. Not once.

I looked back at Dani, watched as she lit the candle inside of the lantern, holding it up to the sky. She took a deep breath, her eyes closed, auburn hair flowing behind her, looking so beautiful it staggered me. And then she released the lantern, the flame flickering in the inky black sky as it rose higher and higher, drifting away.

I looked back at Easy, and if I'd needed any final confirmation about his feelings for Dani, the expression on his face said it all.

He loved her.

One by one, we all repeated Dani's gesture, releasing our lanterns to the sky. I felt a little bit strange, as though I was intruding on a private moment for the people who knew him best, but Dani and Jordan had acted like it was the most natural thing in the world for me to be there alongside them, and Eric had seemed to need it, so I went with it.

When the last person had released their lantern, we all stared up at them—ten flames burning bright overhead. Eric stood next to me, his arm draped around my shoulder.

"You okay?" I whispered.

"Yeah, I am. I feel a little bit better."

Sometimes a little bit was the best you could hope for.

Dani stood at the front, flanked by Jordan and Easy. There was family here, everywhere you looked. Maybe these people weren't bound by blood, but they were bound by a powerful kind of sacrifice.

Dani tilted her head up and said something to Easy, and I watched as his lips curved, a breathtaking smile transforming his face.

Eric stiffened beside me.

"Do you think they'll be okay?" I murmured.

"I don't know. He's not getting over her and I don't think Dani will ever see him as anything other than a friend."

Poor Easy. I knew better than anyone how much it hurt to love someone you couldn't have, who didn't love you back, and I couldn't imagine how tough it must be with the added guilt of her being his friend's widow and the fact that Easy had been there when he died.

I thought of Rachel and the way they'd seemed to hit it off in Columbia and I wondered if anyone really stood a chance with him, if he would call her like she'd hoped, or if he was so hooked by Dani that there wasn't room for anyone else in his life. I'd been there, so on the one hand, I got it; on the other hand, it was a lonely way to live.

When it grew too cold to stand outside anymore and the lanterns had drifted off so far that they were just dim lights in the sky, we walked back into the living room, talking over pumpkin pie and coffee. Eventually the group dwindled down to just me and Eric, Dani, Jordan, and Easy.

"So when do you head back?" Jordan asked between bites of pie.

"Sunday."

We had big plans to spend the rest of my visit holed up in Eric's bed.

"Are you planning on coming out again?"

I grinned at Eric. "Yeah, I am."

Dani smiled. "We should definitely hang out."

"I would like that. A lot."

Easy looked up from his coffee. "How long will you be in town for?" he asked Dani, his voice casual . . . way too casual.

"I'm not sure. I need to get the house ready to put on the market. I'll probably stay here until it sells and then figure something out."

"Have you thought about where you want to go yet?" Jordan asked.

Easy's gaze darted between the two of them.

Dani shook her head. "Not really. I thought I'd go home to Georgia, but after spending several months there . . ." She gave a little laugh. "I love my family, but I think living in the same town—maybe in the same state—is a little too close. After moving every few years and having distance between us, it's an adjustment to imagine staying put in one place."

Jordan nodded. "I know what you mean. I always thought being away from my family would be the hardest part of all of this, but you do start to get used to it after a while."

"How much longer do you have in Oklahoma?" I asked Easy.

"I'm in the same VML as Eric. I have a little over a year left." He shrugged. "I'm staying in. I pin on major next month and I figure with nine years until retirement, it makes the most sense to just keep going."

"Yeah, Noah's the same way," Jordan answered. "You can't beat the benefits."

Eric didn't say anything and I felt a pang of guilt at how easily Dani and Jordan seemed to have accepted the military lifestyle. I wished it could have come more naturally for me, that I wasn't standing between him and his career. What if he couldn't get a spot in the Guard or reserves? What then? I couldn't forget the way he'd spoken about getting out completely, and deep down I knew he wouldn't be happy in the private sector. I just wasn't sure I'd be happy moving all the time and giving up my career.

Eric shifted me on his lap, wrapping his arms more tightly around me, and I said another prayer that we could find a way to make this work.

THOR

We drove back from Jordan and Burn's house, the radio playing Christmas music. Becca had a firm rule that Christmas didn't officially kick off until Thanksgiving ended, and I was surprised she was willing to push it this close, but it gave me an idea.

"I want to spend Christmas with you. In South Carolina. Is that okay with you? Are you cool with me coming out?"

The squadron was deploying in May, and Loco had already decided that we wouldn't fly for the week of Christmas so everyone would have a chance to take leave and see their families. The ops tempo had been high lately, and he had a good pulse on the squadron so he'd realized everyone was dragging a little bit.

The leave I'd taken to go to South Carolina had helped. I hadn't realized how tired I'd been until I'd finally taken a break, and now that I was back in the cockpit, my mind felt clear. I didn't think I'd ever completely forget what had happened with Joker, but now it was a low-level hum in the back of my mind when I flew rather than this overwhelming noise that blocked out all else. And I was surprised by how much it helped to talk to someone who had worked with other guys who suffered from PTSD. It wasn't an overnight fix, but I was getting back to where I needed to be.

"I would love it if you spent Christmas in South Carolina with me," Becca answered. "Or I could come out here if it's too difficult for you to get away. I know you've taken a lot of leave lately. I'm flexible."

"Even with the amount of leave I took to come home, I still have like thirty days left. Opportunities to take vacations have been few and far between these past few years, so trust me, it's fine. I'd like to spend it in Bradbury."

She smiled. "Then we will."

We drove in silence for a few minutes, and then she spoke.

"You know, after listening to everyone talk tonight, I was thinking that maybe I could give this whole active duty military thing a shot. I mean, Dani and Jordan don't seem to think it's so bad. Maybe I wouldn't, either, once I was in it. I could—"

"Don't even think about it."

"What?"

Even when we were younger, I'd struggled with the idea of her giving up her career for mine. I'd always felt guilty about it, like I was taking her away from something she was passionate about. I didn't want her to settle.

"I like Dani and Jordan a lot, but I'm not dating Dani or Jordan. They're happy with the choice they made, but deep down you know it wouldn't be the same with you. I love who you are and I don't want you to be someone you're not. Yeah, they've both adjusted to military life. It's been harder for Jordan; Dani genuinely loved the lifestyle. But you're not either one of them, and I don't want you to feel like you have to change your dreams.

"I don't think you would be happy if we were moving all the time, if you couldn't work, if your life was transient. And that's okay. You've always said you wanted to give our kids the kind of stability we didn't have. You wouldn't find that in active duty, not the way you want. You shouldn't feel guilty for that or apologize for it, either. You shouldn't feel a need to change who you are. I've never wanted that.

"I love that you're on your own path and it's okay if your path isn't the same as mine. We just have to figure out a way to make them go side by side." I made a face. "Which sounds really fucking corny."

She laughed, her voice thick. "I get your point."

"We got this. You just have to have a little faith."

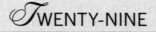

TWENTY-NINE

THOR

I flew into Columbia three days ahead of Christmas. Officially, Becca thought I arrived on the twenty-third. Unofficially I had some work to do, a few meetings, and a question burning a hole in my pocket.

Last time when my flight had landed in Columbia, I'd felt like I was running from something—from all the baggage I'd carried with me for way too long. Now I felt like I was coming home.

I grabbed my luggage from the belt, picked up my rental car, and then I was on the road, driving to McEntire, home of the 169th Fighter Wing, the South Carolina Air National Guard, and a squadron of F-16s that hopefully needed an experienced instructor pilot recovering from a bout of PTSD and looking for a fresh start.

I hadn't told Becca yet, but I'd received my assignment last week—Spangdahlem in Germany. It wasn't a bad assignment—in fact a lot of guys would have given their left nut for it—but Becca wouldn't be able to practice law there, and that had been the deciding factor for me. I'd turned in my paperwork stating my intention to separate from the Air Force. I had a few feelers out with Guard and Reserve bases around the country, but this was the one I wanted.

We could live in Bradbury and I could easily commute in to work every day. The more I thought about it, the more I loved the idea of raising our kids in the town where we'd grown up, of them getting a chance to know my grandmother, of being there for her as she grew older. Becca would get to keep her job—I had no doubt she'd be solicitor one day—and Becca would love being close to Lizzie.

I just had to nail this interview.

Easy had made a few calls for me; he'd managed to get me in to meet with the squadron commander even though the squadron was winding down for the holidays. They had mentioned that there might be an opening for an experienced major type, and considering I'd just pinned on rank, I had high hopes for this one.

It was part one in my two-part plan to give Becca a Christmas that made up for the ten others I'd missed.

I walked out of the 157th Fighter Squadron, also known as the Swamp Foxes, also known as my future squadron, feeling the same adrenaline high I did every single time I got out of the jet.

I'd nailed the interview. Fucking nailed it.

And I owed Easy.

It turned out he knew the commander a lot better than he'd let on, and by the time I walked into the squadron commander's office, he'd already heard an overly inflated account of my skills from Easy.

From there we'd settled into a rapport that had surprised me, as I realized the Guard really was a different beast from active duty. It was clear they still had a high-ops tempo, but it was way more laid back than what I was used to at Bryer, and for the first time in my Air Force career, I felt like I was getting back to my roots and my love of flying rather than a desire to play politics.

I'd explained my intent to extend a few months past my commitment date to see the Wild Aces through their deployment, and as soon as I was back from Afghanistan, I'd transition out of active duty and become a full-time member of the South Carolina Guard.

I celebrated with a drink at the O-Club with the pilots I'd be flying with next year and then I left and texted Becca, fumbling the message twice, nerves jinxing my fingers, before I got it right and hit "Send."

I'd thought about asking her to meet me at Cranberry Lake, but it felt like we needed a fresh start, and I wanted to do things differently this time. Wanted to do everything differently. We were both who we'd been before and something new, something that felt stronger, more resilient, something that would withstand whatever came our way.

I was all in. I just hoped she was, too.

Time for step two.

BECCA

I was sitting at home when my phone pinged with the text from Eric. At first I was convinced I'd read it wrong, that there was some mistake.

I'm at turnoff for the Eggers farm. Can you meet me in an hour?

The last time I'd talked to Eric, he'd told me that he was flying into Columbia tomorrow. I was off the rest of the week and had planned on driving over to pick him up in the morning. Except now he was here. In Bradbury.

Why the Eggers farm?
Trust me.

I shook my head, a smile playing at my lips. This was definitely a new side of Eric; mysterious and romantic hadn't exactly been his modus operandi before.

I'll be there.

I dressed quickly, taking the time to fix my fading makeup, running my fingers through my hair, channeling the tousled look. It was a thirty-minute drive to the Eggers farm on the outskirts of town, so if I left now, I'd be good.

I wanted to call Eric, just to hear his voice, but somehow that felt like cheating, like I'd be ruining the surprise, so I refrained. I listened to Christmas music as I drove, each mile that went by filling me with more and more excitement.

We'd agreed to hold off on celebrating the holidays until we were together, so tomorrow we were putting up a Christmas tree and I'd even gotten him to agree to bake cookies with me. We'd spent enough holidays together that we had our little traditions—ones we were reinstating this year—watching *Christmas Vacation*, his favorite, and *It's a Wonderful Life*, my favorite. I couldn't remember the last time I'd been this excited for the holiday.

I drove to the turnoff for the Eggers farm, pulling off the road when I saw Eric standing next to his rental car.

He wore a pair of dark jeans and a navy blue sweater, and the rest was a blur as I launched myself into his arms.

We kissed for minutes and then I pulled back, my arms wrapped around his neck.

"What are you doing here? I thought you weren't getting in until tomorrow."

He grinned, his breath puffy in the cold.

"I wanted to surprise you."

"Mission accomplished." My gaze darted around our surroundings. "So why are we here, though?"

He grinned. "You'll have to wait and see." He pulled out a blindfold.

"Umm . . ." I made a face. "It's great to see you and all, but I'm thinking it might be a little cold for kinky sex games in the grass. Rain check? When it's not practically snowing?"

He laughed. "This surprise doesn't involve you getting naked. Promise."

"So what's up with the blindfold?"

He cocked his head to the side, a smile playing at his lips, but didn't answer me.

"Fine. I'll put it on." I groaned. "This surprise better be amazing, though."

His smile deepened. "It is. At least, I hope you'll think it is."

He slipped the blindfold over my eyes, his hands lifting my hair out of the way. I felt his lips glide over mine in a kiss that was soft and sweet as he reached down and took my hand.

"I'm going to lead you where you need to go, okay? Just be careful. I promise I won't let you fall."

It was pitch dark, I was getting cold, and the whole thing

reeked of some sort of bizarre sex game, but I went with it. Because I trusted him.

He led me to what I figured out was his rental car, and then I was sliding into the passenger seat with his help, asking questions the whole time until he burst out laughing.

"I forgot how much you need to be in control."

"Yes. Yes, I do."

"I promise. Just a few minutes longer."

I heard the sound of the car engine starting and then we were moving, heading to some unknown destination and my Christmas surprise. I honestly had no clue what it would be, but based on his excitement, I figured it was something big.

He held my hand while we drove, his thumb caressing my skin. Finally, I felt the car come to a stop, listening to the sounds of him turning off the engine and walking around the side to get me. He unhooked my belt, helping me out of the car until I was back outside, standing in the cold.

He guided me over what felt like gravel on the ground and then we stopped and he came to stand behind me, his body brushing against me, his arm wrapped around my waist.

"Ready?"

I nodded, anticipation filling me as his fingers grazed my cheek, and then he lifted the blindfold off my eyes—

I took a deep breath, steadying myself when the view staggered me.

We stood in front of a house. A huge white house decked out in Christmas lights and wreaths. I knew this house.

Oh my God.

"It's my house."

I mean, it wasn't my house. Not anymore. But it had been my home. My parents' land had bordered the Eggers farm.

It was why I'd always loved going there, loved the happy memories it evoked.

Eric's lips curved into a smile that made my breath hitch.

"What? What are we doing here?"

"I put an offer on it today. You know my grandmother—she heard through the grapevine that the owners were thinking of selling and told me. I called them before they'd even had a chance to put it on the market and they accepted my offer a few hours ago. The house is ours if you want it."

Oh my God.

"What?"

My legs felt like rubber, my mind racing as I struggled to understand the words coming out of his mouth, as suddenly he offered me everything I'd always wanted.

"I want to live here with you. You always said this was your dream. Always talked about raising kids here." He gestured to the huge tree where I'd once carved my initials. "I thought I could hang a swing from that branch and the kids could play there. I could take them fishing in the pond out back."

I was still somewhere back at him putting an offer on the house. These images of *children*, of a future together, seemed too good to be true.

"What? How? How did you do this?"

"I got the Guard job. I'll finish out my active duty commitment plus the two months we talked about to help out with the Wild Aces' deployment to Afghanistan. Then I'm out. I figured I could commute to McEntire easily from here. And this way you can keep your job.

"We'll be close to my grandmother as she gets older. And you were right, Bradbury is a great place to raise kids. And the times I do have to deploy, you guys will have a built-in support system in addition to the squadron if you need it."

"Are you—"

I couldn't get my bearings, felt like my heart was beating a million beats a minute. It was everything I'd ever wanted and he was here, offering me the future I'd dreamed of on a silver platter.

And then he smiled. "There's one more thing."

I blinked, convinced I was hallucinating as he got down on one knee in a move I had seen once before, on the version of him that had been in transition, growing into the man he'd become. The man I loved. The man I would grow old with, raise children with.

I'd missed him pulling the box out of his pocket, and it appeared in his palm as if by magic, and my heart skipped and stuttered in my chest.

"Becca Madison, will you marry me?"

He flicked open the box, and I stared down at the ring, then up at him, and for the second time in my life, I gave him the only answer I had to give—

"Yes."

Tears spilled down my cheeks as he slipped the diamond on my finger, his hand trembling as our skin brushed against each other. We didn't speak. The most important words had already been spoken. But I held on to his hand, the bond between us steady. And then he was on his feet, wrapping his arms around me, pulling me in for a kiss, his lips achingly soft, his kiss lighting a fire inside me that warmed me even as the South Carolina winter bore down around us.

We kissed in front of our home, in the yard where I'd played so many times as a kid, where I'd one day watch my kids play. And I didn't know if it was possible or just wishful thinking, but I imagined that my parents were here with us, their hearts full of joy as I started the next chapter in my life, bringing my past and those I'd loved and lost with me.

The road ahead wouldn't be easy. The upcoming deployment, the year he still had to finish out in the Air Force, all of it would test us, all of it would challenge us. But it had taken us ten years to get to this point, to become something stronger than the obstacles thrown our way. And this time, love would be enough.

It was everything.

Turn the page for a sneak peek at
the next Wild Aces Romance,

ON BROKEN WINGS,

coming from Berkley in January 2017.

DANI

"Do you want matte or gloss?"

I blinked, the cans of paint blurring before me. What kind of paint did you use to erase a broken dream?

No fucking clue.

My hands gripped the handle of my cart, filled with painting supplies that had taken me the better part of an hour to assemble. Every time I thought I had what I needed, I realized I'd forgotten yet another thing. Time had ceased to exist here, and I half wondered if I'd finally escape Aisle 12 in order to discover that night had fallen and I'd wasted yet another day not fulfilling the task I dreaded.

The salesman sighed, running his hand through his hair. I couldn't exactly blame him for the frustration—even with the online research I'd done, it was clear that I was pretty clueless on how to repaint an almost-nursery-turned-guest-bedroom in order to make your home more likely to sell.

"What will paint over blue?"

Air Force blue. Baby boy blue.

There will be another baby, Michael had promised when I'd miscarried. *Let's not change the room.*

So we'd kept it—his way of clinging to hope and my way of trying to be a good wife.

Of course, now they were both gone, and I couldn't walk into the room without a chill running down my spine.

The salesman's gaze drifted to my left hand, to the diamond engagement ring that sat there atop a diamond eternity band. I couldn't look at either of those things and yet, like the room, I hadn't quite been ready to cast them off. My husband might have died a year ago, but the memory of him still lingered.

"Ma'am, perhaps it would help if your husband came with you. He might have a better sense of what your needs are."

He would have. He would have repainted the room on one of his free weekends and I wouldn't have had to worry about a thing. Which was part of the problem. I'd always prided myself on having my shit together—being an Air Force wife allowed for nothing less, considering how frequently I was alone—and yet now that Michael was actually gone, I kept realizing how many things I didn't know how to do. And how much I'd grown to depend on him during the five years we were married.

The paint cans became little more than a blur, my eyes filling with tears. Oh God, I was going to lose it in Aisle 12.

The thing about being a widow was that you never knew when the tears would come. You could have a string of good days, and then something could set you off—the scent of your husband's cologne on a stranger, the sound of a jet screaming overhead, your wedding song playing on the radio. Apparently mine had come today. I took a deep breath, steadying myself, struggling to push a response out of my mouth when suddenly a large hand landed behind my back, palm between my shoulder blades, fingers stroking through my ratty T-shirt.

"I got this," a voice rumbled behind me.

I whirled around and came face-to-face with Easy.

As squadron commander of the Wild Aces F-16 squadron, my husband—call sign Joker—had been both boss and mentor to the twenty-something pilots who had flown under his leadership. I'd gotten to know all of the guys and their families pretty well, but there was no doubt that out of all of them, my favorite was Alex "Easy" Rogers.

There were many things to love about Easy—the contagious smile on his face, the compassion in his eyes, the memory of how he'd comforted me when I'd miscarried and Michael had been halfway across the country, how he'd stood next to me at the podium while I delivered Michael's eulogy, the way he'd always treated me with an indulgent affection. He'd been one of my husband's best friends, so for that alone, I'd always love him. But it wasn't just that. He was a big kid with a wild streak ninety percent of the time, but the other ten percent of the time he was one of the best men I'd ever known. He was also one of the last people Michael had spoken to when he was alive—a voice over the radio in their formation of four jets, just before Michael was lost to us forever.

I struggled to get my tears in check as Easy spoke to the salesman, and then the guy was gone and I was staring up into Easy's blue eyes.

"You okay?"

"Just trying to pick out paint."

"What do you need?" he asked, his expression solemn, the usual swagger and amusement drained from his expression.

It had been a rough year for everyone.

"I'm trying to repaint the guest room." *Do not cry.* "The one that was going to be the nursery." The rest of the words came out in a whoosh of pain. "The realtor thinks the house will be more marketable if the rooms are neutral. It's been on the market six months now and we still haven't gotten any interest."

I still hadn't gotten any interest. When you'd been a "we" for seven years, it was hard to switch to the singular.

The days after I'd received the knock on my front door, after the casualty officers had notified me that Michael's F-16 had crashed in Alaska—that he was *gone*—I'd walked through a nightmare. When all the official military events had ended, I'd gone home to Georgia to grieve in private. But at thirty-one, I'd started to feel just a little bit cramped living in my parents' house, so now I was back in Oklahoma, waiting to sell the house I'd lived in with Michael, trying to figure out my next step.

Easy looked down at his feet for a moment, his big body hunched over, and then his gaze was on mine again. "I can do it."

"No. Thanks for offering, but it's too much. I'm fine on my own."

The squadron was deploying to Afghanistan in a month. No way I wanted Easy working in his final weeks before he went to war.

"I can just hire someone to do it. Which I probably should have done all along," I admitted.

Michael's life insurance had taken financial worries off my plate for a few years, but thanks to more than five years of moving all over the world, my résumé wasn't exactly impressive. Luxuries like hiring someone to paint felt incredibly stupid until I found a job. Although if the house didn't sell . . .

"I'll do it." He nudged my shoulder, positioning his big body between me and my cart, studying the items I'd collected so far.

"You have the deployment—"

"It's no big deal," he answered. "It'll take a day. I can come over on Sunday and work on it, if that's okay with you."

It hadn't escaped my notice that the squadron had started stepping in to help out with things, although I hadn't seen Easy for a while. I guessed this was his way of doing the right thing for a buddy's wife, and as much as it made me feel guilty, I couldn't argue with a military man's sense of honor.

"Okay. I really appreciate it. That's really sweet of you." I smiled. "I'll make you a thank-you dinner."

"You don't have to do that," he mumbled, a slight flush covering his cheeks as soon as the word "sweet" fell from my lips.

"I want to." And I did. I hated eating meals alone; half the time I couldn't even be bothered to cook for myself and I ended up eating cereal for dinner. And there was something about Easy that always seemed to need taking care of. He was a confirmed bachelor to the extreme, and while I'd seen him with plenty of girls over the years, I couldn't remember the last time he'd had a girlfriend or anything close to one, had never seen anyone take care of him.

He nodded in response, his Adam's apple bobbing. His hand left my back, running through his thick, blond hair. He looked tired and I wondered how he was really doing. All of the guys who'd been in the air with Michael when he'd died had struggled in the past year.

He turned, his face in profile as he scrutinized the paint cans. And what a beautiful face it was. He was teased mercilessly for the fact that he looked more like an underwear model than a fighter pilot—high cheekbones, full lips, long eyelashes, the kind of blue eyes that people tried to replicate with color contacts.

"So what else do you need?" he asked, his gaze still on the shelf.

I handed him my list, the words scratched there in what might as well have been a foreign language. I'd always handled the finances, but anything related to the house had definitely been Michael's domain.

"I think I got most of it," I managed. "I've never painted before beyond my college dorm room, and I figure this needs to look good if it's going to impress a buyer."

He nodded again, and I realized this was the most economical I'd ever seen Easy be with his words. Ever since Michael's death, things had been . . . strained. He was still polite, still willing to offer a hand if I needed it. But the friendship we'd built years ago seemed to have been replaced by the guilt he felt over the accident.

"How have you been?" I asked, trying to pull the conversation out of him, realizing how much I'd missed our friendship. "I haven't seen you in months." I thought about it for a moment. "Since Thanksgiving?"

That didn't seem right. Had we really let five months slip by? I'd e-mailed him on his birthday in February and he'd responded, but we hadn't seen each other—

"I saw you at the squadron in March. You were leaving with Jordan."

Surprise filled me. "I didn't see you. Why didn't you say hi?"

He shrugged. "You guys were talking; I didn't want to interrupt you."

I'd been walking through a fog for the past few months, and somewhere along the way I'd missed the fact that we'd gotten to this point. And it wasn't just Easy; I'd been so consumed by my grief that life had passed me by. Friends' lives had changed, they'd moved on to other things, and I'd stayed rooted in that day everything changed, in the loss that defined and overshadowed my world. I'd lost touch with people, simply stopped trying, and I'd given up more than I'd realized, and suddenly, I wanted to make up for that, wanted to fix the gap between us.

"Hey." I laid a hand on his arm and his entire body stiffened. A pang hit me, and then another one, piercing the numbness that shrouded me.

My voice cracked. "I miss him, too. If it's too weird to be around me or if I remind you of everything that's happened, and you need to take a step back, that's fine. I know it's been hard for you guys to move on from the accident, and I don't want to make it worse. But if you need someone to talk to, I'm here. I miss our friendship. I miss you."

EASY

Fuck.

I closed my eyes for a beat, trying to drown her out, to throw the wall back up, trying to push her out of the cracks and crevices of my heart where she'd snuck in and taken up permanent residence in my chest.

She smelled like apples. Forbidden-fucking-apples. She looked . . .

My eyes slammed open and my gaze slid over her. I

blinked, not sure if it was the scent of apples or the sight in front of me that had me so fucking hungry.

She wore a pair of white shorts that showed off surprisingly tanned legs. A faded T-shirt that likely harkened back to her days as a cheerleader at the University of Georgia. Her red-gold hair was up in a loose braid, her green eyes staring up at me.

I'd been in detox, figured the months apart would cure this ache inside me every single fucking time I saw her.

They hadn't.

If anything, the time apart had only made the ache worse.

I fisted my hands at my sides, looking away from her again, her words cutting through me as I focused on the paint cans as though my life depended on it. And then I couldn't take it anymore, and my gaze slid down to the spot where she touched me, where her fingers rested on my biceps, her skin a few shades paler than mine.

I swallowed, trying to drag more air into my lungs, that hand suddenly feeling as dangerous as a deadly spider.

I had a pretty solid, you-can-look-but-you-can't-touch policy where Dani was concerned. There had been moments when I bent the rules a little bit, like a few minutes ago when I'd seen her standing there amid all of the painting supplies looking so lost, as though she was drowning and needed a life raft to pull her to shore, but I paid for every fucking moment in spades.

"You don't make it worse," I lied, answering her original question, hating that I'd given her a reason to worry about anyone other than herself. She had more shit on her plate than most people could ever deal with, and the last thing I wanted to do was add to it. I shoved my hands into the pockets of my cargo shorts, breaking the physical connection between us, still not quite able to meet her gaze. Her eyes could bring the most resolute man to his fucking knees.

I swallowed again, wondering if my voice sounded as strained to her ears as it did to mine. "It's good to see you again."

Heaven and hell rolled into a knot in my stomach.

I'd had it bad for her since the moment I first saw her, but as guilty as I'd felt knowing I wanted my friend's wife, the wanting inside me now for his widow felt infinitely worse.

I would have given everything I had to trade places with him, so he could have come back for her.

She smiled, a real smile, one she rarely doled out anymore. "You, too."

Her gaze drifted past me for a moment, her smile deepening, and she stepped forward another foot, close enough that her side brushed against mine, so warm and soft, that apple smell filling my nostrils once again. It had to be her shampoo. Her head came just to my chin, her scent wafting up at me. I bent my head just an inch, barely resisting the urge to inhale, drowning in her, the warmth from her body—

"You have admirers," Dani commented, her teasing voice breaking me from my stupor.

I blinked, following her gaze.

Two girls stood at the end of the aisle—college girls by the look of the youthful glow they sported and the sorority letters stretched across their tits—staring at us, wide, curious smiles on their faces. They both blushed as they caught me staring back, exchanging whispers behind cupped hands.

Dani nudged me, the touch sending another jolt through my body. I was hard as a fucking rock in a home improvement store and it had everything to do with the scent of apples and the allure of soft curves against me, and nothing to do with the sorority girls.

She gifted me with another smile, this one brighter than the last, filling her gaze and spilling over into my heart.

My mouth went dry.

"You can go work your magic," she teased, her words jolting me back to reality. "I'm fine here."

The only thing worse about being utterly and totally in love with the one woman who you absolutely could not fucking have, who saw you more as a brother than a man, was having the same woman, the one who'd ripped your heart out of your chest time and time again, try to set you up with someone else.

I was pretty sure there was some bitter fucking irony here considering my rep, but with my heart lying in the middle of Aisle 12, gushing blood, I wasn't much for humor.

I shook my head, turning away from the girls, Dani once again all I could see.

"I'm okay."

"You sure? I really don't mind. Just think of me as one of the guys. Hell, I can be your wing woman."

"I'm sure," I croaked, pretty sure she'd just slayed me— death by well-meaning matchmaking and the thrust of a sharp blade that accompanied every single one of her words.

I tilted my head, staring back at the girls, wondering if it would help if I did go over there, if I lost myself in two hot bodies. In my younger years, I probably would have gone for it. Now it would be another meaningless fuck in a string of them. And I didn't want that anymore. I'd watched two of my closest friends—Noah and Thor—meet women and fall in love this past year. Noah was now married with a baby on the way, and Thor was engaged to the girl he'd loved and lost and somehow regained. So yeah. Maybe I couldn't have Dani, but that didn't mean I didn't want to meet a woman I could love, who would love me in return. At thirty-three, I might have taken a while to get here, but I was ready for something more. And if my perfect woman bore an uncanny resemblance to Dani, whatever.

Some women slid under your skin so deep, you couldn't carve them out, no matter how hard you tried.

LOVE
ROMANCE
NOVELS?

For news on all your favorite romance authors,
sneak peeks into the newest releases, book
giveaways, and much more—

"Like" Love Always on Facebook!
 **LoveAlwaysBooks**